PENGUIN CLASSICS

A MURKY BUSINESS

ADVISORY EDITOR: BETTY RADICE

Honoré de Balzac was born at Tours in 1799, the son of a civil servant. He spent nearly six years as a boarder in a Vendôme school, then went to live in Paris, working as a lawyer's clerk then as a hack-writer. Between 1820 and 1824 he wrote a number of novels under various pseudonyms, many of them in collaboration, after which he unsuccessfully tried his luck at publishing, printing and type-founding. At the age of thirty, heavily in debt, he returned to literature with a dedicated fury and wrote the first novel to appear under his own name, *The Chouans*. During the next twenty years he wrote about ninety novels and shorter stories, among them many masterpieces, to which he gave the comprehensive title *The Human Comedy*. He died in 1850, a few months after his marriage to Evelina Hanska, the Polish countess with whom he had maintained amorous relations for eighteen years.

Herbert J. Hunt, educated at King Edward VI Grammar School, Lichfield, and Magdalen College, Oxford, was a Tutor and Fellow at St Edmund Hall from 1927 to 1944, Professor of French Language and Literature at London University until 1966, then Senior Fellow at Warwick University until 1971. He published books on the literary history of nineteenth-century France; he was the author of a biography of Balzac and a comprehensive study of Balzac's writings: *Balzac's 'Comédie Humaine'*. He also translated Balzac's *Cousin Pons*, *Lost Illusions*, *History of the Thirteen* and *The Wild Ass's Skin*, for the Penguin Classics. Professor Hunt died in 1973.

Honoré de Balzac

A MURKY BUSINESS

(*Une Ténébreuse Affaire*)

TRANSLATED
AND INTRODUCED BY
HERBERT J. HUNT

PENGUIN BOOKS

Penguin Books Ltd, Harmondsworth, Middlesex, England
Viking Penguin Inc., 40 West 23rd Street, New York, New York 10010, U.S.A.
Penguin Books Australia Ltd, Ringwood, Victoria, Australia
Penguin Books Canada Ltd, 2801 John Street, Markham, Ontario, Canada L3R 1B4
Penguin Books (N.Z.) Ltd, 182–190 Wairau Road, Auckland 10, New Zealand

—

This translation first published 1972
Reprinted 1978, 1981, 1985

—

—

Made and printed in Great Britain by
Cox & Wyman Ltd, Reading
Set in Monotype Garamond

Contents

Introduction

HONORÉ DE BALZAC was the son of a Languedoc peasant who had come to Paris in 1767 and made his career as a government functionary. He had therefore no hereditary right to the supposedly aristocratic particle *de* which he assumed round about 1830. He was born in Tours in 1799 and died in Paris in 1850. A short account of his life, career and literary achievements is given in the present translator's Introduction to the Penguin Classics edition of *Cousin Pons* and, at greater length, in his *Honoré de Balzac, a Biography.*[1]

Here it suffices to recall that Balzac's tremendous novel-cycle, *The Human Comedy*, was begun in 1829 and continued until a year or two before his death. It was probably the most ambitious project any writer ever conceived. Balzac thought of himself as social historian, philosopher and creative artist. As the self-appointed 'secretary' of his own age he published more than ninety novels, short stories and 'studies'; he was still adding to them, and had many others in view, even when his health and vigour were rapidly declining. Thus his work was a snowball growth which, had he not written himself into an early grave, would have reached even more astounding proportions. He divided his books into three main categories: *Studies of Manners*, *Philosophical Studies* and *Analytical Studies.* All three categories, especially the first two, cohere as the expression of a carefully pondered interpretation of life and the scheme of things. The *Studies of Manners* were in turn sub-divided into six compartments or 'scenes'. Balzac had a strong sense of drama and thought of the novel as a form of dramatic entertainment. And so we have the *Scenes of Private Life*, whose ostensible purpose was to study pure and unsophisticated youth in its advance from puberty to maturity, though they were, in fact, more concerned on the whole with the love-life

1. Athlone Press, 1957. Recently reprinted by the Greenwood Press, New York – issued with an indispensable corrigenda slip which more or less rectifies an oversight which caused that Press to omit stipulated emendations and corrections bringing the biography up to date.

of unsatisfied women; the *Scenes of Provincial Life*, showing the transition from the generous impulsiveness of young people of twenty to the hard-headed self-interest they normally reach in their thirties – the most conspicuous feature of these 'scenes' is the depiction of the closed, restricted life of provincial communities; and the *Scenes of Parisian Life*, designed to portray the development or, more accurately, the deterioration of men and women from maturity to the verge of 'decrepitude', which in Balzac's view and that of his contemporaries sets in much earlier than we should admit today. They are the grimmest of these 'scenes': *Old Goriot* (1834–5), Part II of *Lost Illusions* (1839) and *Cousin Pons* (1847) being typical examples.[2] Then come the *Scenes of Political Life*, to which category *A Murky Business* (*Une Ténébreuse Affaire*) belongs.

'These Scenes', a friend and admirer, Félix Davin, wrote on his behalf in 1834,

> cover a wider field of thought. The characters there staged will represent the interests of the masses. They will rise superior to the laws to which the characters of the three previous series were subjected. Here the author is no longer concerned with the play of private interests, but with the formidable activity of the social machine and the clashes produced by the mingling of private and general interests. Up to now, the author has shown individual feeling in constant opposition to society as a whole; but in the *Scenes of Political Life* he intends to show thought coming up against an organizing force; sentiment has no place whatsoever in this conflict. The situations which arise have their own dramatic grandeur, be it comic or tragic. Behind the *dramatis personae* a people and a monarchy are in confrontation: they symbolize the past and the future in its transitions and are at odds, no longer with individuals, but with personified attachments [*affections*], with the resistances of the moment represented by men and women.

The purpose behind this may seem a little vague in detail, but the general idea is fairly clear. One of Balzac's most intense convictions was that in the sphere of political activity principles of private morality go to the wall. 'Rulers must never be hedged round by the principles governing private morality', he was to write in 1846. This questionable maxim lies behind a

2. All three are available in translation in the Penguin Classics.

historical novel – *Sur Catherine de Medicis* – on which he was at work during a long period, from 1830 to 1843. It helps to explain his basic approval, in *A Murky Business*, of such unscrupulous statesmen as Fouché and Talleyrand; also of Napoleon himself, as he appears in his conversation (pages 208–9) with Laurence de Cinq-Cygne; it also explains his virtual acceptance of the sacrifice, abhorrent to us, of the unfortunate Michu as a predestined victim of the sacred principle of 'justice'.

The fifth type of 'scene' which Balzac projected was to be *Scenes of Military Life*. Félix Davin wrote, again as Balzac's spokesman: 'The *Scenes of Military Life* follow on from the *Scenes of Political Life*. Nations are moved by certain interests, and these are formulated by a few privileged men who are destined to lead the masses and, by speaking in their name, set them on their course. And so the purpose of the *Scenes of Military Life* is to give a general picture of the life of the masses as they move forward to combat.' Since Balzac, for various reasons, never succeeded in expanding this category of 'scenes', we need not follow Davin's definition any further. Balzac's greatest scene of military life was to have been *The Battle*, a work which he dreamed about for many years but never managed to write. Consequently, an interesting feature of *A Murky Business* is its final episode – 'The Emperor's Bivouac' – which gives us an idea of what a scene of military life might have been. Of his sixth category, *Scenes of Country Life*, we need say little. They were intended to show a sort of appeasement – men and women tired of or disgusted with the 'struggle for life' and settling down in remote country parts to devote themselves to the betterment of their fellow-beings: an important category, but having little relevance to the present work in spite of its country setting.

It is not a matter for surprise that *A Murky Business* takes us away from Balzac's normal fields of interest. Most of his fictions give us his vision, based on acute observation but also heightened by his prodigious creative imagination, of contemporary society, mainly that of the Restoration period (1814–30) and the July Monarchy (the reign of Louis-Philippe, 1830–48), groping its way in a new and bewildering world, with the rivalry of classes – the old aristocracy, the new bureaucracy, more or less ennobled by Napoleon (like Malin de Gondreville), and the industrial, commercial-minded bourgeoisie, very much to the fore in an age when modern capitalism was just beginning to take shape and move slowly on towards its ultimate triumph. The picture which generally emerges from Balzac's novels is one of a human nature 'red in tooth and claw', struggling anarchically for wealth, position and power, with money as the only god worshipped during a period when time-honoured values and institutions had gone to the four winds. Society had become predominantly acquisitive, and Balzac, very conservative in his political beliefs – he rarely missed an opportunity to sneer at forms of constitutional government – was convinced that only a return to a strongly disciplined political order supported by the Catholic Church could halt the downward rush of the Gadarene swine. That is why the picture he gives us of political intrigue and jobbery at the moment when Napoleon was forcing his way to autocracy is an extremely interesting one. *A Murky Business* has for its time and setting the years 1803–6, a period when disgruntled republicans, resentful aristocrats and a mixed multitude of time-servers were engaged in strange plots and conspiracies which were doomed to failure because they entailed unnatural alliances between factions which in reality were working against one another. So the main theme of the book is the 1803 conspiracy against the First Consul, in which an aristocratic family becomes dangerously involved. It manages to extricate itself, but by so doing excites the vengeful hatred of a wily and implacable police agent: Corentin, who already in Balzac's novel of 1829 (*The Chouans*) had succeeded in destroying the leader of royalist guerilla forces in Western France. Consequently the second episode of the novel shows him avenging himself on the Simeuses and the d'Hauteserres by his unfathomable machinations.

The obscure story of these machinations makes *A Murky Business* an early example of what the French call a *roman policier* and the English a detective story. We must consider it later as such. But this novel is more important from the historical point of view because of the light it casts on those troubled times when Napoleon was exploiting the still dynamic revolutionary fervour for his own ends, when republicans were smarting from a sense of defeat, and when the aristocrats – both those who had stayed in France and those who were waiting at Coblenz in the vain hope of reinstating the monarchy by main force – fondly believed that they could either come to an understanding with Napoleon or bring about his downfall. It is evident throughout the novel that Balzac's sympathies lie with the aristocracy, although he never tries to minimize the genius of Napoleon nor indeed the resourcefulness of his dubious supporters. The novelist's admiration for the Simeuses, the d'Hauteserre brothers and his intrepid heroine – modelled, as he himself admits, on Diana Vernon in Scott's *Rob Roy* – is almost unbounded. Yet, no doubt involuntarily, he has depicted them in such a way as to diminish our respect for them. Could one in fact conceive anything more unconsciously arrogant than Laurence's patronizing remark to the excessively loyal Michu (page 86): 'You are worthy to be a noble!'? Or anything more insolently tactless than the refusal of the Simeuses and the d'Hauteserres to return Malin's bow at the end of the trial (page 197), after he has shown a surprising amount of generosity in casting doubt on their guilt?

The 'murky' aspect of Balzac's story is by no means pure invention. The mysterious abduction of Malin de Gondreville is based on a curious episode which actually occurred in 1800 on the eve of Napoleon's decisive victory at Marengo. Malin's prototype was one Clément de Ris, a member of the Consulate Senate who, without being so thorough-going a time-server as Malin, was implicated in the conspiracy then being hatched against Napoleon by those slick statesmen Talleyrand and Fouché and their not so slick allies Sieyès and Carnot. Balzac's own father, at that time an administrative official at Tours, had been in contact with Clément de Ris and was able to give his son some information about this 'ténébreuse affaire'. Honoré, a very talkative man, had repeated some of this to his one-time mistress the Duchesse d'Abrantès (widow of one of Napoleon's generals, Junot), and she had stolen some of his thunder by recounting the affair (inaccurately) in her *Mémoires* (1831–5). This act of piracy stirred his bile. But whatever may be the rights or wrongs of the case, Balzac mingles fact and fiction in accordance with the exigencies of artistic creation. He postdates certain events, postpones the Clément de Ris abduction and the burning of the compromising documents, and gives them as a sequel to the first episode in his narrative, which, quite accurately, he places in 1803–4, on the eve of Napoleon's self-promotion from First Consul to Emperor. The events of his second episode are made to happen in 1805–6, on the eve of another Napoleonic victory, that of Jena. He also changes the scene of action. Clément de Ris had been abducted from his château in Beauvais, in Touraine. The scene of the attack made on Malin – the château of Gondreville – is transferred to Champagne. Of course a competent novelist fuses fact and fiction, and no one would dream of blaming Balzac for making such changes of time and locality.

A Murky Business is then, in the first place, a historical novel, and the tribute Balzac pays (page 58) to Sir Walter Scott, to whom he owed so much, has its significance. It raises the question of Balzac's psychological intentions in this novel. He brings both historical and imagined characters on to his stage. Adhering to Scott's practice, he allows his great historical figures to appear only momentarily and in the background: effectively, I think. His admiration of Fouché, Talleyrand and Napoleon does not prevent him from showing their essential selfishness and ruthlessness. We may feel that Fouché and Talleyrand must stand by the verdict of history. This is not necessarily true of Napoleon. Balzac fully reveals his egoism and ambition. But there is something else: the mythical Napoleon is visible in this work. He himself had contributed much to the Napoleonic legend, especially in his *Country Doctor* of 1833. In this novel of 1841 he gives it further corroboration.

Malin, half fictitious, half historical, is not, I think, entirely convincing. Balzac seems to be intent on making him more contemptible than he actually shows him to be. His French version of Diana Vernon, Laurence de Cinq-Cygne, is a curious creation. Like the Simeuses and the d'Hauteserres, she can only be completely accepted if the reader whole-heartedly plunges himself into the passions and prejudices of the times. At any rate we should perhaps be grateful to Balzac for dwelling upon her 'ovine profile' and thus refraining from making a classical beauty of her. D'Hauteserre senior is useful as a specimen of the more pusillanimous brand of aristocrat of the period. The Abbé Goujet is one of Balzac's most congenial clerical figures – he showed more sympathy with the clergy as he grew older and the *Human Comedy* progressed.

Corentin and Peyrade are well worth their place in fiction as perfect examples of the cunning and malevolent police spy. As for the rank and file in this story, they are convincing enough. But what of Michu? Can we accept him as a fanatical adherent of the aristocratic and royalist cause, a man who has resorted to terrorism in support of it? We ourselves live far from those times, and perhaps we must be willing to accept Balzac's testimony that such self-devotion was possible, even though it may have been exceptional.

The love-interest, usually so prominent in Balzac's novels, is quite subordinate here. Balzac castigated Scott for creating heroines who were too chaste and too cold. Laurence is far from cold, but she is unusually chaste for a heroine of the *Human Comedy*. The effect of sexual passion in determining the course of historical events, which is the essential theme of *The Chouans*, is absent here. Balzac has here preferred to follow a psychological side-issue and to study the case of two identical twins in love with one and the same woman, who in turn is unable to decide which of them she wants to marry. Balzac is so intrigued with this situation that he makes (page 132) the naïve suggestion that in medieval times papal power might have provided a solution to such an impasse. But he himself eludes the problem by subordinating it to his political drama. And this drama brings us back to Balzac the social and political philosopher. Here, as everywhere else in his works, he presents himself as a commentator on social conditions. He gives a scrupulous account of judicial principles and procedure in the transitional period between Consulate and Empire. In doing so he was looking back from a *cause célèbre* in which he had become passionately interested in 1839: the trial at Bourg of a notary, Peytel, who was accused of murdering his wife and his manservant, and was guillotined in spite of Balzac's efforts to save him. Balzac not unnaturally carried back the interest thus conceived in criminal justice to the Napoleonic era, and in consequence two interesting features emerge from his presentation of the 1805 trial: his dubious attitude to the jury system borrowed from England, and the admission of the public to trials in court – a psychological but none the less rational objection: the possibility, or rather the likelihood, of emotional factors intervening to divert the strict course of justice.

It may thus be seen that *A Murky Business* is no less wide in the interests it arouses than the more normal run of Balzacian novels. But reference has been made above to the detective-story element in this novel. How does *A Murky Business* stand up to the somewhat rigorous tests we nowadays apply to so highly developed a genre as the 'whodunit'? We may find some fault with Balzac in this respect, particularly since, as we have seen, his investigation of the Peytel case had given him some experience.

Here are a few objections:

(1) Senator Malin, once released from captivity, tells the court that, when Marthe Michu brought him food, he recognized her by the ring she wore – one given her by Laurence de Cinq-Cygne. How could he have known that Laurence had given it to Marthe?

(2) At Michu's second cross-examination, when a fragment of the forged letter to Marthe had been produced, referring to a prison warder whom Michu was supposed to have enlisted in his service because of his obligations to Michu's late father-in-law, why did counsel for the defence not take two steps: (*a*) have the fragment collated with specimens of Michu's genuine handwriting in order to establish the document as a forgery, and (*b*) look into the identity of the alleged warder? It should have been easy to show that no such man existed.

(3) Michu's conviction is mainly founded on the supposition that only he, his wife, Laurence and her kinsmen knew of the existence of the subterranean vault. But Corentin and Peyrade had discovered it. Michu had met them at the entrance to the vault after the four noblemen had vacated it. Why did not Michu, in mere self-defence, divulge this fact at the trial?

We may feel that counsel for the defence, skilled as they are made out to be, fall short in these respects. None the less *A Murky Business* may be accepted as a fair example of an early mystery story; we must, however, repeat that it is more than that: it is a historical novel which brings into vivid relief the subtleties of political intrigue at a very important moment in the history of France and Europe.

This novel was first printed in serial form in *Le Journal du Commerce* (14 January to 20 February 1841). It was published in book form by Henri Souverain in 1842. In that edition it was divided into a score of chapters. Then, in the first edition of *The Human Comedy*, the publication of which began in 1842, this novel being placed in it in 1846, these short chapters were dropped, since Balzac had taken to the habit of suppressing chapter-divisions and presenting his novels in continuous narrative. The original chapter titles have no particular value, but the chapter-divisions are useful as a means of breaking up the narrative: therefore, in this translation, they are indicated by the use of asterisks.

Devotees of Balzac (there are some even in England) will know of his device of 'reappearing characters', which helped him to confirm the impression that his invented world was a real and convincing one. Malin de Gondreville is one of these reappearing characters, but perhaps the most important of them is Monsieur de Granville, who plays a major role in *A Double Family* (1830), where he appears as an unhappy husband and father, a lesser one in *Honorine* (1843), and more or less minor roles in other novels. Corentin, who had been a central figure in *The Chouans* (1829), has also an important part to play – one consistent with his character – in *Splendour and Misery of Courtesans*[3] (1838–47). Most of the characters gathered together in the Conclusion of *A Murky Business* are familiar to assiduous readers of *The Human Comedy*. Henri de Marsay is the pliable politician and cynical man of the world. Rastignac is the 'go-getter' characteristic of the Monarchy of July period. The Princesse de Cadignan is a lady of meretricious charm with numerous adventures to her credit.

3. Translated in the Penguin Classics as *A Harlot High and Low*.

Since there are repeated allusions in this novel to various 'Revolutionary days' and *coups d'état*, it may be useful here to list those mentioned in the text, and also to add a note on a few other relevant events. Many of the dates recorded are those of the Revolutionary Calendar, which was deemed to have begun in September 1792 and was in use from 1793 to 1806.

9 Thermidor, Year II (27 July 1794). The revolt in the National Convention which overthrew the Terrorist leaders Robespierre, Couthon and Saint-Just, who were guillotined the next day. Both extreme republicans (the party of the 'Montagne') and moderate ones took part in this revolt. Those who engineered or supported it are known as 'Thermidorians'. Under the 'Thermidorian reaction' (August 1794 to October 1795) the 'Montagnards' became weaker and weaker, and in November 1795 a new government – the 'Directory' – was set up, despite the fact that on 5 October (13 Vendémiaire, Year IV) a rising against the moribund Convention had been bloodily suppressed with the aid of Bonaparte.

18 Fructidor, Year V (4 September 1797). A military *coup d'état* which frustrated royalist plots to destroy the Directory.

18 Brumaire, Year VII (9 November 1799). The Bonapartist *coup d'état* which abolished the Directory and founded the Consulate (Bonaparte, Sieyès and Ducros; then Bonaparte, Cambacérès and Carnot), of which Bonaparte was of course the dominant member.

There are several allusions in the novel to the attempted assassination of Bonaparte in the rue Saint-Nicaise (24 December 1800) by means of an infernal machine.

16 Thermidor, Year X (3 August 1802). The date of the *Senatus-consultum* which made Bonaparte Consul for life. By another *Senatus-consultum* (18 May 1804) he constituted himself Emperor. In the meantime (21 March 1804) he had committed one of the most ruthless acts of his career by swooping on the Duc d'Enghien (the sole remaining heir of the Condé family) at Baden, rushing him into France and having him court-martialled and shot at Vincennes. The Duc d'Enghien was an important representative of the Bourbon dynasty. Napoleon's grounds for this high-handed act were that the duke was implicated in the conspiracy of 1803. As the novel indicates, this put Napoleon beyond the pale as far as the Bourbons were concerned. It was in fact preliminary to his establishment of himself as Emperor of France.

Napoleonic victories. The plots against Napoleon in 1800, related in the Conclusion to the novel, were frustrated by the victory he gained against the Austrians at Marengo (14 June 1800), preceded by his brilliant feat in taking his army over the Mont Saint-Bernard pass. His victory against Austria and Russia at Austerlitz (2 December 1805) was almost simultaneous with the break-up of the camp at Boulogne from which he had hoped to invade England. What Balzac calls 'the disaster of Trafalgar' (21 October) had put an end to this scheme. These events are all mentioned in the novel.

Napoleon's victory against the Prussians at Jena, partly witnessed by Laurence de Cinq-Cygne and the Marquis de Chargebœuf, was won on 14 October 1806.

The occasional footnotes in the text are of course those of the translator.

A MURKY BUSINESS

To Monsieur de Margonne
His grateful guest at the Château de Saché
DE BALZAC

1. The Vexations of the Police

THE autumn of 1803 was one of the finest in the early years of our century, the Napoleonic period. In October occasional rain had revived the meadows, and the trees were still green and leafy in the middle of November. Consequently the populace was beginning to believe that there existed, between the firmament and Bonaparte, who had recently been declared Consul for life, an understanding to which he owed some part of his glamour; and, strange to say, on that day in 1812 when sunshine failed him, his prosperity came to an end.

On 15 November, then, about four o'clock in the afternoon, the sun was casting a kind of red haze on the age-old tops of the four rows of elms down a long seignorial avenue, and flooding with radiance the sand and herb-tufts in a vast, round clearing, the meeting-place of convergent tracks, such as is found in country regions where formerly land was cheap enough to be devoted to ornamental purposes. The air was so pure, the atmosphere so mild, that it was still possible for a family to sit out in the cool of the evening as in the summer. A man dressed in a green twill hunting-jacket with green buttons and breeches of the same material, and wearing twill gaiters up to his knees, was cleaning a carbine with the care which skilled huntsmen give to this occupation in their moments of leisure. This man had neither game nor game-bag, nor indeed any equipment indicative of departure for or return from the chase. Two women sitting near him were watching him in what seemed to be a state of ill-concealed terror. Anyone hiding behind a bush and contemplating this scene would undoubtedly have felt as apprehensive as this man's elderly mother-in-law and his wife. Clearly, in the department of the Aube, a huntsman would not take such minute precautions in order to kill game; nor would he use a heavy, rifled carbine.

'Are you going out after roe-deer, Michu?' asked his beautiful young wife, doing her best to put on a cheerful air.

Before replying, Michu gazed at his dog lying in the

sunlight with his muzzle resting on his outstretched paws in the charming gesture that hunting-dogs adopt. The animal now raised his head and sniffed in alternative directions towards the mile-long avenue in front of him and towards a cross-track which entered the clearing from the left-hand side.

'No,' Michu answered. 'I'm after a beast I don't want to miss – a lynx.'

The dog, a magnificent white spaniel speckled with brown, growled.

'Ha!' said Michu, as if talking to himself. 'Spies! The country's swarming with them.'

Madame Michu dolefully raised her eyes to heaven. Beautiful and fair-haired, with blue eyes, as shapely as an antique statue, pensive and withdrawn, she seemed to be in the grip of some dark and bitter affliction. The husband's appearance might to some extent explain the terror manifested by the two women. The laws of physiognomy are precise, not only in their application to character, but also in relation to the destinies which govern human existence. There is such a thing as prophetic physiognomy. If it were possible – such a vital statistic could be of import to society – to obtain the exact lineaments of those who perish on the scaffold, the science of Lavater and also that of Gall would conclusively prove that there had been strange portents in the skulls of all these people, even the innocent ones. Fate does indeed set its mark on the faces of those who are destined to die some kind of violent death. Now such a seal, visible to an observant eye, was imprinted on the expressive countenance of the man with the carbine. Small and stocky, as swift and as agile in movement as a monkey, although he was calm in temperament, Michu had a white face injected with blood, and his fuzzy red hair lent a sinister expression to his features, which were squat like those of a Kalmuk. His eyes, as clear and yellow as those of a tiger, had such inner depth that anyone who looked right into them lost his bearings, and he would discern no movement or warmth in them. These eyes were so fixed, luminous and rigid that in the end they inspired fear. The contrast between Michu's unflickering gaze and his physical restlessness added still more to the icy impression he gave at the very first glance. Action was prompt with him and was directed to a single purpose, just as, with animals, the vital urge is unreflectingly subject to the bidding of instinct. Since 1793 he had cut his beard to the shape of a fan. Even if, during the Reign of Terror, he had not been the chairman of a Jacobin club, these distinctive features alone would have made him fearsome to look at. His Socratic, snub-nosed face was crowned with a very fine forehead, but one so bulging that it seemed to beetle over the rest. His ears stood out and had a kind of mobility like those of wild animals, always on the alert. His mouth, half-open as is quite common among country folk, revealed strong teeth, as white as almonds but irregularly set. Thick and gleaming side-whiskers served as a framework to his countenance, white, but mottled in patches. His hair was close-cropped in front but grew long over his temples and the back of his head; with its tawny redness it threw into perfect relief everything in his physiognomy that was uncouth and fateful. His short, thick neck offered temptation to the guillotine-blade of the law.

At this moment the sunlight, bearing slantwise on this group, was giving full illumination to the trio of heads on which the dog gazed every now and then. Moreover, this scene was being enacted on a splendid theatre. The *rond-point* in question stands at the farther end of the Gondreville parkland, one of the richest domains in France and incontestably the finest in the Aube department: splendid avenues lined with elms, a château built to Mansard's design, a fifteen-hundred-acre walled park, nine big farms, a forest, mills and meadows. Before the Revolution this almost royal domain belonged to the Simeuse family. Ximeuse is a fief situated in Lorraine. It was pronounced Simeuse and had come to be spelt the way it was pronounced.

The great wealth of the Simeuses, noblemen attached to the house of Burgundy, goes back to the time when the Guises were threatening the Valois dynasty. Richelieu first of all, and then Louis XIV remembered the loyalty shown by the Simeuses to the factious house of Lorraine and rebuffed them. The then Marquis de Simeuse, a dyed-in-the-wool Burgundian, henchman of the Guises, Leaguer and Frondeur (he had inherited this four-fold rancour of the nobility against the monarchy) came to live at Cinq-Cygne. Spurned at Court, he had married the widow of the Comte de Cinq-Cygne, who belonged to the junior branch of the famous house of Chargebœuf, one of the most illustrious families in the old province of Champagne. This junior branch became as famous as, and more opulent than, the elder branch. The Marquis, one of the richest men of his time, instead of ruining himself at Court, built Gondreville, made a large demesne of it and accumulated estates round it merely in order to provide himself with extensive hunting-grounds. He also built the Simeuse mansion at Troyes in close proximity to the Cinq-Cygne mansion. These two old town-houses, with the Bishop's palace, were for a long time the only stone-built houses. The Marquis sold Simeuse to the Duke of Lorraine. During the reign of Louis XV his son squandered his savings and a considerable part of this great estate; but this same son became first of all a squadron-commander and then vice-admiral, and compensated for his youthful follies by brilliant service in the Navy. The Marquis de Simeuse who succeeded this sailor had perished on the scaffold at Troyes, leaving twin sons who emigrated and were now abroad, having thrown in their lot with the house of Condé.

The circular clearing was the spot where the meet had formerly gathered in the time of the 'Great Marquis', the name by which the Simeuse who had erected Gondreville was known inside the family. Since 1793 Michu had been living at this rendezvous inside the park in what was called the Cinq-Cygne pavilion, built during the reign of Louis XIV. The village of Cinq-Cygne stood at the other end of the forest of Nodesme (a corruption of Notre-Dame), and the avenue with four rows of elms in which Couraut was scenting out spies led up to it. Since the death of the Great Marquis the pavilion had fallen into total disrepair. The vice-admiral spent much more of his time at sea and in Court than in Champagne, and his son gave this dilapidated pavilion to Michu as a lodge.

This once noble structure is made of brick decorated with vermiculated stone at its quoins, doors and windows. Access to it is gained through a double gateway of fine ironwork, though corroded with rust. Beyond it stretches a wide, deep ha-ha with sturdy trees springing up from it, and its parapets bristle with iron arabesques which threaten marauders with their innumerable spikes.

The park walls only begin beyond the circumference of the clearing. Outside it is a magnificent demilune demarcated by embankments planted with elms, and the corresponding one inside the park is formed by plantations of exotic trees. Thus the pavilion occupies the centre of a circle traced by these two crescents. Michu had converted the old rooms of the ground floor into a stable, a byre, a kitchen and a woodshed. The only relic of ancient splendour is an anteroom with black and white marble tiles which is entered from the park by French windows glazed with small panes, such as still existed at Versailles before Louis-Philippe turned the palace into an alms-house for the bygone glories of French art. Inside, the pavilion is divided in two by an old wooden staircase, worm-eaten but full of character, leading up to the first floor, which has five bedrooms with somewhat low ceilings. Above this runs a vast attic. Over this venerable edifice extends a roof structure in four sections whose arris is adorned with finials in lead. Four bulls-eye windows are let into it – for these Mansard had a justifiable preference, since in France attic windows and flat Italian roofs are an absurdity against which our climate protests. There Michu stored his forage.

All that part of the park which surrounds this old pavilion follows the English style. A hundred yards away, what was a lake but is now simply a well-stocked fish-pond makes its presence known as much by a slight mist above the trees as by the twilight croaking of innumerable frogs, toads and other voluble amphibians. A thousand details – the general decrepitude, the deep quiet of the woods, the view along the avenue, the distant forest, the rusty ironwork, the masses of stone with their velvety mosses – give a poetic aura to this still existing structure.

At the moment when this story begins, Michu was leaning on one of the moss-covered parapets, on which lay his powder-flask, cap, scarf, screw-driver and swabs, in fact all the utensils he needed for the dubious operation he had in hand. His wife's chair was leaning against the outer door of the pavilion, above which still stood the Simeuse coat of arms with its proud device: *Si meurs!*[1] Madame Michu's mother, who was wearing a peasant costume, had placed her chair in front of her daughter in order to keep her feet on one of its rungs, away from the damp.

'Where's the boy?' Michu asked his wife.

'He's roaming round the pond,' the child's mother replied. 'He's mad about frogs and insects.'

Michu gave a startling whistle. The rapidity of his son's approach bore witness to the despotism with which the bailiff of Gondreville ruled his family. Since 1789, and above all since 1793, Michu had had this estate practically under his control. The awe he inspired in his wife, his mother-in-law, his young farm-hand Gaucher, and a servant named Marianne, was shared by other people for more than twenty miles round. It will perhaps be well to wait no longer before explaining the reasons for this feeling. They will moreover add the finishing touches to Michu's moral portrait.

The old Marquis de Simeuse had disposed of his property in 1790, but events had moved too fast for him to entrust his fine estate of Gondreville to loyal hands. Accused of corresponding with the Duke of Brunswick and the Prince of Cobourg, the Marquis de Simeuse and his wife were put in prison and condemned by the revolutionary tribunal of Troyes, presided over by Marthe Michu's father. And so this fine domain was confiscated and sold as national property. At the time when the Marquis and Marquise were executed, it was noticed with some horror that the bailiff of the Gondreville estate, who was now chairman of the Jacobin club at Arcis, came to Troyes to witness the event. Michu, the orphaned son of a simple peasant, upon whom the Marquise had heaped benefits, bringing him up in the château and giving him the post of bailiff, was looked upon as a Brutus by the hotheads; but throughout the region he was shunned by everybody after this apparent act of ingratitude. The purchaser of Gondreville was a man of Arcis named Marion, grandson of a steward of the Simeuse house. This man, who had been an advocate since before the Revolution, was afraid of Michu and made him his bailiff with a salary of three thousand francs

1. *Cy meurs*: 'Here I die' (a pun on the name *Simeuse*).

and a commission on the sale of produce. Michu, who was already reputed to possess some ten thousand francs, married, by virtue of his reputation as a patriot, the daughter of a tanner in Troyes, who was the apostle of revolution in this town and president of the revolutionary tribunal. This tanner, a man of conviction who resembled Saint-Just in character, later became involved in the Babeuf conspiracy and committed suicide in order to escape condemnation. Marthe was the most beautiful girl in Troyes. And so, despite her touching modesty, she had been forced by her redoubtable father to figure as the Goddess of Liberty in a republican ceremony. After purchasing Gondreville, Marion did not visit it three times in seven years. Since his grandfather had been the Simeuses' steward, all Arcis believed that Citizen Marion was acting for Messieurs de Simeuse. Whilst the Terror lasted the new bailiff of Gondreville, an ardent patriot, son-in-law of the president of the Troyes revolutionary tribunal, was made much of by Malin (surnamed *de l'Aube* because he was one of the Parliamentary representatives for that department) and was to some extent an object of respect. But when the Montagne party was defeated, after his father-in-law's suicide, he became a scapegoat: everybody was in a hurry to blame him and his father-in-law for deeds in which he himself had taken no part. Michu stood firm against the injustice of the mob, steeled himself, adopted a defiant attitude and became bold of speech. However, since Napoleon's *coup d'état* of 18 Brumaire, he had been maintaining the deep silence which is the philosophical recourse of a strong-minded man. He no longer struggled against general opinion but contented himself with action, and this wise conduct earned him the reputation of an artful schemer, for he owned lands to the value of about a hundred thousand francs. For one thing he spent nothing; for another this fortune had been legitimately acquired, since it came from his father-in-law's inheritance and also from the six thousand francs a year which his post brought him in profits and salary. Although he had been managing the estate for a dozen years, and although it was open to anyone to compute his savings, when at the beginning of the Consulate he bought a farm for fifty thousand francs the former Montagnard incurred much censure and the people of Arcis credited him with the intention of regaining respectability by piling up a large fortune. Unfortunately, just when he was beginning to be forgotten by all and sundry, a stupid affair, envenomed by the cackle of country gossip, revived the general belief in the ferocity of his character.

One evening, as he was leaving Troyes in the company of several peasants, including the man who farmed Cinq-Cygne, he let a paper fall on to the highroad; this farmer, who was walking behind the others, stopped and picked it up. Michu turned round, saw the man holding the paper, immediately drew a pistol from his belt and, knowing that the farmer could read, threatened to blow his brains out if he opened the paper. Michu's action was so swift, so violent, his tone of voice so intimidating, he had such blazing eyes that everyone went cold with fear. The Cinq-Cygne farmer was naturally hostile to Michu, for his landlady, Mademoiselle de Cinq-Cygne, a cousin of the Simeuses, had no other property than this one farm and her château of Cinq-Cygne. She lived only for her cousins, with whom she had played as a child at Troyes and Gondreville. Her only brother, Jules de Cinq-Cygne, who had emigrated before the Simeuses, had died at the siege of Mainz, but thanks to a somewhat rare privilege of which we shall speak hereafter, the race of Cinq-Cygne did not die out for lack of male issue. This squabble between Michu and the Cinq-Cygne farmer caused a frightful stir in the *arrondissement* and gave a more sombre tint to the veil of mystery surrounding Michu; but this was not the only occurrence which made him a man to be feared. A few months after this scene took place, Citizen Marion came to Gondreville with Citizen Malin. Rumour had it that Marion was selling the estate to Malin, whom political events had well served and whom the First Consul had just promoted to the Council of State in reward for his services on 18 Brumaire. Politically-minded people in the small town of Arcis then guessed that Marion had acted on behalf of Malin and not for the Simeuses. The all-powerful Councillor of State was the most prominent person in Arcis. He had had one of his political cronies appointed Prefect in Troyes, and obtained exemption from military service for the son of one of the Gondreville farmers, one Beauvisage by name. He rendered services to everybody. In consequence this transaction was not destined to meet with opposition in the locality, where Malin reigned and still reigns supreme. The Empire was dawning. Those who today read the history of the French Revolution will never know what vast intervals popular opinion then interposed between the closely succeeding events of the time. The general craving for peace and quiet after a period of violent commotion engendered complete forgetfulness of the gravest recent occurrences. History was very promptly receding into the past since events were constantly being ripened by new and avid self-interest. Thus it was that no one except Michu looked back to the origins of the Gondreville transaction, which was regarded as a quite simple affair. Marion, who some time ago had bought Gondreville for six hundred thousand francs in *assignats*, sold it for about three million in coin; but the only sum Malin now had to disburse was the registration fee. One Grévin, who had been a crony of Malin when they were both lawyer's clerks, naturally lent a hand in this fiddling, and the Councillor of State rewarded him by getting him appointed notary at Arcis. When the news of this reached the Cinq-Cygne pavilion, brought by a farmer named Grouage whose farm lay between the forest and the park to the left of the fine avenue, Michu turned pale and left the house. He went looking for Marion and finally came upon him in one of the park lanes. 'So you are selling Gondreville?'

'Yes, Michu, yes. You'll have an influential man as your master. The Councillor of State is a friend of the First Consul. He has close connections with all the ministers and will protect your interests.'

'So you were keeping the property for him?'

'I don't say that,' Marion replied. 'At that time I didn't know how to invest my money, and for safety's sake I put it into national property. But it's not right for me to keep an estate which belonged to the family in which my father – '

'Was a servant, a steward,' Michu interjected with violence. 'But you shall not sell it. *I* want it and can pay for it.'

'You?'

'Yes. I'm quite serious and will pay you eight hundred thousand francs in solid gold – '

'Eight hundred thousand francs? How did you lay hands on them?' asked Marion.

'That's no concern of yours,' Michu replied. Then, in a milder tone, he whispered: 'My father-in-law saved many people from the scaffold!'

'You're too late, Michu, the deal is made.'

'You'll unmake it, Monsieur,' exclaimed the bailiff, taking Marion by the hand and squeezing it as in a vice. 'People hate me. I want to be rich and powerful. I must have Gondreville! Mark my words: I'm not so keen on living, and either you'll sell me the estate or I'll blow your brains out.'

'But at least I must have time to get things straight with Malin. He's an awkward customer.'

'I'll give you twenty-four hours. And if you breathe a word about this, I'd make no more bones about lopping off your head than I would about topping a turnip.'

Marion and Malin left the château during the night. Marion was alarmed and told the Councillor of State about the encounter and advised him to keep an eye on the bailiff. It was impossible for Marion to wriggle out of the obligation of handing the estate over to the man who had really put up the money for it, and Michu was not the sort of man who would either understand or accept such an argument. Moreover, the service rendered to Malin by Marion was to be, and in fact turned out to be, the starting-point in his political career and that of his brother . . . In 1806 Malin had the advocate Marion appointed First President of an Imperial court of justice, and once General Tax-Collectors were brought into existence he obtained the post of Receiver-General in the Aube department for the advocate's brother. The Councillor of State told Marion to stay in Paris and informed the Minister of Police, who put the bailiff under surveillance. All the same, so as not to push him to extremities, and perhaps to watch him more closely, Malin kept Michu on as bailiff under the control of the notary of Arcis. From then on Michu, becoming more taciturn and pensive, acquired the reputation of a man capable of some desperate deed. As Councillor of State, a function which the

First Consul then put on a par with that of a Minister, and as one of those who drafted the Civil Code, Malin was playing an important role in Paris, where he had bought one of the finest mansions in the Faubourg Saint-Germain after marrying the only daughter of Sibuelle, a rich Government contractor of dubious reputation whom he had made a partner with Marion's brother in the taxation department of the Aube. Consequently he had not visited Gondreville more than once; in any case he was relying on Grévin to deal with everything in which his interests were involved. After all, what had he, a former representative of the Aube, to fear from a former chairman of the Arcis Jacobin Club? In the meantime the already definitely unfavourable opinion of Michu held by the lower classes was naturally shared by the middle-class citizens; and Marion, Grévin and Malin, without explaining their motives or compromising themselves, singled him out as an exceedingly dangerous man. Public officials, obliged by the Minister of General Police to keep the bailiff under surveillance, did nothing to undermine this belief. Throughout the region, people were now astonished that Michu was still in his post, but they regarded this leniency as a result of the terror he inspired. Who then could fail to understand the profound melancholy in which Michu's wife was plunged?

To begin with, Marthe had been piously brought up by her mother. Both were Catholics and had suffered from the tanner's opinions and conduct. Marthe never remembered without blushing that she had been paraded round the town of Troyes dressed up as a goddess. Her father had forced her to marry Michu, whose reputation was going from bad to worse and whom she feared too much ever to be able to appraise him. Nevertheless she sensed that he loved her; deep down in his heart this terrifying man was stirred with the truest affection for her. She had never seen him do an unjust action; he never used harsh words, not to her at any rate; in short, he made every effort to anticipate all her desires. This unfortunate man, shunned by all, believing that his wife disliked him, stayed almost always out of doors. Thus Marthe and Michu lived in misunderstanding of each other, in what today is called a state of 'armed peace'. Marthe never saw anyone and suffered keenly from the reprobation which for the last seven years had fallen upon her as the daughter of a terrorist and on her husband as a traitor. More than once she had heard the people from the Bellache farm, which stood in the plain below the avenue and was tenanted by Beauvisage, a man attached to the Simeuses, say as they passed in front of the lodge: 'That's where Judas lives!' The striking resemblance between the bailiff's physiognomy and that of the thirteenth Apostle, a resemblance he seemed intent on making complete, had earned him this odious nickname throughout the district. And so Marthe's unhappiness and her vague, persistent apprehensions for the future made her pensive and withdrawn. Nothing causes deeper sadness than an unmerited fall into ill repute from which it is impossible to rise again. A painter could have made a fine picture of this family of outcasts living in one of the prettiest sites in Champagne, a country where on the whole the landscape is dreary.

'François!' the bailiff called out in order to hurry up his son.

François Michu, a boy of fourteen, enjoyed the park and the forest, on which he levied his small toll as if he owned it. He ate the fruit, went round looking for small game and knew neither grief nor care. He was the only happy member of the family, which was geographically isolated in this area between the park and the forest and morally so thanks to the general odium from which it suffered.

'Pick up all that stuff there,' said the father to the son, pointing to the parapet, 'and put it away. Look me in the face. Do you love your father and mother?' The child threw his arms round his father's neck to embrace him; but Michu turned round in order to move his carbine and thrust him back. 'Good! You have sometimes chattered about what goes on here,' he said, gazing fixedly on him with eyes as fearsome as those of a wild cat. 'Bear this well in mind: if you told Gaucher, the people from Grouage or Bellache, or even Marianne who is fond of us, about the slightest thing we do, you might cause your father's death. Don't ever do that again, and I'll forgive you for the way you blabbed yesterday.' The child began to cry. 'Don't cry. But whenever anyone asks you a question, say what the peasants say: "I don't know". There are people skulking about these parts that I don't like. Off you go! – Did you hear, you two?' Michu said to the women. 'You too must keep your mouths shut.'

'My dear, what are you going to do?'

Michu, who was carefully measuring out a charge of powder and pouring it into the muzzle of his gun, leaned his weapon against the parapet and said to Marthe: 'Nobody knows I have this carbine. Stand in front of it.'

Couraut, who had got up on his four paws, was barking furiously.

'What a fine, intelligent animal!' Michu exclaimed. 'I'm sure there are spies about.'

One can sense the presence of spies. Couraut and Michu seemed to think and feel alike and lived together like an Arab and his steed in the desert. The bailiff recognized every modulation in Couraut's growl and every idea it expressed, just as the dog read his master's thought in his eyes and scented it in the exhalations of his body.

'What do you make of those people?' Michu asked his wife in a whisper as he pointed to two sinister-looking persons who came into view in a side-lane as they approached the clearing.

'What's happening round here? Are they people from Paris?' the old woman asked.

'Ah! Maybe they are,' cried Michu. 'Hide my carbine,' he whispered to his wife. 'They're coming this way.'

*

The two Parisians coming across the clearing presented figures which painters would certainly look on as types. One of them, who apparently played second fiddle to the other, was wearing fairly short top-boots which showed that he had meagre calves, and shadowed silk stockings of doubtful cleanliness. His apricot-coloured corduroy breeches with metal buttons were a little too wide. They were of a loose fit, and the fall of their well-worn creases indicated that their owner was a man of sedentary occupation. His ribbed cotton waistcoat with its showy embroidery, gaping open, buttoned only at the top of his stomach, gave this character an appearance of slovenliness enhanced by the way his black hair with its corkscrew curls concealed his forehead and fell along his cheeks. Two steel watch-chains hung down over his breeches. His shirt was adorned with a blue and white cameo breast-pin. His coat of cinnamon colour was of the kind that appeals to caricaturists because its long tail, viewed from the back, was so exactly like a codstail that it went by that name: a fashion which lasted for ten years, almost as long as Napoleon's Empire. This individual's loose neckcloth with its multiple folds enabled him to bury his face in it right up to his nose. Many details which might have passed for grotesque – a spotty complexion, a long, thick, brick-red nose, flushed cheek-bones, a mouth with few teeth, but menacing and greedy, ears decked with large gold ear-rings, a low forehead – drew a terrifying quality from two close-set pig-like eyes aglint with implacable avidity and a bantering, almost jovial cruelty. They were prying and perspicacious, of a frigid, frosty blue, and might have served as a model for the famous Eye adopted as a fearsome police emblem during the Revolution. He wore black silk gloves and carried a cane. He evidently had some official status, for one discerned in his bearing and his way of taking snuff from his snuff-box and thrusting it up his nostrils the bureaucratic self-importance of a man of secondary rank, but one who is drawing a State salary and on whom orders from above confer temporary omnipotence.

The other person, whose costume was in the same taste but elegant and worn with a swagger, was well-groomed down to the slightest detail. His Souvorov boots, pulled on over close-fitting trousers, creaked as he walked along. He wore a spencer over his coat – an aristocratic fashion which had been adopted by members of the Clichy Club[2] and the gilded youth of the period and was destined to outlive both Club and gilded youth, for in those times certain modes lasted longer than political parties: a symptom of the anarchy which we have seen recurring in 1830. This perfect dandy appeared to be about thirty. There was a smack of good breeding in his manners and he wore expensive jewelry. His shirt-collar reached the top of his ears. His foppish and almost impertinent demeanour suggested a hidden sense of superiority; his pallid face seemed to be

2. A more or less royalist club founded in Directory times.

drained of blood; his sharp, turned-up nose gave him the appearance of a death's-head and his green eyes were inscrutable: the look they gave was as uncommunicative as his thin, pinched mouth undoubtedly was. The first of the two men looked quite amiable in comparison with this lean, desiccated young man, who was thrashing the air with a Malacca cane whose gold pommel was gleaming in the sunlight. The first man might well cut off somebody's head, but the second was capable of entangling innocence, beauty and virtue in a net of calumny and intrigue, of cold-bloodedly drowning or poisoning them. The ruddy-faced man would have consoled his victim with buffoonery, the other would not even have let himself smile. The first was forty-five, and obviously loved good cheer and women. Men of this sort are the slaves of passion, and that makes them slaves to their calling. But the younger man had neither passions nor vices. He was a spy, but at the diplomatic level: a votary of art for art's sake. He conceived, the other executed; he was the idea, the other its embodiment.

'Are we at Gondreville, my good woman?' the young man asked.

'We don't say "my good woman" round here,' Michu replied. 'We are still simple enough folk to call one another "citizen" and "citizeness"!'

'Indeed?' said the young man, quite at ease and seemingly unperturbed.

Gamblers, especially at écarté, have often felt as it were inwardly demoralized on seeing, when the cards are going their way, another gambler settle down at the gaming-table – one whose manners, look, tone of voice and mode of shuffling the cards predict defeat for them. At the sight of this young man Michu experienced a nervous collapse of this prophetic kind. He was seized with a mortal presentiment and he caught a confused foreglimpse of the scaffold. A voice cried out to him that this fop would bring doom upon him, even though as yet they had had no dealings with one another. That was why he had been gruff of speech: he intended to be rude and he was rude.

'Aren't you Councillor Malin's man?' the second Parisian asked.

'I am my own master,' answered Michu.

'Well now, ladies,' said the young man with a great show of politeness. 'Are we at Gondreville? Monsieur Malin is waiting for us there.'

'There's the park,' said Michu, pointing to the open gateway.

'And why are you hiding that carbine, my beautiful child?' asked the young man's jovial companion, having spotted the muzzle of it as he passed through the gate.

'Always on the job! Even in the country!' the young man exclaimed with a smile.

Both of them came back, for a suspicion had taken hold of them which the bailiff understood in spite of their expressionless faces. Marthe let them look at the carbine while Couraut went barking round their legs, for she was convinced that Michu was planning some desperate deed: she was almost glad that the strangers had been so observant. Michu cast a look at his wife which made her tremble. Then he took up the carbine and set about ramming a bullet into it, accepting the fatal hazard of this discovery and this encounter. He seemed no longer to value his life, and at that moment his wife well understood his baleful resolution.

'So you have wolves around here?' the young man said to Michu.

'Where there are sheep there are always wolves. You're in Champagne, and yonder there's a forest. But we have wild boars too. We have animals both small and large. We have pretty nearly everything,' said Michu with a mocking air.

'I bet you, Corentin,' said the elder of the two men after exchanging a glance with the other, 'that this is my friend Michu.'

'Friend? You and I have never kept pigs together,' said the bailiff.

'No, but we've both sat in the chair at Jacobin meetings, citizen,' the old cynic retorted. 'You at Arcis, and I elsewhere. You still have the polite manners of a *sans-culotte*. But that's gone out of fashion, young man.'

'The park seems to be a big one; we might get lost. If you are the bailiff, get someone to show us the way to the château,' said Corentin in a peremptory tone.

Michu whistled for his son and continued to ram his bullet home. Corentin was gazing at Marthe with an indifferent eye, whereas his companion seemed charmed by her beauty; but the former discerned in her traces of anguish which escaped the notice of the elderly rake whom the sight of the carbine had startled. This significant trifle gave a complete picture of the difference between these two characters.

'I have to meet someone on the other side of the forest,' said the bailiff, 'and cannot do you this service myself. But my son will take you to the château. By what route did you come to Gondreville? Did you pass through Cinq-Cygne?'

'Like you, we had business in the forest,' said Corentin, without any visible irony.

'François,' cried Michu. 'Take these gentlemen to the château along the bypaths so that they won't be seen. They don't take the beaten tracks. But first come here!' he said as he saw that the two strangers had turned their backs on him and were walking along talking quietly together. Michu took hold of his child, embraced him with almost religious fervour and an expression on his face which confirmed his wife's apprehensions. A chill ran down her spine and she looked at her mother with dry eyes, for she was unable to weep. 'Off you go!' said Michu. And he followed him with his eyes until he was quite out of sight. Couraut barked, with his muzzle pointing towards the Grouage farm. 'Oh, it's Violette,' Michu went on. 'This is the third time he's been along this way today. What's in the air? Lie down, Couraut!'

A few instants later a horse's slow trot could be heard.

Violette, on one of the nags used by farmers in the regions around Paris, brought into view, under a round, broad-brimmed hat, his nut-brown face, so deeply puckered that it seemed browner still. His grey eyes, bright and sprightly, gave no inkling of his treacherous character. His spindly legs, cased in white duck gaiters reaching to the knees, hung down stirrup-less, and his balance seemed to be maintained by the weight of his stout hob-nailed shoes. Over his blue cloth jacket he wore a rough woollen cloak in black and white stripes. His frizzy grey hair fell back behind his head. Everything about him – the clothes he wore, his grey horse with its short little legs, his way of sitting it with his belly forward and the upper part of his body leaning backwards, his big, chapped, grimy hand holding a mean, worn-out and tattered bridle – depicted a grasping and ambitious peasant, greedy for land and buying it at whatever cost. His blue-lipped mouth, cleft as if some surgeon had slashed it with a lancet, and the countless wrinkles on his face and forehead prevented his features from showing any play, so that they were expressive only in their general effect. These harsh, rigid traits gave a menacing impression, despite his humble mien – one which practically all country people assume in order to conceal their emotions and calculations, just as orientals and Red Indians hide theirs behind a mask of imperturbable gravity. He had begun as a simple day-labourer, then he became the farmer of Grouage by following a policy of increasing malevolence, and he kept this up after acquiring a position which went beyond his early ambitions. He bore hearty ill-will to his neighbours and was always delighted to do them harm. He was undisguisedly envious, but in all his spiteful deeds he remained within the bounds of legality, very much like opposition parties in Parliament. He believed that his own prosperity depended on other people's ruin, and regarded everyone above him as an enemy to be dealt with by fair means or foul. This is a very common characteristic among peasants. His great concern at the moment was to obtain from Malin an extension of the lease of his farm, which had only six years to run. Jealous of Michu's prosperity, he was watching him closely. The country people around were at odds with him for keeping in touch with the Michus, but he did this in the hope of getting his lease renewed for another twelve years, for this cunning farmer was looking for an opportunity to render service to the Government or Malin, who mistrusted Michu. With the help of the Gondreville under-bailiff, the rural policeman and a few faggot-cutters, Violette kept the police superintendant at Arcis informed about Michu's slightest activities. This official had tried, though in vain, to persuade Marianne, Michu's servant-girl, to work with the authorities; but Violette and his spies drew all their information from Gaucher, the young farm-hand on whose loyalty Michu counted but who betrayed him for trifling rewards – waistcoats, buckles, cotton stockings and gifts of sweets. For that matter, the lad had no idea of the importance of his pratlings. Violette blackened all Michu's deeds and invented the most absurd suppositions to give them a criminal twist. The bailiff was ignorant of this; nevertheless he was aware of the odious part Violette was playing when he came to the house, and took pleasure in fooling him.

'You must have lots to do at Bellache,' said Michu, 'since you've come this way again!'

'Again! That's a nasty thing to say, Monsieur Michu.' Then he pointed to the gun. 'You're not reckoning on whistling at sparrows with a clarinet like that! I didn't know you had a carbine . . . '

'It came from one of my fields where carbines do well,' Michu replied. 'Look! This is how I plant them.'

The bailiff took aim at a viper's bugloss and cut it clean off at the stalk.

'Do you keep this bandit's weapon to protect your master? Perhaps he made you a present of it.'

'He came straight from Paris to bring it to me,' Michu replied.

'The fact is that there's a good deal of talk going on round these parts about his visit here. Some say he's in disgrace and wants to retire; others say he wants to clear things up here. Why indeed does he come here without a word of warning, just like the First Consul? Did you know he was coming?'

'I'm not on good enough terms with him to be told what he's doing.'

'So you haven't seen him yet?'

'I didn't know he was here until I'd done my round in the forest,' Michu rejoindered as he reloaded his carbine.

'He has sent to Arcis for Monsieur Grévin. They must want to put their heads together over something.'

'If you're making for Cinq-Cygne,' the bailiff said to Violette, 'take me with you. I'm going there.'

Violette was too apprehensive to have a man of Michu's strength behind him on horseback; he galloped off.

'What's wrong with Michu?' Marthe asked her mother.

'Since he heard of Malin's arrival he's been in a very black mood,' she replied. 'But it's getting damp. Let's go in.'

When the two women had sat down in front of the fire, they heard Couraut barking. Michu was in fact coming upstairs. His wife anxiously followed him into their bedroom.

'Make sure there's no one about,' he said in a troubled tone of voice to Marthe.

'There's nobody,' she answered. 'Marianne is in the fields with the cow, and Gaucher . . .'

'Where *is* Gaucher?'

'I don't know.'

'I distrust that little rascal. Go and search the attic and look for him in every corner of the house.'

Marthe did as she was told. When she came back she found Michu on his knees in prayer.

'What's the matter?' she asked in alarm.

The bailiff put his arm round his wife's waist, drew her to him, kissed her forehead and answered in a moved tone of voice: 'If we never see each other again, remember, my dear wife, that I loved you very much. Follow in every detail the instructions which are written in a letter buried at the foot of the larch in that clump of trees,' he added after a pause, pointing to the tree in question. 'It's in a metal tube. Don't touch it until after my death. In any case, whatever happens, just believe that in spite of the injustice of men my hand has served the justice of God.'

Marthe turned gradually paler and paler until she became as white as a sheet. She gazed steadily at her husband with eyes which were wide open with fright. She tried to speak, but her throat was parched. Michu slipped away like a shadow. He had tied Couraut to the foot of the bed, and the animal began to howl as dogs do when they are in distress.

*

Michu had grave reasons for being angry with Monsieur Marion; but his anger had turned against the man who in his view was much more of a criminal, namely Malin, whose secret plans had become clear to him, since he was in a better position than anyone to understand what the Councillor of

State was about. So far as politics were concerned Michu's father-in-law had had the confidence of Malin once the latter had been chosen to represent the Aube department on the National Convention, thanks to the support Grévin gave him.

It would perhaps be pertinent to relate the circumstances which had brought the Simeuses and the Cinq-Cygnes into contact with Malin, for they were to bear on the destiny of the twins and Mademoiselle de Cinq-Cygne, and still more on that of Marthe and Michu. The Cinq-Cygne mansion in Troyes stood opposite that of the Simeuses. When the populace, unleashed by skilful but cautious intriguers, had pillaged the Simeuse mansion, laid hands on the Marquis and Marquise, who were accused of corresponding with the enemy, and delivered them to the national guards who haled them off to prison, the crowd quite logically shouted: 'Now for the Cinq-Cygnes!' It could not conceive that the Cinq-Cygnes might not be guilty of the same crime. The worthy and courageous Marquis de Simeuse, in order to save his two eighteen-year-old sons, whose bravery might well land them into trouble, had put their aunt, the Comtesse de Cinq-Cygne, in charge of them shortly before the storm broke. Two servants attached to the Simeuse family kept the young men indoors. The old man did not want his name to die out, so he had recommended that his sons should be kept in ignorance in case the worst happened. Laurence, a girl of twelve, was loved in equal measure by the two brothers, and she loved them equally in return. As with many twins, the two Simeuses were so like each other that for a long time their mother gave them clothes of different colours in order to distinguish them. The first one to be delivered was called Paul-Marie, the other Marie-Paul. Laurence de Cinq-Cygne had been told how the situation stood, and she played her feminine part very well: she coaxed and wheedled her cousins and kept them with her until the moment the mob was encircling the Cinq-Cygne mansion. The two brothers simultaneously realized the danger they were in and with one look at each other came to an immediate decision. They armed their two servants and the Cinq-Cygne servants barricaded the door, closed the shutters and posted themselves at the windows with the five men-servants and the

Abbé d'Hauteserre, a relation of the Cinq-Cygnes. These eight valiant defenders directed a terrible fire at the mob. Every shot killed or wounded one of the assailants. Laurence, instead of wringing her hands, loaded the rifles with extraordinary coolness and handed bullets and powder to those whose ammunition was spent. The Comtesse de Cinq-Cygne had fallen on her knees. 'What are you doing, Mother?' asked Laurence. 'I am praying,' she replied, 'both for them and for you!' A sublime remark, made also by the mother of the Principe de la Paz in Spain on a similar occasion. In no time eleven people were killed; dead and wounded lay mingled together. Events of this kind either cool a mob down or inflame it; it either becomes exasperated or gives up. Those in the forefront were terror-stricken and surged back, but the main body, those who had come to kill, rob and murder, when they saw the corpses, shouted: 'Assassins! Murderers!' The more cautious ones went to find the people's representative on the National Convention. The two brothers, now informed about the dreadful events of the day, suspected that this representative, Malin, was out to destroy their family, and this suspicion soon became a conviction. In a vengeful state of mind, they posted themselves at the street door with their rifles loaded in order to kill Malin immediately he came in sight. The countess was beside herself. She could see her house being burnt to ashes and her daughter assassinated, and blamed her kinsfolk for this heroic defence, which the whole of France talked about for a week. At Malin's summons, Laurence half opened the door; seeing her, the people's representative put his faith in his own redoubtable reputation and the girl's frailty, and came in. 'What, Monsieur,' she replied to the first word he spoke as he asked why they were putting up such resistance, 'you want France to be free and yet you don't protect people in their houses! The mob is out to demolish our house and murder us, and we haven't the right to meet violence with violence!'

Malin stood stock-still.

'You, the grandson of a mason the Great Marquis employed for the building of his château,' Marie-Paul said to him, 'have given ear to slanders against our father and let him be dragged off to prison!'

'He shall be set at liberty,' said Malin, thinking his end had come as he saw each of the young men clutching his rifle.

'Your life depends on this promise,' Marie-Paul said in solemn tones. 'But if you don't keep it by this evening we shall be able to find you again!'

'As for this howling mob,' said Laurence, 'if you don't send it away, the first shot will be for you. Now, Monsieur Malin, out you go!'

The member of the Convention went out and harangued the multitude, talking of the sacred rights of the home, the *habeas corpus* and the inviolability of domiciles in England. He said that the Law and the People were sovereign, that the Law was the people, that the people ought to act only through the Law, and that the Law would prevail. Necessity gave him eloquence and the gathering dispersed. But he never forgot either the contemptuous look the two brothers gave him, or Mademoiselle de Cinq-Cygne's 'Out you go!' Therefore, when the question arose of selling the estates of the Comte de Cinq-Cygne, Laurence's brother, as national property, the partition was carried out according to the letter of the law. The official appraisers only left Laurence the château, the park, the gardens and the farm which went by the name of Cinq-Cygne. According to Malin's statement of the case, Laurence was only entitled to her legal portion, the Nation standing in the stead of the *émigré*, the more so since he was bearing arms against the Republic.

On the evening of this angry tumult, Laurence, fearing that they might be betrayed and entrapped by the people's representative, entreated her cousins to depart so pressingly that they leapt on their horses and made straight for the outposts of the Prussian army. At the very moment when the two brothers reached the forest of Gondreville, the Cinq-Cygne mansion was surrounded. The people's representative came in person with armed men to arrest the heirs of the house of Simeuse. He did not dare to lay hands on the Comtesse de Cinq-Cygne, then in bed with a horrible nervous fever, or on the twelve-year-old Laurence. The servants, in fear of harsh treatment from the Republic, had disappeared. The next morning the news of the resistance offered by the two brothers and their reported flight to Prussia spread through the neighbourhood; three thousand people assembled round the Cinq-Cygne mansion and it was demolished with astonishing rapidity. Madame de Cinq-Cygne had been removed to the Simeuse house, and she died there of an intensified attack of fever. It was only after these events that Michu appeared on the political stage, for the Marquis and his wife remained in prison for about five months. In the meantime the representative for the Aube was sent on a mission. But when Marion sold Gondreville to Malin, now that everybody in the vicinity had forgotten the havoc wrought by the seething mob, Michu saw through Malin completely – or at least thought he did, for Malin, like Fouché, was a man of many facets, with much depth behind each of them. Such men are inscrutable while they are playing their hands and can only be fathomed long after the game is over.

At all the turning-points of his career, Malin never failed to consult his faithful friend, Grévin the notary, one who looked at men and things in perspective, so that the judgements he formed were sharp, clear and precise. To make a habit of this is prudence itself, and second-rate men draw their strength from it. Now in November 1803 the combination of circumstances was so critical for the man who was now Councillor of State that an exchange of letters between the two friends might have been compromising for both. Malin was about to become a senator and was afraid of talking things over in Paris. So he left the capital and came to Gondreville, giving the First Consul only one of his reasons for wishing to go there – one which made him appear to be full of zeal in Bonaparte's eyes, whereas in reality he was only concerned with his own interests and not those of the State. And so, while Michu was stalking him in the park and waiting, like a Red Indian, for an opportunity to take vengeance on him, the wary Malin, accustomed to exploiting events for his own advantage, was taking his friend to a small meadow in the 'English garden', a secluded spot, ideal for a secret conference. There, standing in the middle of this meadow and keeping their voices low, the two friends were too isolated to be overheard, and could switch the subject of their conversation if any eavesdropper came along.

'Why didn't we meet inside the château?' asked Grévin.

'Haven't you seen the two men sent me by the Prefect of Police?'

Although Fouché, when dealing with the conspiracy of Pichegru, Georges Cadoudal, Moreau and Polignac, was the moving spirit in the First Consul's cabinet, he was not yet Minister of Police: he was then only a Councillor of State like Malin.

'These two men are Fouché's right and left arm. One of them, the dandified young fellow with a face as sour as a lemon, vinegar on his lips and verjuice in his eyes, only needed a fortnight to wreck the 1799 insurrection in Western France. The other was trained by Lenoir, the Lieutenant General of Police, and is the only man well versed in traditional police methods. I had asked for an unimportant agent and a police official to support him, and I've been landed with these two characters. Obviously, Grévin, Fouché wants to see what cards I hold. That's why I have left the two of them at dinner in the château. Let them do their ferreting; they won't find any trace of my dealings with Louis XVIII.'

'Come now,' said Grévin, 'what are you up to?'

'Well, my friend, double-dealing is very dangerous. But as far as Fouché is concerned it's triple-dealing, and he has perhaps some scent of my secret understanding with the Bourbons.'

'What? You?'

'Yes, I,' Malin rejoindered.

'Have you forgotten what happened to Favras?'[3]

This question made some impression on the Councillor.

'How long have you been doing this?' Grévin asked after a pause.

'Since Napoleon became Consul for life.'

'Is there any evidence against you?'

'Not so much as that!' said Malin, snapping his fingers.

Then, briefly, Malin gave a clear picture of the critical position in which Bonaparte was putting England by the

3. A nobleman hanged in 1790 for trying to rescue the imprisoned Louis XVI.

deadly menace of the Boulogne camp, and showed Grévin the purport, unknown to France and Europe, of this project of invasion. Then he unfolded the critical position in which England was about to put Bonaparte: an impressive coalition, Prussia, Austria and Russia, subsidized with English gold, was to launch an army of seven hundred thousand men. At the same time a formidable conspiracy was casting a wide net inside France. Montagnards, Breton rebels, Royalists and their princes alike were taking part in it.

Malin continued: 'So long as Louis XVIII saw three Consuls in power, he believed that anarchy would continue and that some rising or other would enable him to take his revenge for 13 Vendémiaire and 18 Fructidor. But now that Bonaparte is Consul for life his designs are unmasked: he will soon proclaim himself Emperor. The former second lieutenant wants to found a dynasty! Now therefore they are planning to kill him, and the plot against him is being more skilfully hatched than that of the rue Saint-Nicaise. Pichegru, Georges Cadoudal, the Duc d'Enghien, Polignac and Rivière, the Comte d'Anjou's two friends, are in it.'

'A mixed bag!' Grévin exclaimed.

'France is being silently invaded. There will be a general upheaval: no holds will be barred. A hundred determined men, with Georges at their head, are to make a bodily attack on the Consular Guard and the Consul himself.'

'Very good. Inform against them.'

'For the last two months the Consul, his Minister of Police, the Prefect and Fouché have had some of the threads of this vast conspiracy in their hands. But they don't know how widespread it is, and at present they are leaving almost all the conspirators at liberty in order to get full knowledge.'

'Legally speaking,' said the notary, 'the Bourbons have a much greater right to plan, conduct and carry through an attempt against Bonaparte than Bonaparte had to conspire on 18 Brumaire against the Republic which had brought him into being. He was assassinating his mother, and all these people merely want to get their homes back. I can well see that when our erstwhile princes saw the list of *émigrés* being closed, the names of the proscribed being crossed off, the

Catholic religion being re-established and counter-revolutionary decrees being multiplied, they realized that Bonaparte was making it difficult if not impossible for them to return to France. He is now the only obstacle to their re-establishment: they want to remove that obstacle – naturally enough. If the conspirators are defeated, they will be treated as brigands. If they win, they will be heroes. So I can understand your hesitation.'

'This is the question,' said Malin. 'Either we make Bonaparte toss the Duc d'Enghien's head at the Bourbons in the same way as the National Convention tossed the head of Louis XVI at the reigning monarchs, in order to involve him as deeply as we are ourselves in the continuance of the Revolution. Or we overturn the present idol of the French people and its future Emperor, and set up the legitimate throne on the ruins. I'm at the mercy of events: a well-aimed pistol-shot, or an infernal machine like that of the rue Saint-Nicaise. But this time it must be successful. I'm not entirely in the know. It has been proposed that I should assemble the Council of State at the critical moment and direct legal procedure for the restoration of the Bourbons.'

'Better wait,' the notary replied.

'But I can't! I have to decide straight away.'

'Why?'

'The two Simeuses are in the conspiracy and are already in France. I must either have them hounded down, let them compromise themselves and get rid of them, or support them in secret. I had asked the Prefect for underlings, and he has sent me first-class bloodhounds who have enlisted the support of the Troyes gendarmerie.'

Grévin gave his reply: 'Gondreville is the *bird in hand* and the conspiracy is the *bird in the bush*. Neither Fouché nor Talleyrand, your two partners, are in it. Play straight with them. Just think. All the men who voted for Louis XVI's execution are in the Government. France is full of people who have bought the confiscated estates, and you want to bring back the men who will claim Gondreville back from you! Unless they're imbeciles, the Bourbons are sure to wipe out everything we've done. Warn Bonaparte.'

'A man of my status can't be an informer,' Malin sharply retorted.

'Your status?' said Grévin with a smile.

'They are offering me the Great Seal.'

'I can understand you being dazzled, but it's my business to see through the political fog and find a way out for you. I can see no possibility of the Bourbons coming back when a man like General Bonaparte has eighty warships and four hundred thousand troops. The most difficult thing in a game of political "wait-and-see" is to know when a tottering power is about to fall. But, my friend, Bonaparte's power is in the ascendant. Might it not be that Fouché is having you sounded so as to find out what's at the back of your mind and get rid of you?'

'No, I have Talleyrand on my side. Besides, Fouché wouldn't have given the job to two jokers like that. I know them too well not to smell a rat.'

'They alarm me,' said Grévin. 'If Fouché doesn't distrust you and isn't trying you out, why did he send them? He doesn't play tricks like that just for the fun of it ...'

'This is the decisive factor,' Malin exclaimed: 'I shall never have any peace of mind while the two Simeuses are about. Perhaps Fouché, who knows how I stand with them, intends to lay hands on them and reach the Condés through them.'

'Anyway, my friend, the owner of Gondreville needn't be afraid of dispossession while Bonaparte is in power.'

Malin raised his eyes and caught sight of a rifle muzzle through the foliage of a big lime-tree.

'I wasn't mistaken, I had heard the click of a rifle being cocked,' he said to Grévin after taking cover behind a big tree-trunk, where the notary joined him, disturbed by his friend's sudden movement.

'It's Michu,' said Grévin. 'I can see his red beard.'

'Don't let's look as if we were afraid,' Malin went on, slowly moving away and saying several times: 'What is the grudge this man bears against the purchasers of Gondreville? He surely wasn't aiming at you. If he overheard us, I must certainly take drastic steps against him. We ought to have had our talk in more open country. But who on earth would have thought we were running any risk in the open air?'

'One lives and learns!' said the notary. 'But he was a fair distance away and we were talking almost in a whisper.'

'I shall have a word with Corentin about this,' Malin replied.

*

A few minutes later, Michu returned home, with pale and drawn face.

'What's the matter?' his wife asked in great alarm.

'Nothing,' he replied, thunderstruck at seeing that Violette was there.

Michu took a chair, sat down calmly in front of the fire and threw a letter into it which he drew from a metal cylinder of the sort given to soldiers to keep their papers in. This action, which enabled Marthe to breathe again like a person with an enormous weight off her mind, puzzled Violette greatly. The bailiff placed his carbine on the mantelpiece with admirable coolness. Marianne and Marthe's mother were spinning in the lamplight.

'Come on, François,' said the father. 'Time for bed, off you go!'

Roughly, he seized his son round the waist and took him off. 'Go down to the cellar,' he whispered once they were on the stairs. 'Get two bottles of Mâcon, pour a third of each away and fill them up with the brandy which is on the bottle-rack. Then mix one bottle of white wine with brandy half and half. Be careful how you do it and put the three bottles on the empty cask just inside the cellar. When I open the window, leave the cellar, saddle my horse, get on it and wait for me at the Poteau-des-Gueux.'

'The little scamp never wants to go to bed,' said the bailiff as he came in again. 'He wants to do what grown-ups do – see, hear and know everything. You are spoiling my family for me, Violette.'

'God save us! God save us!' cried Violette. 'What has loosened your tongue? You've never spoken so many words before!'

'Do you suppose I let people spy on me without noticing it? You're on the wrong side of the fence, Papa Violette. If you stood by me instead of serving those who are out for my skin, I'd do more for you than renewing your lease.'

'What more would you do?' asked the greedy peasant with round open eyes.

'I'd sell you my property cheap.'

'Nothing's cheap when it has to be paid for,' said Violette sententiously.

'I'm leaving the district, and I'll let you have my Mousseau farm, buildings, seed and cattle for fifty thousand francs.'

'You mean that?'

'Would that suit you?'

'Well, that depends.'

'Let's talk it over . . . But I want something in advance.'

'I've got nothing.'

'All I want is one word.'

'What word?'

'Tell me who sent you here.'

'I was coming back from where I went just now. I only wanted to say good evening.'

'You came back without your horse. What sort of a fool do you take me for? You're lying, you won't get my farm.'

'All right, it was Monsieur Grévin, so there! He said: "Violette, we need Michu, go and look for him. If he's not there, wait for him." I could see I had to spend the evening here.'

'Were those blackguards from Paris still at the château?'

'That I don't really know; but there were people in the salon.'

'You will get my farm. Let's settle the terms. Wife, go and get some wine for the contract. Bring the best Roussillon wine, the ex-marquis's wine . . . Our heads can stand it. You'll find two bottles on the empty cask just inside the cellar and a bottle of white wine.'

'That's fine!' said Violette, who had a hard head. 'Let's drink.'

'You have fifty thousand francs under your bedroom floor, right underneath your bed: you can pay them over to me a fortnight after the contract is signed in Grévin's office . . . ' Violette looked hard at Michu and turned pale. 'Ah! You come sneaking round a hardened Jacobin who had the honour of presiding over the Arcis club, and you think you can get past him? I have eyes. I noticed that the tiles had been set in with fresh mortar, and I reckoned you hadn't prised them up to sow wheat under them. Drink up.'

In his confusion Violette gulped down a large glass of wine without noticing how strong it was. Terror, so to speak, had thrust a red-hot poker into his stomach and avarice had burnt up the brandy. He would have given a lot to be back at home to put his hoard in a fresh hiding-place. The three women were smiling.

'That suit you?' said Michu to Violette, refilling his glass.

'Of course.'

'You'll be quite at home there, you old scoundrel.'

After half an hour's animated discussion over the date of completion and the innumerable captious objections usual with peasants striking a bargain, punctuated with asseverations, copious draughts, wordy promises, protestations and exclamations – 'Not really?' – 'Yes, really!' – 'I give you my word!' – 'Just as I say!' – 'Cut my throat if I . . . ' – 'Let this wine poison me if I'm not speaking gospel truth!' etc. – Violette fell forward with his head on the table, not merely tipsy but dead-drunk. As soon as Michu saw that his eyes were blurred, he rushed to the window and opened it.

'Where's that rascal Gaucher?' he asked his wife.

'In bed.'

'You, Marianne,' the bailiff said to his faithful servant, 'post yourself outside his bedroom door and keep watch on him. – You, Mother, stay downstairs, keep guard on that spy; be alert and only open the door when you hear François's voice. – It's a matter of life and death,' he added. 'As far as everyone under my roof is concerned, I have not left it this night, and you will stick to this story even with your heads on the block. – Come,' he said to his wife, 'come, my girl. Put on your shoes and bonnet and let's be off! No questions. I'm coming with you.'

For the last three quarters of an hour, this man, by his gestures and looks, had wielded despotic, irresistible authority, drawn from the same secret spring whence all exceptional people draw their exceptional power: great generals spurring masses of troops to action on the battlefield, great orators carrying assemblies off their feet and – let us say this too! – great criminals bringing off their audacious *coups*. On such occasions it seems as if some compelling influence is emitted from the brain and conveyed in the words uttered, and that a man's will-power is pumped into others by his very gestures. The three women knew that a terrible crisis had arisen; they had not been warned of it, but it was strongly borne in on them by the speed of this man's actions: his face shone, his brow was eloquent with unspoken thoughts, his eyes were glittering like stars. They had noticed the sweat at the roots of his hair, and more than once his voice had trembled with rage and impatience. And so Marthe gave him passive obedience. Armed to the teeth, rifle on shoulder, Michu dashed into the avenue with his wife following him, and they swiftly reached the crossroad where François was hiding in the bushes.

'The lad has his wits about him,' said Michu when he spotted him. It was the first time he had spoken, for so far he and his wife had hurried along without being able to utter a word.

'Go back to the pavilion, hide in the leafiest tree, and keep an eye on the fields and the park,' he said to his son. 'Remember this: we are all in bed. We're letting nobody in. Your grandmother's on the watch and won't stir until she hears your voice. The police must never know we have spent the night out.' On hearing these whispered instructions François slipped through the woods like an eel into the mud. Michu said to his wife: 'Get behind me on the horse and pray that God may be on our side. Hold steady. We may ride the horse to death.'

No sooner were these words uttered than the horse, whom Michu gave a couple of prods in the flanks and who was squeezed hard between Michu's strong knees, shot off with the speed of a thoroughbred. It was as if he understood his master's intentions, and they crossed the forest in a quarter of an hour. Michu had taken the shortest cut, and they were now on the edge of the wood from which the moonlit roofs of the Cinq-Cygne château were visible. He tethered the horse to a tree and leapt up the hillock which looked out over the Cinq-Cygne valley.

The château which Marthe and Michu gazed at together for a moment is a charming feature in the landscape. It has no great dimensional or architectural importance, yet it is not without archaeological interest. It is an ancient fifteenth-century edifice, perched on a height, surrounded by deep, wide and still full moats, built of pebble and mortar, but with walls seven feet thick. In its simplicity of structure it admirably recalls the rude and warlike existence of feudal times. Quite primitive in style, it consists of two huge towers of reddish hue, connected by a long main building with mullioned windows, whose cross-bars are crudely fashioned to resemble vine-shoots. The staircase stands outside in the middle, and is set in a pentagonal tower with a little Gothic door. Over the ground floor, modernized during the reign of Louis XIV, and the first storey, is an extensive roofage broken by casements with carved tympana. An immense lawn, recently denuded of trees, stretches in front of the château. On each side of the bridge over the moat are two ramshackle buildings which house the gardeners; a meagre, nondescript, obviously modern railing bars them from the drive. To the right and left of the lawn intersected by the paved drive run the stables, byres, barns, woodshed, bakery, henhouses, and also the offices and outbuildings no doubt cut out of the remains of two wings similar to the present château. It must formerly have been a square-based castle fortified at its four quoins, defended by an enormous tower with an arched porch, at the foot of which was a drawbridge where the gateway now is. The two sturdy towers with their pepperpots still intact, and the bell-turret in the middle, gave character to the village of Cinq-Cygne. Nearby, a church of the same period displayed its pointed steeple, which was in keeping with the massive blocks of this stronghold. All its crests and cones were resplendent in the moonlight which was playing and sparkling around them.

Michu gazed at this seignorial residence in such a way as to upset all his wife's previous ideas, for his face, now calmer, showed an expression of hope and a kind of pride. He scanned the horizon with a certain wariness and listened for noises in the country around. It must have been about nine o'clock.

Moonlight was streaming over the edge of the forest, and the hillock itself was flooded with light. He felt that he was in a dangerous position, and climbed down as if he were afraid he might be seen. And yet no suspicious sounds were disturbing the peace of this lovely valley girded about on this side by the forest of Nodesme. As for Marthe, exhausted and trembling, she was expecting something dramatic to happen after their headlong course. What was it to lead to? A good deed or a crime? Just then Michu whispered in his wife's ear:

'You'll go to the Comtesse de Cinq-Cygne and ask to speak to her. When you see her, you'll beg her to step aside with you. If there's no one listening you'll say: "Mademoiselle, your two cousins are in danger of their lives, and the man who will explain why and how is waiting for you." If she's frightened or mistrustful, add this: "They are conspiring against the First Consul and the conspiracy has been discovered." Don't tell her who you are – they are too suspicious of us.'

Marthe Michu looked up at her husband and said, 'So you are in their service?'

'Well, what of that?' he asked, knitting his brows and thinking he was being blamed.

'You don't understand me,' cried Marthe, taking hold of Michu's broad hand, falling on her knees before him and kissing it until it became wet with her tears.

'Run along; you can cry afterwards,' he said, giving her a sudden and rough embrace.

When the sound of his wife's footsteps had died away, this man of iron had tears in his eyes. He had distrusted Marthe because of her father's opinions and had concealed his secret from her. But he had suddenly come to realize the beauty and simplicity of his wife's character, just as the grandeur of his own had suddenly become apparent to her. Marthe was passing from the profound humiliation caused by the abasement of a man whose name she bore to the rapture which came from knowing how splendid he was. There had been no transition between these two states of mind: no wonder she was in a daze! A prey to the deepest anxiety, she had felt, as she told him later, as if she were walking through pools of blood from the pavilion to the château, and then, in a twinkling, she had felt herself caught up to heaven with angels all around her. Likewise, in an instant, Michu, who had felt he was unappreciated, who had taken his wife's grief-stricken and melancholy attitude to mean a lack of affection, who had left her to herself and lived out in the open air, showering all his tenderness on his son, had realized what his wife's tears stood for: she was bitterly regretting the part that her beauty and her father's will had forced her to play. So, like a flash of lightning in the midst of the storm, effulgent happiness had descended on them. And it was to be as brief as a flash of lightning! Each of them pondered over the ten years of misunderstanding between them, and each accepted the blame for it. Michu stood there, motionless, his elbow leaning on his carbine and his chin on his elbow, lost in deep reverie. A moment like that compensates for all past suffering, however painful.

Her mind in a turmoil with similar thoughts, Marthe's heart sank as she thought of the risk the Simeuse brothers were running. For now she understood everything, even the look on the faces of the two Parisians, though she still could not make out what the carbine was for. She ran like a deer along the path to the château. Then she was surprised to hear a man's footsteps behind her. She gave a cry, but Michu's broad hand stopped her mouth.

'From the top of the knoll I saw the gleam of silver on men's hats. Go in through the breach in the moat between Mademoiselle's tower and the stables. The dogs won't bark at you. Slip into the garden, call the countess through the window, have her horse saddled and tell her to walk it to the moat. I shall be there once I have studied the Parisians' tactics and found a means for getting away from them.'

This new danger, rolling down on them like an avalanche, had to be circumvented. This thought lent wings to Marthe.

*

The Frankish name common to the Cinq-Cygnes and the Chargebœufs is Duineff. The younger branch of the Chargebœufs had taken the name of Cinq-Cygne after their father's castle had been defended, in his absence, by his five daughters, all of them of remarkably swan-white complexion, of whom no one could have expected such heroic conduct. One of the early Counts of Champagne decided to perpetuate the memory of it, by means of this pretty name, so long as the family subsisted. Ever since this singular deed of arms, the daughters of this family had taken pride in it, though perhaps they were not always so pale-complexioned. The last one, Laurence, had inherited the name, coat of arms and fiefs in spite of the Salic Law, for the King of France had confirmed the Count of Champagne's charter by virtue of which, in this family, nobility and title of succession were conferred through the female line. And so Laurence was Comtesse de Cinq-Cygne, and when she married her husband would take both her name and her escutcheon, on which was inscribed, as a motto, the sublime reply made by the eldest of the five sisters when summoned to surrender the castle: 'We sing as we die!' Laurence was a worthy descendant of those fair heroines, and chance seemed to have made a point of giving her the same whiteness of skin. The delicate tracery of her blue veins showed through the fine, close texture of her skin. Her lovely blond hair went marvellously well with eyes of the deepest blue. She was of dainty build, but her frail body, despite her slim waist and milky complexion, housed a soul tempered like that of a man of sturdiest character; yet not even the most observant person would have guessed this from her mild countenance and her oval face, whose profile was vaguely reminiscent of a ewe's head. This excessive though noble gentleness did indeed seem to suggest the innocent simplicity of a lamb. 'I look like a dreamy sheep!' she would sometimes say with a smile. A girl of few words, she seemed dormant rather than dreamy. But once a grave circumstance arose, the Judith under the surface was instantly revealed and she became transfigured. Alas, such circumstances had not been rare in her life. At thirteen, after the events already related, Laurence found herself an orphan, having lost her home in the market-square of Troyes where previously the Hôtel de Cinq-Cygne had stood, one of the most interesting examples of sixteenth-century architecture. Monsieur d'Hauteserre, one of her kinsmen, now her guardian, immediately took the heiress away into the country. This estimable country gentleman, terrified at the murder of his brother the Abbé d'Hauteserre, who had been shot dead in the market-square while escaping in peasant costume, was in a poor position for defending his ward's interests: two of his children had joined the army of the emigrant princes, and every day, when the slightest disturbance occurred, he imagined that the municipal authorities of Arcis were coming to arrest him. Laurence, who was proud of having withstood a siege and of possessing the historic paleness of her ancestresses, scorned the prudent timidity of this old man who bowed his head before the storm: she thought only of adding lustre to her name. And so, in her poorly furnished drawing-room at Cinq-Cygne, she boldly set up a portrait of Charlotte Corday with a garland of oak-leaves round it. She exchanged express letters with the twins in defiance of the law and the death penalty this involved. The messenger who brought back their replies was also risking his life. Since the catastrophes at Troyes, Laurence lived only for the triumph of the royalist cause. After having coolly judged Monsieur and Madame d'Hauteserre and recognized that they were honest but unenterprising souls, she put them outside her field of vision. She had too much intelligence and genuine indulgence to resent their lack of determination: she was kind, amiable and affectionate with them, but did not let them into any of her secrets. Nothing moulds character more than constant reticence within the bosom of a family. At twenty-one Laurence still allowed the worthy d'Hauteserre to manage her affairs as in the past. Provided that her favourite mare was well groomed, her maid Catherine dressed to her taste, and her little page-boy Gothard suitably clad, she cared about little else. She was setting herself too high a goal to stoop to occupations which in different times would no doubt have given her pleasure. She gave little thought to dress: why should she, since her cousins were away? She had a bottle-green habit for riding, a dress of common material with a frogged lace jacket for walking, and a silk morning-dress to wear in the house. Gothard, her little groom, a bold and agile boy of fifteen, escorted her on her rides, for she spent most of her time out of doors and hunted over the Gondreville estates without either Michu or the farmers objecting. She was an admirable horsewoman and her skill in the chase was superlative. Through the whole region she was never called anything but Mademoiselle, even during the Revolution.

Anyone who has read that fine novel, *Rob Roy*, will remember Diana Vernon, an exception among Scott's female characters because in conceiving her he departed from his habitual coldness. The memory of Diana may help for an understanding of Laurence, if one adds to the qualities displayed by the Scottish huntress the restrained exaltation of a Charlotte Corday while suppressing the amiable vivacity which makes Diana so attractive. The young countess had seen her mother die, the Abbé d'Hauteserre struck down by a bullet, the Marquis and Marquise de Simeuse perish on the scaffold. Her only brother had died of wounds, her two cousins serving in Condé's army were liable to be killed at any moment; finally, the fortune of the Simeuses and the Cinq-Cygnes had been devoured by the Republic without the Republic being any the better for it. Her gravity, which made her seem sunk in torpor, can well be imagined.

For that matter Monsieur d'Hauteserre proved a most honest and resourceful guardian. Under his management Cinq-Cygne began to look like a real farm. The good man, who had less in him of the doughty champion than of the landowner exploiting his property, had made good use of the park and gardens, whose extent was about two hundred acres and from which he drew forage for the horses, food for the servants and wood for heating. By the time she was twenty-one, thanks to the strictest economy, the countess had recovered enough money to live on from her investments in State bonds. In 1798 she had an income of twenty thousand francs from the funds – though in fact payments were in arrears – and twelve thousand francs from her farm-leases, which had been renewed with considerable increases in rent. Monsieur and Madame d'Hauteserre had retired to the country with annuities of three thousand francs coming from the Lafarge tontines; and since this remnant of their fortune did not allow of their living elsewhere than at Cinq-Cygne, Laurence's first step was to give them a life tenancy of the pavilion they occupied in it. The d'Hauteserres, who had become parsimonious for their ward's sake as well as their own, and who every year hoarded up their three thousand francs with a thought for their two sons, brought the heiress up on very short commons. Total expenditure at Cinq-Cygne did not exceed five thousand francs a year. But Laurence never went into details and was quite satisfied. Her guardian and his wife, unconsciously dominated by the imperceptible influence her character exerted even in the most trifling matters, had come to admire the girl they had known since childhood – a rare enough attitude; but in her manners, her low voice and imperious gaze there was an indescribable something, the sort of authority which always imposes itself even when there is nothing behind it, for with stupid people mere vacuousness may pass for depth of character. Such depth is incomprehensible to ordinary people: hence perhaps the admiration of the populace for anything it cannot fathom. Monsieur and Madame d'Hauteserre, struck by the young countess's habit of silence and impressed by her lack of sociability, remained in constant expectation of some manifestation of greatness in her. By doing good with discernment, and not letting herself be imposed upon, Laurence obtained great respect from the peasants, even though she was an aristocrat. Everything, her sex, her name, her misfortunes, her unusual way of life, contributed to her ascendancy over the inhabitants of the Cinq-Cygne valley. Sometimes she would go off for a day or two in company with Gothard. On her return, neither Monsieur nor Madame d'Hauteserre asked for an explanation of her absence. Not that there was anything eccentric about Laurence. Her Amazonian qualities were concealed behind a mask of utter femininity and fragility. She had great sensibility of heart but mentally she was a woman of virile determination and stoical firmness. One rarely saw a tear in those clear-sighted eyes. Looking at her white and delicate wrist, tinted with blue veins, no one would have imagined that it could outrival that of the most hardened horseman. Her hand, so soft, so fluid, wielded a pistol or a rifle with the vigour of a practised shot. Outside the house, she never wore any other headgear than women wear when they go riding – a neat little beaver hat with its turned-down veil. And so her delicate complexion and her white throat wrapped in a black scarf had never suffered from her rides in the open air.

Under the Directory and the early years of the Consulate, Laurence had been able to behave in this way without anyone being concerned about her; but now that government was becoming more settled, the new officials, the Prefect of the Aube, Malin's friends and Malin himself were seeking to bring her into discredit. Laurence's only thought was for the fall of Bonaparte, whose ambition and triumph had excited rage in her – a cold and calculated rage. As an obscure and unknown enemy of this man covered with glory, she watched him, from the depths of her valley and forests, with a terribly steady gaze, and sometimes was minded to go to the environs of Saint-Cloud or Malmaison and kill him. The execution of this design would have sufficed to explain her habits and mode of life; but after the breach of the Peace of Amiens, having been initiated into the conspiracy of the men who were attempting to stage a new 18 Brumaire which would destroy the First Consul, she had from then on harnessed her energy and hatred to the very wide-spread and well-concerted plan whose aim was to strike at Bonaparte from outside – through the vast coalition of Russia, Austria and Prussia which as Emperor he was to defeat at Austerlitz – and inside the country through a coalition of men who were diametrically opposed to one another but united by a common hatred, some of whom, like Laurence, intended to encompass the man's death without shrinking from the word 'assassination'. And so this girl, so fragile in appearance but of such fortitude to those who knew her well, was at this juncture the faithful and sure guide of the nobles who came from Germany to take part in this very serious attack. Fouché was to avail himself of this collaboration among *émigrés* beyond the Rhine in order to involve the Duc d'Enghien in the plot. The latter's presence in the Baden territory, quite near Strasbourg, later lent weight to his suspicions. The great question whether the Duc d'Enghien was really cognizant of the enterprise and whether he was intending to enter France when it had succeeded is one of the secrets about which, as about so many others, the princes of the House of Bourbon have maintained the deepest silence. As in due course the history of those times recedes into the past, impartial historians will find that it was imprudent, to say the least, for the prince to approach the frontier at a moment when an immense conspiracy, which the whole royal family certainly knew about, was afoot.

Such prudence as Malin had just displayed in his open-air conference with Grévin, Laurence applied in her slightest relationships with the conspirators. She received emissaries and conferred with them either on the various borders of the forest of Nodesme or beyond the valley of Cinq-Cygne between Sézanne and Brienne. She often covered more than thirty-five miles at a stretch with Gothard and returned to Cinq Cygne without her fresh cheeks showing the slightest trace of fatigue or anxiety. In early days she had detected in the eyes of this little cow-herd, then nine years old, the naïve admiration children feel for what is out of the ordinary; she made him her stable-boy and taught him to groom horses with all the care and attention that the English give to this task. She discovered in him the desire to acquit himself well, intelligence and complete unselfishness; she tried out his devotion and found that he had not only readiness of wit but also nobility of heart: he never expected any reward. She gave much attention to the boy, showed him kindness while treating him with dignity, and attached him to herself by attaching herself to him, by taking it upon herself to polish this rough diamond without robbing him of his freshness and simplicity. When she had sufficiently tested the almost canine fidelity she had nurtured in him, Gothard became her ingenious and ingenuous accomplice. The little peasant, whom no one was likely to suspect, would go from Cinq-Cygne to Nancy and sometimes return without anybody knowing he had been away. He practised all the tricks used by spies, yet the extreme wariness which his mistress had taught him in no way spoiled his nature. He possessed at once the artfulness of a woman, the naïvety of a child and the constant alertness of a conspirator, and these admirable qualities were hidden under the peasant's mask of ignorance and torpor. The little fellow seemed to be stupid, weak and clumsy, but once he set to work he was as agile as a fish and as slippery as an eel. Like a dog, he could take the meaning of a look and sniff out a thought. His good homely face, round and red, his sleepy brown eyes, his hair close-cropped in peasant style, his clothes and his stunted growth gave him the appearance of a child of ten.

Under the protection of their cousin, who took charge of their journey from Strasbourg to Bar-sur-Aube, Messieurs d'Hauteserre and Messieurs de Simeuse, accompanied by various other *émigrés*, passed through Alsace, Lorraine and Champagne, while other equally courageous conspirators landed in France from the cliffs of Normandy. Dressed as workmen, the d'Hauteserres and the Simeuses had tramped from forest to forest, guided from stage to stage by persons whom Laurence had picked out in each department from among people most devoted to the Bourbon cause but the least liable to be suspected. These *émigrés* slept by day and travelled by night. Each had with him two loyal soldiers, one of whom went ahead to reconnoitre while the other remained in the rear to protect their retreat in case of mishap. Thanks to these military precautions, the precious detachment had without misadventure reached the forest of Nodesme, which had been chosen as a rendezvous. Twenty-seven other noblemen also came through Switzerland and crossed Burgundy, being guided towards Paris with similar cautiousness. Monsieur de Rivière was reckoning on having five hundred men, including a hundred young nobles who were the officers of this dedicated battalion. Monsieur de Polignac and Monsieur de Rivière, whose conduct as leaders was truly remarkable, kept the identity of all their accomplices a dead secret and they were never found out. It can therefore be stated today, in accordance with the revelations made during the Restoration, that Bonaparte did not know the dangers he then ran, any more than England realized the peril in which she stood from the camp at Boulogne; and yet at no other time were the police under more intelligent or more skilful direction. At the moment when this story begins – such a thing always happens in conspiracies which are not restricted to a small band of equally resolute men – one coward, a conspirator who was brought face to face with death, gave some information which was precise enough about the purpose of the enterprise, but happily insufficient regarding its scope. And so, as Malin had told Grévin, the police kept the conspirators under supervision but allowed them freedom of action so that all the threads of the plot could be gathered together. Nevertheless, to some extent the Government had its hand forced by Georges Cadoudal, a man of action who consulted nobody but himself and had gone into hiding in Paris with twenty-four Chouans in order to strike at the First Consul.

Hatred and love were at work together in Laurence's mind. To destroy Bonaparte and restore the Bourbons was to recover Gondreville and make a fortune for her cousins. The two sentiments, one the counterpart of the other, were strong enough in this girl of twenty-three to bring all her moral faculties and all her vital strength into play. That is why, during the last two months, Laurence seemed more beautiful to the occupants of Cinq-Cygne than she had ever been. Her cheeks now had a touch of colour and there were times when hope brought a glow of pride to her countenance. However, when the *Gazette* was read out in the evenings with the list of the First Consul's conservative measures, she let her eyes droop so that no one should read in them the menacing conviction that the enemy of the Bourbons was nearing his downfall. Consequently nobody suspected that the countess had seen her cousins again the previous night. Monsieur d'Hauteserre's two sons had spent the night in the countess's own bedroom under the same roof as their parents. In order not to arouse suspicion, as soon as the two d'Hauteserres had retired, between one and two o'clock in the morning, Laurence had gone to rejoin her cousins at the rendezvous and taken them to the heart of the forest, where she had hidden them in the deserted hut of a timber-merchant's agent. Sure of seeing them again, she gave no sign at all of joy or the emotion born of expectation; in short she managed to wipe out all traces of her pleasure at meeting them again and remained impassive. Her nurse's pretty daughter, Catherine, and Gothard, both of whom had been let into the secret, modelled their behaviour on hers. Catherine was nineteen. At that age, as at Gothard's, a girl is fanatical and will let her head be cut off rather than utter a word. As for Gothard, one whiff of the perfume which the countess put on her hair and clothes would have made him go through the torture-chamber without opening his mouth.

*

While Marthe, forewarned of imminent danger, was gliding like a shadow towards the breach in the moat which Michu had indicated, the drawing-room in the château of Cinq-Cygne presented a most peaceful spectacle. Its occupants were so far from anticipating the storm about to burst over them that their attitude would have aroused compassion in anyone alive to their situation. In the lofty fire-place surmounted by a pier-glass adorned with dancing shepherdesses in hoop-petticoats blazed such a fire as is seen only in a château bordering on woodlands. In the chimney corner, on a large, square sofa of gilded wood trimmed with magnificent green lampas, the young countess lay practically sprawling in a state of complete exhaustion. Not until six o'clock had she returned from the confines of Brie after reconnoitring the country ahead of the band in order to bring the four noblemen safely to the spot which was to be their last halt before Paris, and she had found Monsieur and Madame d'Hauteserre just finishing dinner. Pressed by hunger, she had sat down to table in her muddy riding-habit and ankle-boots. After dinner, instead of changing, she had felt so spent with fatigue that she had leaned her shapely head, with its profusion of fair ringlets, against the back of the capacious sofa and stretched out her legs on a stool while she dried her spattered habit and boots at the fire. Her deerskin gloves, her little beaver hat, her green veil and riding-whip lay where she had flung them on a console-table. She was glancing alternately at the antique Buhl clock which stood on the mantlepiece between two candelabras wrought with floral motifs – to see if by this time the four conspirators were likely to be in bed – and at the card-table in front of the hearth at which Monsieur d'Hauteserre, his wife, the Cinq-Cygne curé and his sister were sitting.

Even if these persons had not a vital part to play in the ensuing drama, their physiognomy would still have the merit of presenting one aspect of the life led by aristocrats since their defeat in 1793. In this respect a description of the Cinq-Cygne drawing-room can give the savour of history seen in undress.

The country gentleman, Monsieur d'Hauteserre, then fifty-two, tall, spare, rubicund and robust, would have looked like a potentially energetic man had it not been for his china-blue eyes and the extreme simplicity their glance betokened. He had a long, pointed chin and an aesthetically disproportionate space between nose and mouth which suggested a submissiveness well in keeping with his character. Every detail of his physiognomy confirmed this impression. His grey hair, crammed under a hat which he wore practically the whole day long, sat like a skull-cap on his head and defined its pear-shaped outline. His forehead, deeply lined by his cares as a landlord and his constant anxiety, was flat and expressionless. His aquiline nose gave some relief to his features; but only his shaggy eyebrows, still black, and his high colouring, showed any indication of strength: a reliable indication, for this gentleman, simple-minded as he was, clung to the monarchy and the Catholic faith, and for no consideration would he have changed his party allegiance. Yet this docile man would have let himself be arrested without firing a shot at the municipal guards and would have gone quite meekly to the scaffold. His annuity of three thousand francs, his only means of subsistence, had debarred him from emigrating. So he obeyed the *de facto* government but still loved the royal family and hoped for its restoration. He would, however, have refused to compromise himself by participating in an attempt to reinstate the Bourbons. He belonged to that section of royalists who never forgot that they had been drubbed and robbed but from then on remained mute, parsimonious, resentful and inert, incapable either of abjuring their faith or of sacrificing themselves to it; eager to hail the monarchy once it triumphed, pious and well-disposed to the clergy, but resolved to endure all the humiliations of misfortune. Such people cannot be said to hold an opinion, but merely to be opinionated: action is the essence of partisanship. Unintelligent but loyal, as miserly as a peasant while preserving the manners of a noble, cherishing audacious hopes but discreet in word and deed, making the best of any eventuality and even ready to accept office as

Mayor of Cinq-Cygne, Monsieur d'Hauteserre was a typical representative of those honourable noblemen on whose brow God has written the word *mites*.[4] They allowed the revolutionary storm to pass over their head and homesteads, stood erect again under the Restoration – all the richer for their clandestine economies, proud of their cautious loyalty – and retired to their country estates after 1830.

His costume, an appropriate envelope for his person, gave a picture both of the man and of the times. He wore the kind of nut-brown, short-collared greatcoat which had been brought into fashion by the late Duke of Orleans on his return from England and which, during the Revolution, struck a compromise between the hideous costumes of the plebs and the elegant frock-coats of the aristocracy. His velvet waistcoat, striped with silk, recalling a fashion favoured by Robespierre and Saint-Just, disclosed the upper part of the finely pleated frill of his shirt-front. He still wore breeches, though they were of coarse blue cloth with burnished steel buckles. His black, floss-silk stockings fitted tightly round his legs, as slender as those of a stag, and these were shod with heavy shoes supported by black cloth gaiters. He had kept to the outmoded muslin collar with multiple pleats, fastened with a gold buckle at the neck. The good man had not intended to give proof of political eclecticism by adopting this manner of dress, at once rustic, revolutionary and aristocratic: he had, in all innocence, conformed to circumstances.

The careworn Madame d'Hauteserre, aged forty, had a withered face which always seemed to be posing for a portrait, and her lace cap, adorned with satin bows, singularly enhanced this air of solemnity. She still applied powder despite her white neckerchief and her puce-coloured dress with its flat sleeves and skirt: such a costume as Marie-Antoinette wore in her last, sad days. She had a pinched nose, a pointed chin, an almost triangular face and grey eyes which much weeping had robbed of their lustre; but she brightened up her appearance with a touch of rouge. She took snuff, and at every pinch she practised those dainty gestures which elegant ladies overdid in former times; the studied details of her snuff-taking

4. This is of course the Latin word for 'meek'.

amounted to a ceremony which one fact can explain: she had pretty hands.

Two years before, the former tutor of the Simeuse twins, a friend of the Abbé d'Hauteserre named Goujet, a member of the Order of Minims, had retired to the living of Cinq-Cygne out of friendship for the d'Hauteserres and the young countess. His sister, Mademoiselle Goujet, joined her income of seven hundred francs to her brother's meagre stipend and kept house for him. Neither the church nor the presbytery, being of so little value, had been put up for sale by the State, and so the Abbé Goujet was lodged a few yards away from the château, for in some places the presbytery garden and the park shared a common wall. Consequently, twice a week, the Abbé and his sister dined at Cinq-Cygne, and they came in every evening to play cards with the d'Hauteserres. Laurence had no knowledge of card-games. The Abbé Goujet, an old man with white hair and a complexion as white as that of an old woman, was gifted with an amiable smile and a gentle, persuasive voice; the insipidity of his somewhat babyish features was redeemed by his shrewd eyes and a forehead instinct with intelligence. Of medium height and good proportions, he still wore the black habit of the French clergy, knee-breeches and shoes with silver buckles, black silk stockings and a black waistcoat with his clerical bands over it. This gave him a grand air without detracting from his dignity. This Abbé, who became Bishop of Troyes at the Restoration, had spent his life weighing young people up and had discerned the loftiness of character in Laurence. He appreciated her at her true worth, and from the very beginning had paid the girl a respectful deference which did much to assure her independence at Cinq-Cygne and make the austere lady and the worthy gentleman bend to her will, even though convention would certainly have required that she should bend to theirs. For the last six months the Abbé had been observing Laurence with the keen eye of a priest, and priests are the most perspicacious of men. Although he had no idea that this girl of twenty-three, while her delicate hands were untwisting a loose frog in her riding-habit, was plotting Bonaparte's overthrow, he none the less conjectured that some great design was stirring in her head.

Mademoiselle Goujet was one of those spinsters who can be portrayed in a single phrase which will enable even the least imaginative reader to picture her: she belonged to the tall and gawky species. She knew she was ugly and was the first to make a joke of it by displaying her long teeth, as yellow as her complexion, and her bony hands. She was thoroughly kind and good-humoured. She wore the good old jacket of former times, a very ample skirt with the pocket always bulging with keys, a cap with ribbons and a hair-piece. She had reached her forties before her time, but made up for it, as she used to say, by staying at forty for twenty years more. She venerated the nobility, but knew how to keep her dignity while paying them due respect and deference.

Having their company at Cinq-Cygne had been a godsend to Madame d'Hauteserre, who had not any rural occupation like her husband or, like Laurence, the tonic of hatred, to relieve the burden of solitude. And so life had in some measure improved for her during the last six years. The re-establishment of the Catholic religion enabled her to perform her religious duties, and these are of much greater consequence in country life than anywhere else. Monsieur and Madame d'Hauteserre, reassured by the First Consul's conservative measures, had been able to correspond with their sons, receive news of them, cease trembling for their safety and urge them to apply for their names to be struck off the proscription list so that they might return to France. The Treasury had settled the overdue interest on the national debt and was paying regularly every half-year, so that the d'Hauteserres were now drawing eight thousand francs' income in addition to their annuity. The old man was congratulating himself on having made wise provision for the future, for he had invested all his savings – twenty thousand francs – and those of his ward, before 18 Brumaire, an event which, as is well-known, had advanced the funds by as much as twelve or eighteen francs.

For a long time Cinq-Cygne had remained bare, empty and stripped. During the revolutionary commotions Laurence's prudent guardian had been reluctant to renovate it. But after the Peace of Amiens he had journeyed to Troyes in order to retrieve some remnants of furniture from the two pillaged mansions and had bought them from the secondhand dealers; by so doing he had been able to refurnish the drawing-room in which these people were at that moment assembled. Its six casement windows were now adorned with fine white lampas curtains embroidered with green floral patterns. The immense room was completely relined with wainscoting laid out in panels, with beaded moulding and bas-reliefs at the angles, painted in two tones of grey. Over the lintels of the four doors were monochrome designs such as had been in vogue under Louis XV. At Troyes he had picked up some gilt consoles, a set of chairs in green lampas, a crystal chandelier, an inlaid card-table and all sorts of things useful for the redecoration of Cinq-Cygne. In 1792, when the sacking of town-houses had its repercussions also in the valley, all the furniture in the château had been carried off. Every time the old man went to Troyes he came back with some relics of its former splendour, perhaps a fine carpet like the one with which the drawing-room parquet was laid, or some job-lot of plates and dishes, or old Saxe or Sèvres porcelain. Only six months before this he had ventured to dig up the Cinq-Cygne silver plate which the chef had buried in a little house he owned at the further end of one of the straggling suburbs of Troyes.

This faithful servant, Durieu by name, and his wife always stood by their young mistress. Durieu was the château factotum and his wife was housekeeper. He had Catherine's sister to help him in the kitchen; he was teaching her his art, and she was becoming an excellent cook. An old gardener, his wife, his son who was paid by the day, also their daughter who looked after the cattle, completed the domestic staff. Six months ago Durieu's wife had secretly had a livery made in the Cinq-Cygne colours for Gothard and the gardener's son. Monsieur d'Hauteserre had roundly scolded her for this piece of imprudence, but it procured her the pleasure of seeing dinner served almost in the old style on the feast of Saint Laurence, which was Laurence's birthday. This slow and painful restoration of amenities brought joy to the two d'Hauteserres and the Durieu couple. Laurence smiled at what she called such childishness. However, the good d'Hauteserre gave his mind also to practical things. He went on repairing buildings, rebuilt walls, planted trees wherever they had a chance of growing, and did not leave one square inch of ground untilled. For that reason the valley of Cinq-Cygne looked on him as an oracle in agricultural matters. He had been able to recover a hundred acres of disputed land which the commune had left unsold and absorbed into its common lands; he had turned them into artificial meadows for the château cattle to graze on and had surrounded them with poplars which had grown marvellously in six years. He intended to buy back various bits of land, make use of all the manorial buildings, and establish a second farm which he proposed to run himself.

Life at the château had then become almost happy during the last two years. Monsieur d'Hauteserre set out at daybreak and went to supervise his workmen, for at all times he had some in his employ. He returned for lunch, and after that mounted his farm nag and made his rounds like a farm bailiff; then, back for dinner, he ended his day playing boston. Everyone in the château had his own allotted task, and life was as strictly regulated as in a monastery. Laurence alone disturbed its even tenor with her sudden journeys and absences, which Madame d'Hauteserre referred to as her rovings. And yet there were two opposing policies pursued at Cinq-Cygne, and hence grounds for dissension. In the first place, Durieu and his wife were jealous of Gothard and Catherine, who were on a more intimate footing than they were with their young mistress, who was the idol of the house. In the second place, the two d'Hauteserres, supported by the curé and Mademoiselle Goujet, wanted both their own sons and the Simeuse twins to return home and share their happy, tranquil life instead of living in hardship abroad. Laurence stigmatized such an odious compromise and stood out for militant and implacable royalism. The four elderly people, unwilling to see their peaceful existence jeopardized or to forfeit this plot of earth reconquered from the angry waters of the revolutionary flood, tried to win Laurence over to their undoubtedly sensible viewpoint, divining that she was largely responsible for the obduracy of the four exiles in refusing to return to France. Poor souls, they were dismayed by their ward's proud disdain and had good grounds for fearing that she might commit some impulsive act. Disagreement had flared up at the time of the explosion of the infernal machine in the rue Saint-Nicaise, the first royalist attempt directed against the victor of Marengo after his refusal to treat with the house of Bourbon. The d'Hauteserres considered it fortunate that Bonaparte had escaped a hazard which they believed the Republicans had engineered. Laurence had wept with rage on seeing the First Consul emerge unscathed. Despair got the better of her customary dissimulation and she accused God of betraying the sons of Saint-Louis.[5] 'I myself would have succeeded!' she exclaimed.

'Have we not the right', she said to the Abbé as she observed their profound stupefaction after she had made this remark, 'to attack usurpation by all possible means?'

'My child,' the Abbé Goujet replied, 'the Church had indeed been attacked and censured by the *philosophes* for having formerly held that the weapons which usurpers use for their own ends may be turned against them. But today the Church owes too much to the First Consul not to shield and protect him from this maxim – which, by the way, the Jesuits invented.'

'So the Church abandons our cause,' she mournfully replied.

From that day on, every time these four elderly people talked about bowing to the decrees of Providence, the young countess left the drawing-room. For some time the Abbé, more tactful than her guardian, instead of discussing principles, emphasized the material advantages arising from the Consular government, less in order to convert the countess than to catch expressions in her eyes which might enlighten him about her projects. Many things, Gothard's absences, Laurence's numerous excursions and the preoccupation which in these latter days was plainly written on her face, in short a multitude of little signs which could not escape attention in the silence and calm of life at Cinq-Cygne – particularly the anxious attention of the d'Hauteserres, the Abbé Goujet and the Durieu couple – had reawakened the fears of these submissive royalists. But since nothing seemed to be happening, since of

5. i.e. the legitimate Kings of France.

late there had been perfect quiet in the political sphere, life had regained its tranquillity in the little château. Everyone had attributed the countess's long rides to her passion for the chase.

We may imagine the profound silence which reigned in the château, and outside in the gardens and courtyards, at nine o'clock that evening, since there was such a harmony of tone between people and things: the deepest peace prevailed, abundance was returning, and the good, cautious gentleman was hoping that an uninterrupted series of happy results would convert his ward to his own policy of obedience. These royalists went on playing their boston, a game which, as a frivolous pastime, spread the idea of independence throughout France. It had been invented in honour of the American insurgents, and every term of it was a reminder of their struggle, encouraged by Louis XVI. While they declared their *independences* or their *misères*, they were watching Laurence who, soon overcome with sleepiness, dozed off with an ironic smile on her lips. Her last waking thought had taken in the peaceful picture of the card-players, whom a single word would have thrown into the liveliest trepidation by informing the d'Hauteserres that their sons had slept under their roof the previous night. What girl of twenty-three would not have been proud, as Laurence was, to think she was an instrument of destiny, or would not have felt, as she did, a slight impulse of pity for people who fell so short of her own standards?

'She's asleep,' said the Abbé. 'I've never seen her so tired.'

'Durieu told me her mare is practically dead-beat,' Madame d'Hauteserre affirmed. 'Her gun has not been fired, the priming-pan is not fouled, so she has not been out shooting.'

'My goodness!' said the curé, 'that's a bad sign.'

'Nonsense!' Mademoiselle Goujet exclaimed. 'When I was only twenty-three and saw that I was doomed to spinsterhood, I rushed about and tired myself out far more. But I understand why the countess goes riding over the countryside without thinking of killing game. It will soon be twelve years since she saw her cousins, and she loves them. Well, in her place, if I were young and pretty as she is, I'd dash straight off to

Germany! The poor darling probably feels drawn to the frontier.'

'Mademoiselle Goujet,' said the Abbé with a smile, 'are you not letting your tongue run away with you?'

'Well,' she retorted, 'since you're worrying about the comings and goings of a girl of twenty-three, I'm just giving you a reason for them.'

'Her cousins will come back,' said the simple-minded d'Hauteserre. 'She'll find out she is rich. She'll calm down in the end.'

'God grant it be so!' his wife exclaimed, producing her gold snuff-box, which she had taken to again when Bonaparte was made Consul for life.

'Something's happening round about,' d'Hauteserre said to the curé. 'Malin has been at Gondreville since yesterday evening.'

'Who? Malin?' Laurence exclaimed, roused from her sleep by the mention of this name.

'Yes,' the curé replied. 'But he's going back tonight, and people are lost in speculation as to why he made this sudden visit.'

'That man', said Laurence, 'is the evil genius of our two houses.'

She had just been dreaming of her cousins and the d'Hauteserres and the threat hanging over them. Her fine eyes became fixed and dull as she thought of the risk they would be running in Paris. She rose abruptly and went up to her bedroom without a word. She occupied the state-room, next to which were a dressing-room and private chapel situated in the turret overlooking the forest. She had no sooner left the drawing-room than the dogs began to bark, the bell of the little gateway rang, and Durieu, looking alarmed, came into the drawing-room and said, 'The mayor is here! There's something afoot.'

The mayor, once whipper-in for the Simeuses, sometimes came to the château, and as a matter of policy the d'Hauteserres paid him a deference to which he attached great value. His name was Goulard. He had married a rich tradeswoman of Troyes whose property lay inside the commune of Cinq-Cygne. He had enlarged it by applying all his economies to the purchase of a rich abbey, the vast abbey of Le Val-des-Preux, less than a mile away from the château, which provided him with a habitation almost as splendid as Gondreville: he and his wife rattled about in it like two peas. 'Goulard, you've been greedy!' Mademoiselle Goujet had said to him smilingly the first time she saw him at Cinq-Cygne. Although a keen supporter of the Revolution and coldly received by the countess, the mayor still felt attached by bonds of respect to the Cinq-Cygnes and the Simeuses, and consequently he kept his eyes shut to everything happening at the château. What he meant by keeping his eyes shut was not noticing the portraits of Louis XVI, Marie-Antoinette and the royal children – the Comte de Provence and the Comte d'Artois – Cazalès and Charlotte Corday, which adorned the panels of the drawing-room; also not taking it amiss that, even in his presence, they expressed their hopes for the downfall of the Republic, jeered at the five Directors and all the political shufflings of the period. The two-faced position of this man who, like many upstarts once their fortune is made, was recovering his faith in the old families and was ready to rally to them, had just been exploited by the two personages whose profession Michu had so promptly divined and who, before going to Gondreville, had made inquiries in the neighbourhood.

*

Peyrade, the man who maintained the time-honoured traditions of the pre-revolutionary police, and Corentin, that phoenix among spies, were on a secret mission. Malin had not been mistaken in crediting these two artists in tragic farce with a double role. Therefore, perhaps, before we see them at work, a picture should be given of the man whose instruments they were. When Bonaparte became First Consul, he found Fouché in charge of the general police. The Revolutionary government had boldly and with good reason created a special Ministry of Police. But Bonaparte, on his return from Marengo, set up a Prefecture of Police, made Dubois head of it, called Fouché to the Council of State and appointed as his successor at the Ministry of Police a former member of the Convention – Cochon, who later became Comte de Lapparent. Fouché, who regarded the Ministry of Police as the most important one in a government with far-reaching intentions and settled policy, looked on this transference as a kind of disgrace, or at any rate as a mark of distrust. Afterwards, when Napoleon had recognized the immense superiority of this great statesman from the way he dealt with the infernal machine affair and the conspiracy with which this story is concerned, he reinstated him as Minister of Police. Then later, alarmed by the talent displayed by Fouché during his absence at the time of the Walcheren expedition, the Emperor handed the Ministry over to the Duke of Rovigo and sent Fouché, now Duke of Otranto, to govern the Illyrian provinces. This was tantamount to exile.

The outstanding genius of this man, which inspired something like terror in Napoleon, only became manifest by degrees. He had been inconspicuous as a member of the Convention, and it was only the Revolutionary storms that shaped him as one of the most extraordinary – also the most ill-judged – men of his times. During the Directory he reached the sort of vantage-ground from which a man of profound mind is able to foresee the future by weighing up the past; then, like certain second-rate actors whom a sudden flash of insight converts into excellent ones, he gave the measure of his dexterity during the rapid revolution of 18 Brumaire. This sallow-faced man, who had been trained in dissimulation while still a monk, who had secret relations with the Montagnards, to whom he belonged, and with the Royalists, whom he was to join in the end, had patiently and silently studied men and events and the imbroglios of the political scene; he saw through Bonaparte's secret intentions, gave him useful advice and valuable information. Content to have thus demonstrated his capability and usefulness, Fouché had taken good care not to show his hand completely, since he wanted to remain at the head of affairs; but Napoleon's attitude towards him induced him to take an independent line in politics. The Emperor's ingratitude, or rather his distrust after the Walcheren affair, explains the conduct of a man who, unfortunately for himself, was not of aristocratic rank and whose tactics were modelled on those of Talleyrand. At present neither his erstwhile nor his new colleagues suspected the wide scope of his genius, which was purely ministerial, essentially administrative, accurate in all its forecasts and incredibly sagacious. Today, certainly, any impartial historian sees that Napoleon's excessive self-importance was one of the numerous causes of his downfall, which in itself was a cruel expiation for the mistakes he had made. The acts of this distrustful sovereign were determined by two motives: a jealous concern for his newly-acquired power and an underlying hatred for the talented men – a precious legacy from the Revolution had he but known it – whom he might have used to form a junta to which he could have entrusted the furtherance of his designs.

Talleyrand and Fouché were not the only men to give him umbrage. Usurpers are unfortunate in having two kinds of enemies: those who have put the crown on their heads, and those from whose head it has been removed. Napoleon never entirely established his sovereignty over those who had been his superiors or his equals, nor over those who clung to their legal rights: that is why no one felt bound by the allegiance they had sworn him. Malin, a mediocre man incapable either of appreciating the genius latent in Fouché or of suspecting how quick-sighted he was, was singed like a moth in a candle when he went confidentially to ask him to send some police agents to Gondreville, where, he said, he hoped that light might be thrown on the conspiracy. Fouché did not alarm his friend by questioning him, but he did wonder why Malin was going to Gondreville and why he did not divulge immediately, in Paris, any information he might have. The former Oratorian, well versed in knavery and aware of the double role played by many members of the Convention, asked himself: 'How has Malin come by his knowledge, when as yet we ourselves know very little?' Fouché therefore assumed some hidden or anticipated complicity on Malin's part, though he took care not to say anything to the First Consul, since he preferred to use Malin as a cat's-paw rather than bring him to ruin. In this way he could keep to himself a large part of the secrets he might discover and get a tighter grip than Bonaparte could on the persons concerned ... Such duplicity was one of Napoleon's grievances against his minister. Fouché knew that Malin had laid hands on Gondreville by sharp practice and was therefore obliged to keep close watch on the Simeuse brothers. They were serving in Condé's army, Mademoiselle de Cinq-Cygne was their cousin, and so they were likely to be lurking in the neighbourhood and taking part in the conspiracy. This participation would mean that the house of Condé, to which they were devoted, was implicated.

Monsieur de Talleyrand and Fouché were anxious that light should be cast on this very obscure aspect of the 1803 conspiracy, and Fouché made a rapid and lucid survey of the situation. But there were connections between Malin, Talleyrand and himself which forced him to use the greatest circumspection and made him desire to know exactly what was going on inside the château of Gondreville. Corentin was unreservedly attached to Fouché, in the same way as Monsieur de la Besnardière was attached to Prince Talleyrand, Gentz to Monsieur de Metternich, Dundas to Pitt, Duroc to Napoleon, and Chavigny, in former times, to Cardinal Richelieu. He was not Fouché's confidant, but rather his willing tool, in secret a Tristan l'Hermite to this small-scale Louis XVI: consequently Fouché had naturally kept him in the Ministry of Police so as to have an eye on it and someone working for him inside it. It was said that this individual belonged to Fouché through some kind of unavowed kinship, for he gave him lavish reward every time he availed himself of his services. Corentin had made friends with Peyrade, who had learnt his trade under the pre-revolutionary Lieutenant of Police; but there were none the less secrets which he kept from Peyrade. Corentin had instructions from Fouché to explore the château of Gondreville, to engrave the plan of it in his memory and spy out all the hiding-places it contained. 'We shall perhaps be obliged to come back to it,' the ex-minister told him, in exactly the same way as Napoleon, in 1805, told his lieutenants to make a close survey of the battlefield of Austerlitz, to which he intended to fall back. Corentin was also to study Malin's behaviour, take stock of his influence in the neighbourhood and watch the men he was employing there. Fouché was certain that the Simeuses were somewhere in the region. By skilfully spying on these two officers, who were well in favour with the Prince de Condé, Peyrade and Corentin might well throw valuable light on the ramifications of the plot which was being hatched on the right bank of the Rhine. In any case, Corentin had at his disposal the funds, orders and agents needed for drawing a cordon round Cinq-Cygne and combing out the whole countryside from Nodesme to Paris. Fouché had recommended the greatest circumspection and sanctioned a domiciliary visit to Cinq-Cygne only if Malin furnished some positive facts. Finally, as a piece of further information, he told Corentin about the enigmatic Michu, who had been under surveillance for the last three years. Corentin had the same idea as his chief: 'Malin knows all about the conspiracy! – But,' he asked himself, 'who knows whether Fouché isn't in it too?'

Corentin had left Troyes before Malin, had come to an arrangement with the major of the gendarmerie, made his choice of the most intelligent men and put an able captain in charge of them. To him he assigned the château of Gondreville as a rendezvous and told him to send a picket of a dozen men, after dark, to four different points in the Cinq-Cygne valley, sufficiently far apart to avoid giving the alarm. The four pickets were to draw a square and close in round the Cinq-Cygne château. By leaving Corentin in possession of the Gondreville château during his consultation with Grévin, Malin had given him an opportunity to fulfil one part of his mission. On returning from the park, the Councillor of State had so positively assured Corentin that the Simeuses and the d'Hauteserres were in the vicinity that the two agents sent off the captain; but he, very fortunately for the four nobles, crossed the forest through the avenue while Michu was plying the spying Violette with drink. The Councillor of State had begun by telling Peyrade and Corentin about the ambush from which he had just escaped. Then the men from Paris had told him about the episode of the carbine, and Grévin had sent Violette to find out what was going on in the pavilion. Corentin told the notary to take his friend the Councillor of State, for greater security, to sleep in his house in the little town of Arcis. And so, just as Michu was speeding through the forest to Cinq-Cygne, Peyrade and Corentin set out from Gondreville in a rickety basket-gig drawn by a post-horse and driven by the corporal of mounted police of Arcis,[6] one of the wiliest men in the detachment, whom the major at Troyes had advised them to take with them.

'The best way of catching the lot is to let them know we're coming,' said Peyrade to Corentin. 'When we've got them scared and they try to salvage their papers or escape, we'll drop down on them like a ton of bricks. The cordon of gendarmes will close in on the château like a net, and that way we shall get every one of them.'

'You can send the mayor to them,' said the corporal. 'He goes easy with them, wishes them no harm, and they won't be suspicious of him.'

And so, just as Goulard was going to bed, Corentin, halting the gig in a small wood, had come to tell him in confidence that in a few moments a government agent was going to require him to have the château of Cinq-Cygne surrounded in order to lay hold of the d'Hauteserres and the Simeuses. If, however, they had disappeared, he was to find out if they had slept there the previous night, go through Mademoiselle de Cinq-Cygne's papers and perhaps put the occupants of the château, masters and servants, under arrest.

'Mademoiselle de Cinq-Cygne', said Corentin, 'no doubt has important protectors, for my secret instructions are to forewarn her of this visit and do everything to save her without compromising myself. Once I'm there I can't help her, for I'm not alone. So hurry along to the château.'

The mayor's visit half-way through the evening astonished the card-players, the more so because distress was plainly written on his countenance.

'Where is the countess?' he asked.

'In bed,' Madame d'Hauteserre answered.

The mayor, incredulous, began to listen to the sounds coming from the first floor.

'What's wrong with you this evening?' said Madame d'Hauteserre.

6. The French gendarmerie was a body of mounted police, and this officer is called a *brigadier* in the text. A *brigadier* is a corporal of a mounted regiment. In the British police force the rank of corporal does not exist; but the term 'sergeant' would not meet the case.

Goulard was deeply bewildered as he studied their faces, which registered the complete innocence one may have at any period of life. Seeing them so calm despite the interruption of their harmless card-game, he could not imagine why the police officials from Paris were so suspicious. At this moment Laurence was on her knees in her chapel, praying fervently for the success of the conspiracy. She was asking God to grant aid and succour to Bonaparte's would-be assassins! She was beseeching Him to destroy the man of destiny! This heroic girl, of such virginal purity, was possessed with the fanaticism of Harmodius, Judith, Jacques Clément, Amkarstroëm, Charlotte Corday, Limoëlan. Catherine was getting her bed ready while Gothard was closing the shutters; thus he was able to descry Marthe Michu, who was standing under Laurence's window and throwing pebbles at it.

'Mademoiselle, something's happening,' said Gothard, seeing an unknown figure below.

'Quiet!' Marthe called in a low voice. 'Come down and speak to me.' Gothard reached the garden in less time than it would have taken a sparrow to flit down from a tree.

'In a minute or two the gendarmes will put a cordon round the château,' she said to Gothard. 'Will you quietly saddle Mademoiselle's horse and lead it down through the breach in the moat between this tower and the stables?'

Marthe gave a start as she saw that Laurence, who had followed Gothard, was a few paces away from her.

'What is it?' she asked, calmly and unperturbed.

'The plot against the First Consul has been discovered,' Marthe whispered to the countess. 'My husband, whose purpose is to save your cousins, has sent me to ask you to come and have a talk with him.'

Laurence took a few steps backwards and looked at Marthe. 'Who are you?' she asked.

'Marthe Michu.'

'I can't think what business you can have with me,' Mademoiselle de Cinq-Cygne coldly rejoindered.

'Come now, do you want the Simeuses to die? For their sake, follow me!' said Marthe, falling on her knees and stretching out her hands to Laurence. 'Have you no papers here, nothing which might compromise you? From a height in the forest my husband has seen the braided hats of the gendarmes, and rifles gleaming in the moonlight.'

Gothard had begun by climbing to the attic and had spotted the embroidered accoutrements of the gendarmes in the distance. In the profound country silence he had heard the trot of their horses. He ran down to the stables, saddled his mistress's mare and, at his prompting, Catherine tied cloths round its hooves.

'Where am I to go?' Laurence asked Marthe, impressed by the unmistakable sincerity in her looks and speech.

'Through the breach,' she said, leading Laurence along. 'My noble husband is there. You will learn what a Judas is worth!'

Catherine dashed up to the drawing-room, took up her riding-whip, gloves, hat and veil and ran out again. Her sudden appearance and action provided so eloquent a commentary on the words the mayor had spoken that Madame d'Hauteserre and the Abbé Goujet exchanged a look which showed both had the same terrible thought: 'Good-bye to all our happiness! Laurence is conspiring. She has sealed the doom of her cousins and the d'Hauteserres!'

She resumed the conversation with Goulard. 'What do you mean?' she asked.

'Just this: the château is surrounded, and you are about to undergo a domiciliary visit. In short, if your sons are here, make them take to their heels, and Messieurs de Simeuse as well.'

'My sons!' cried the stupefied Madame d'Hauteserre.

'We've seen no one here,' said Monsieur d'Hauteserre.

'So much the better!' said Goulard. 'But I am too attached to the Cinq-Cygne and Simeuse families to let disaster come upon them. Listen: if you have any compromising papers...'

'Papers...?'

'Yes, if you have any, burn them,' the mayor continued. 'I will go and keep the police agents occupied.'

Goulard, bent on running with the hares – the Royalists – and hunting with the hounds – the Republicans – left the room, and the dogs began barking furiously.

'It's too late,' said the curé. 'They're here. But where's the countess and who will warn her?'

'Catherine didn't come and fetch Laurence's whip, gloves and hat to make a donation of them to the Church,' said Mademoiselle Goujet.

Goulard tried to delay the agents for a few minutes by assuring them that the occupants of the château knew nothing about what was going on.

'You don't know those customers,' said Peyrade, laughing in Goulard's face. Thereupon these two smoothly sinister men went into the drawing-room with the Arcis corporal and a gendarme behind them. The sight of them gave a chill of fright to the four peaceable card-players, who remained frozen to their seats, appalled by such a display of force. The noise made by a dozen gendarmes, whose horses were pawing the ground, resounded on the lawn.

'Everyone's here except Mademoiselle de Cinq-Cygne,' said Corentin.

'But no doubt she's asleep in her bedroom,' Monsieur d'Hauteserre replied.

'Come with me, ladies,' said Corentin, darting into the anteroom and from there to the staircase. Madame d'Hauteserre and Mademoiselle Goujet followed him.

'Rely on me,' Corentin continued in a whisper to the elderly lady. 'I am on your side, that's why I sent the mayor along. Don't trust my colleague, but trust in me. I will save all of you.'

'But what's the trouble?' asked Mademoiselle Goujet.

'It's a matter of life and death. Don't you know that?' Corentin replied.

Madame d'Hauteserre fainted. To Mademoiselle Goujet's great astonishment and Corentin's great disappointment, Laurence's suite of rooms was empty. Certain that no one could escape into the valley either from the park or from the château, Corentin posted a gendarme in every room, ordered a search through all the outbuildings and stables, and returned to the salon, to which Durieu, his wife and all the domestic staff had rushed in a state of panic. Peyrade, the only person who remained calm and cold in the midst of this commotion, was scanning every face with his beady blue eyes. When Corentin reappeared alone – Mademoiselle Goujet was attending to Madame d'Hauteserre – they heard the clatter of horses' hooves mingled with the sound of a child sobbing. The horses came in through the smaller gateway. Amid the general anxiety, a corporal of gendarmes appeared, pushing Gothard forward with his hands tied, and Catherine, whom he brought before the police agents.

'Prisoners,' he said. 'This little scoundrel was getting away on horseback.'

'You fool!' Corentin whispered to the corporal. 'Why didn't you let him go? We could have followed him and found out something.'

Gothard's tactics were to burst into tears like a village idiot. Catherine maintained an attitude of innocent simplicity which gave Peyrade food for reflection. The pupil of Lenoir, after looking the two youngsters up and down, after studying the old gentleman, whose air of inanity he thought was assumed, the sprightly curé, who was fiddling with the counters, the stupefied servants including the Durieu couple, turned to Corentin and whispered: 'We're not dealing with simpletons!' Corentin's immediate reply was to point to the card-table. Then he added: 'They were playing boston. The lady of the house was having her bed made. She has slipped away. We have taken the rest of them by surprise. We'll press them hard.'

*

A breach in a moat is no accident and it can prove useful. This is the why and wherefore of the breach between the tower, now called 'Mademoiselle's tower', and the stables: as soon as the good d'Hauteserre settled at Cinq-Cygne, he turned a long gully which carried the forest waters into the moat into a road separating two large tracts of land belonging to the château preserve, for the sole purpose of lining it with a hundred or so walnut-trees bought from a nursery. After eleven years, these walnuts had spread out and almost entirely overhung the road, which was already enclosed by banks six feet high and led to a small thirty-acre wood recently purchased. Once the château had its full quota of inhabitants, everyone preferred to cross the moat and take the communal road which skirted the walls of the park and led to the farm, rather than go round by the entrance-gate. The habit of trampling across the breach inevitably widened it on either side, but no one worried about this since, in the nineteenth century, moats have no purpose; and in fact Laurence's guardian often talked of putting this one to some other use. This constant wear and tear brought down soil, gravel and stones which in the end filled up the dyke. The water contained by this sort of causeway only covered it up in very rainy seasons. Nevertheless, despite this wearing away to which everybody, including the countess, made their contribution, the breach was steep enough to make it difficult to take a horse down it, and more so still to get it up on to the communal road. But it seems that, in times of danger, horses are aware of their masters' intentions. While the young countess was hesitantly following Marthe and asking for explanations, Michu, who from the top of his hillock had been watching the gendarmes' manoeuvres and taking in their plan of action, despaired of success when he saw no one coming. One picket of gendarmes was lining the park wall in open formation like sentries, with just enough distance between man and man for them to communicate by voice and look, listen to take stock of the slightest sounds and movements. Michu was lying down flat, his ear to the ground, calculating the time left to him by the volume of sound, like a Red Indian. 'I have come too late!' he was saying to himself. 'Violette shall pay for this. What a time it took to get him drunk! What can I do?' He heard the picket which was coming down the road from the forest pass in front of the gateway and close in by executing a similar manoeuvre to that followed by the picket coming from the communal road. 'We've still five or ten minutes!' he told himself. At this instant the countess came in sight. Michu caught her in a vigorous grasp and pushed her into the covered road.

'Go straight ahead,' he said to his wife. 'Take her to where my horse is tethered, and remember that gendarmes have ears.'

On seeing Catherine with the whip, gloves and hat, but above all on seeing Gothard with the mare, Michu, a man of quick resource in danger, resolved to trick the gendarmes as successfully as he had tricked Violette. As if by magic, Gothard had forced the mare to climb across the moat.

'You've muffled the horses' hooves? . . . Good lad!' said the bailiff, clasping Gothard in his arms. He let the mare go to her mistress and took the gloves, hat and whip.

'You're a bright boy and you'll understand me,' he continued. 'Get your horse too over the road, ride him bareback and draw the gendarmes after you by galloping hard over the fields towards the farm, and gather this straggling picket into a bunch.' He made his meaning clear by a gesture showing him which way to go. 'As for you, my girl,' he said to Catherine, 'there are other gendarmes coming along by the road from Cinq-Cygne to Gondreville. Dash off in the opposite direction to Gothard, and draw them away from the château towards the forest. In short, do what you can to prevent us being disturbed in the sunken road.'

Catherine and the splendid boy, who was to give so much proof of intelligence in this affair, executed this manoeuvre in such a way as to make each file of gendarmes believe that their quarry was slipping away. The moonlight was too deceptive for them to distinguish either the figure, clothes, sex or number of those they were pursuing. They rushed after them in obedience to the false axiom *arrest all runaways*, the tactical stupidity of which had just been brutally pointed out by Corentin to the corporal of gendarmes. Michu, who had reckoned on this instinctive reaction, was able to reach the forest shortly after the countess, whom Marthe had escorted to the spot indicated.

'Run to the pavilion,' he said to Marthe. 'The Parisians will have set a guard over the forest and it's dangerous to stay here. We shall certainly need all the freedom of action we can get.'

He untethered his horse and begged the countess to follow him.

'I won't go a step further,' said Laurence, 'unless you give me tangible proof of the interest you take in me, for, after all, you are Michu.'

'Mademoiselle,' he replied in a gentle tone of voice, 'it won't take me long to explain the part I have been playing.

Without the Simeuse gentlemen knowing it, I am the caretaker of their fortune. In this matter I received instructions from their late father and their dear mother, my patroness. And so I played the part of a rabid Jacobin in order to serve my young masters: unfortunately I began it too late and was unable to save their parents.' Michu's voice faltered. 'Since the young men took flight I have had passed on to them the sums needed for them to live according to their rank.'

'Through Breintmayer, the Strasbourg bankers?'

'Yes, Mademoiselle. They are working with Monsieur Girel of Troyes, a royalist who made his way as I did, by pretending to be a Jacobin. The paper your farmer picked up one evening as we were leaving Troyes was connected with all this and might have compromised us: my life was no longer my own, but theirs – you understand? I was not able to buy back Gondreville. A man in my position would have been asked where he had got so much money and been sent to the guillotine. I preferred to buy it back a little later, but that scoundrel Marion was acting for another scoundrel, Malin. Never mind. Gondreville will come back to its rightful owners – I'll see to that. To think that four hours ago I had Malin in the sights of my carbine: he was as good as done for! Anyway, once he's dead, Gondreville will be put up for auction and you'll be able to buy it. In the event of my death, my wife would have handed you a letter providing you with the means to do it. But this brigand was telling his crony Grévin, another blackguard, that Messieurs de Simeuse were conspiring against the First Consul, that they were in the region and that it would be better to hand them over and get rid of them in order to live in peace in Gondreville. Now as I had seen two master spies coming this way, I uncocked my carbine and lost no time hurrying along here, thinking that you would know where and how to warn the young men. That's all there is to it.'

'You are worthy to be a noble,' said Laurence, offering her hand to Michu who tried to get down on his knees to kiss it. She forestalled this movement and said: 'Stand up, Michu!' in such a tone of voice and with such a look as atoned, at that instant, for all the unhappiness he had suffered for the last twelve years.

'You are rewarding me as if I had already done what I still have to do,' he said. 'Do you hear them, the hussars of the guillotine? Let us go elsewhere and talk.' Taking the mare's bridle and drawing up to the right of the countess in order to escort her, he said: 'Think only of holding steady, using your whip and shielding your face from tree-branches likely to lash at you.' Then for half an hour he guided the girl at a fast gallop, making many twists and turns and cutting across his route by taking to clearings in order to baffle pursuit, until they came to a spot where he halted.

'I no longer know where I am,' said the countess, looking around her. 'And yet I know the forest as well as you do.'

'We are right in the middle of it,' he replied. 'There are two gendarmes after us, but we have shaken them off!'

The picturesque spot to which the bailiff had brought Laurence was destined to be a fateful one for the chief actors in this drama and for Michu himself: it is therefore our duty as a historian to describe it. Moreover this landscape, as we shall see, has become famous in the judiciary annals of the Empire.

The forest of Nodesme once belonged to a monastery dedicated to Our Lady. It had been captured, looted, demolished and had entirely disappeared, monks and chattels alike. The much-coveted forest was added to the domains of the Counts of Champagne, who later mortgaged and then sold it. In half a dozen centuries nature had covered the ruins with its rich and luxuriant green mantle and had so completely obliterated them that there was nothing left to show where one of our finest monasteries had been, except a piece of gently rising ground shaded with lordly trees and encircled by thick, impenetrable bushes which, from 1794 onwards, Michu had elected to make still more dense by planting thorny acacias in the gaps between them. There was a pond at the foot of this rise, attesting the existence of a now undiscoverable spring which originally, no doubt, had determined the site of the monastery. The owner of the title-deeds of the forest of Nodesme had alone been able to recognize the etymology of its name, which went back eight centuries, and to discover that there had indeed once been a monastery in the centre of the forest. On hearing the first rumblings of the Revolutionary storm the Marquis de Simeuse, obliged to consult his title-deeds in the course of a legal dispute, and thus apprised by chance of this interesting historical fact, started to search for the monastic site with an easily understandable ulterior motive. His ranger, who knew the forest well, had naturally aided his master in the task, and his forest lore enabled him to locate the site. Noting the direction taken by the five main tracks in the forest, several of which had become overgrown, he saw that they all ended at the hummock and the pond: a point of convergence in former times for people coming from Troyes and three villages, Arcis, Cinq-Cygne and Bar-sur-Aube. The marquis intended to excavate this hillock, but could have entrusted the operation only to people from outside the locality. Under the pressure of circumstances he gave up the quest, but left Michu with the idea that under it was concealed either buried treasure or the Abbey foundations.

Michu went on with these archaeological researches. He discovered that the ground sounded hollow on a level with the pond, in between two trees, at the foot of the one and only point where the hillock sloped sharply downwards. One night he came along with a pick and uncovered the opening to a vault, to which stone steps led down. The pond, nowhere more than three feet deep, forms a spatula whose handle seems to emerge from the hummock, and one might suppose that from this artificial cliff came a spring which oozed away into the vast forest. This swamp, surrounded by aquatic trees, alder, willow and ash, is a place where many paths meet – all that remains of ancient roads and forest alleys nowadays untrodden. The water is running although it looks stagnant; it is covered with wide-leaved plants and cress. Its surface is entirely green and its edges of fine thick grass are not easy to detect. It is too remote from any habitation for any but wild animals to drink from it. Under-keepers and huntsmen, quite certain that there could be nothing under this swamp, and repelled by the difficulty of access to the knoll, had never visited, investigated or explored this nook in the forest, which contained the oldest timber for felling and which Michu intended to fell when it reached maturity.

At the further end of the vault is a small arched cellar in freestone, clean and sanitary, of the kind that is known as an *in pace* – the monastery dungeon. The healthy condition of the vault and the sound state of the remnant of stairway and the wagon-roof were due to the spring with which demolishers had not interfered, and a wall, probably of great thickness, built in brick and cement like that used by the Romans, which prevented the water from seeping through from above. Michu blocked the entrance to this retreat with huge stones, and in order to keep the secret to himself and deter any intruders, he made it a rule to climb up the wooded rise and go down to the cellar by way of the bluff instead of approaching it from the pond. At the moment when the two fugitives reached it, the moon was throwing its lovely silvery beams on to the tops of the century-old trees surmounting the hillock, and playing its light among the magnificent clusters in the tongues of woodland cut into diverse shapes by the convergent tracks – some rounded, some pointed, this one terminating in a single tree, that one in a clump of trees.

From this eminence the eye was irresistibly drawn to receding perspectives, and one's gaze followed the curve of a footpath, or the splendid view of a long forest alley, or a wall of dark green verdure. The moonlight filtering through the intertwining boughs at this junction of tracks brought a sparkle of diamonds to this placid, secluded sheet of water in the patches which were clear of cress and water-lilies. Only the croaking of frogs disturbed the deep silence of this lovely forest nook, where the scents of wild nature awakened the soul to thoughts of liberty.

'Have we really shaken them off?' asked the countess.

'Yes, Mademoiselle. But we each have a job to do. Will you tether our horses to the trees at the top of that little hill and tie a handkerchief round their jaws?' he said, handing her his neck-cloth. 'They are both intelligent and will know they are not to neigh. When you have done that, come straight down to the pond along that steep slope, and mind your riding-habit doesn't get caught in the branches. You'll find me down below.'

While the countess was hiding, tethering and gagging the horses, Michu cleared away the stones and laid bare the entrance to the cellar. The countess, who thought she knew her forest well, was much astonished to find herself under a barrel-vault. With a mason's skill, Michu replaced the stones archwise over the entrance. When he had finished, the trot of horses and the voices of gendarmes echoed through the silence of the night. Nevertheless he calmly struck his flint, set light to a twig of fir and led the countess into the *in pace*, where there was still a candle-end which he had used to explore the little vault. He had repaired the iron door, which was half an inch thick but had rusted through here and there: it was closed from the outside by bars which fitted into slots on either side. Tired out, the countess sat down on a stone above which there was still a ring embedded in the wall.

'Here is a drawing-room where we can chat,' said Michu. 'Now the gendarmes can prowl round as long as they like. The worst that could happen would be for them to steal our horses.'

'To steal our horses', said Laurence, 'would mean the death of my cousins and Messieurs d'Hauteserre! Tell me all you know.'

Michu repeated what little he had overheard of the conversation between Malin and Grévin.

'They are making for Paris. They will get there in the morning,' the countess told him when he had finished.

'Then they're lost!' Michu exclaimed. 'You realize that watch is kept at the barriers on people coming in and going out? It's very much in Malin's interest to let my masters get thoroughly implicated and so get them executed.'

'And to think I knew nothing about the general plan of the conspiracy!' cried Laurence. 'How can we warn Georges, Rivière and Moreau? Where are they? Anyway, let's think only of my cousins and the d'Hauteserres. Get through to them at all costs.'

'The semaphore travels quicker than the fastest horses,' said Michu, 'and of all the nobles mixed up in this conspiracy, your cousins will be the most mercilessly tracked down. If I can find them we must bring them here and keep them here until all is over. Perhaps their poor father had a foreboding when he put me on the track of this hiding-place: he had a presentiment that his sons would find safety in it.'

'My mare comes from the Comte d'Artois's stables and was sired by his finest English stallion; but she has done ninety miles and would die before you reached your destination.'

'Mine is a good one,' said Michu, 'and if you have done ninety miles I shall have only forty-five to do.'

'Sixty by now,' she replied, 'for they have been on the march for five hours. You'll find them at Coupvrai, beyond Lagny, which they are to leave at dawn disguised as bargees – they're proposing to get into Paris by boat. Here', she added, taking the half of her mother's wedding-ring from her finger, 'is the only token they will trust in – I gave them the other half. The Coupvrai keeper, the father of one of their soldiers, is hiding them this night in a charcoal-burner's abandoned hut in the middle of the woods. There are eight of them all told: my cousins, Messieurs d'Hauteserre and four soldiers escorting my cousins.'

'Mademoiselle, the soldiers won't be pursued. Let us bother only about Messieurs de Simeuse, and let the others look out for themselves. Isn't it enough to give them warning?'

'Abandon the d'Hauteserres? Never!' she cried. 'They must all perish or escape together.'

'Minor gentry?' Michu rejoindered.

'I know they're no more than knights,' she replied. 'But they're relations of the Cinq-Cygnes and the Simeuses. So bring back my cousins and the d'Hauteserres after discussing with them the best way of getting to this forest.'

'The gendarmes are here! Can't you hear them? They're holding a council of war.'

'Anyway, you've already been lucky twice this evening. Fetch them here, hide them in this cellar and they'll be quite safe from pursuit. I can't be of any use to you,' she said furiously. 'I should be like a beacon light for the enemy. If the police see I am calm they won't imagine that my kinsmen could be returning to the forest. So the whole problem is to find five good horses to do the six-hour journey from Lagny to here, five horses to ride to death and leave in a thicket.'

'What about money?' asked Michu, who had been doing some deep thinking while listening to the countess.

'I gave my cousins a hundred louis last night.'

'I will answer for their safety,' Michu exclaimed. 'Once they are in hiding you must do without seeing them: my wife or my youngster will take them food twice a week. But as I can't answer for my own safety, Mademoiselle, let me tell you in case of disaster that the main rafter in the attic of my pavilion has had a hole drilled in it, with a big plug to stop it up. In the hole is a plan of a corner of the forest. The trees marked with a red dot on the plan have a black mark at their foot at the actual site. Each of these trees serves as a sign-post. At the third old oak, on the left of each sign-post, two feet in front of the trunk, tubes of metal buried seven feet down are concealed, and each of them contains a hundred thousand francs in gold. These eleven trees – there are only eleven of them – constitute the whole fortune of the Simeuses now that they have been robbed of Gondreville.'

'It will take a hundred years for the nobility to recover from the blows dealt them!' said Mademoiselle in measured tones.

'Is there a password?' asked Michu.

'"France and Charles!" for the soldiers. "Laurence and Louis!" for Messieurs d'Hauteserre and Messieurs de Simeuse. My God! To think that I saw them yesterday for the first time in eleven years and to know that today they are in danger of death – and such a death! Michu,' she continued with a melancholy look, 'be as cautious during these fifteen hours as you have been great and devoted for the last twelve years. I should die if harm came to my cousins . . . No,' she added, 'I would live long enough to kill Bonaparte!'

'There will be two of us to see to that, on the day when all is lost.'

Laurence took Michu's rough hand and clasped it firmly in English fashion. He drew out his watch: it was midnight.

'We simply must get out of here,' he said. 'Bad luck to the gendarme who gets in my way! And you, Madame la Comtesse,

I don't want to give you orders, but ride back at full speed to Cinq-Cygne. The policemen are there. Keep them occupied.'

When the entrance to the hiding-place had been cleared, Michu could hear nothing. He lay down, put an ear to the ground, and got up again in a hurry. 'They are on the edge of the forest facing Troyes,' he said. 'I'll lead them a dance.'

He helped the countess to get out and replaced the stones. When he had finished, he heard Laurence gently calling him – she wanted to see him on horseback before mounting her own horse. This rugged man had tears in his eyes as he exchanged a last look with his young mistress. But her eyes were dry.

'Keep them occupied, he's right!' she told herself when all was quiet again. And she galloped back to Cinq-Cygne.

*

Knowing that her sons were threatened with death, Madame d'Hauteserre, who did not believe the Revolution was over and knew how summary was the justice of those times, recovered her senses and strength through the very violence of the suffering which had caused her to lose them. Her intense curiosity took her back to the drawing-room, and the picture which met her eyes was one truly worthy of an artist's brush. The curé, still sitting at the card-table, was mechanically toying with the counters while stealthily watching Peyrade and Corentin, who were standing at the corner of the chimney-piece and talking together in low tones. Several times Corentin's sharp gaze met that of the curé, which was no less sharp; but like a pair of duellists who find they are equally matched and return to the guard position after crossing swords, each of them promptly looked away. The worthy d'Hauteserre, planted on his two legs like a heron, was standing beside the tall, stout, avaricious Goulard, who was still registering stupefaction. The mayor, though dressed as a bourgeois, always looked like a lackey. Both men were gaping at the gendarmes, who had the still weeping Gothard between them, his hands having been so tightly tied that they had become blue and swollen. Catherine had not abandoned her pose of utter innocence and naïvety, but she was still inscrutable. The corporal of gendarmes, after what Corentin had called his act of stupidity in arresting these harmless young people, was uncertain whether to go or stay. He was lost in thought in the middle of the drawing-room, his hand resting on the hilt of his sword, eyeing the Parisians. The flabbergasted Durieu and all the servants formed a group admirably expressive of anxiety. But for Gothard's sobs one could have heard the flies buzzing.

When the pale, terrified mother opened the door and appeared on the threshold, practically dragged along by Mademoiselle Goujet, whose eyes were red with weeping, every face turned towards the two women. The two agents were hoping to see Laurence come in, while the inhabitants were trembling lest she should. The spontaneous movements of both servants and masters might have been produced by some mechanism, the sort which jerks the limbs or eyes of puppets into action.

Madame d'Hauteserre took three quick, long strides towards Corentin and said to him in broken but vehement tones: 'For pity's sake, Monsieur, of what are my sons being accused? And do you really think that they have come here?'

The curé, who as he saw the old lady come forward looked as if he expected her to do something stupid, lowered his eyes.

'My duties and the mission I am carrying out do not allow me to tell you,' Corentin replied with an air that was at once gracious and mocking. This refusal, rendered even more implacable by his odiously foppish politeness, petrified the old lady. She collapsed into an armchair next to the Abbé Goujet, clasped her hands and uttered a prayer.

'Where did you arrest this sniveller?' Corentin asked the corporal, pointing to Laurence's little groom.

'In the road along the park wall leading to the farm; the little rascal was making for the Closeaux woods.'

'And the girl?'

'The girl? It was Olivier who grabbed her.'

'Where was she going?'

'Towards Gondreville.'

'They were off in opposite directions?' asked Corentin.

'Yes,' the gendarme replied.

'Are they not the page and chambermaid of Citizeness Cinq-Cygne?' Corentin asked the mayor.

'Yes,' Goulard replied.

After exchanging a few words in a whisper with Corentin, Peyrade immediately left the room and took the gendarme with him.

At this moment the corporal from Arcis came in, went up to Corentin and told him in a low voice: 'I know my way about here. I've searched all the outbuildings. Unless the young chaps have got themselves buried, there's nobody about. We're now sounding the floors and walls with our rifle-butts.'

Peyrade returned, beckoned to Corentin and took him out to show him the breach in the moat and pointed to the sunken road communicating with it. 'We've guessed what their tactics were,' he said.

'So have I!' Corentin retorted. 'I'll tell you what they were: the little rascal and the girl side-tracked those idiotic gendarmes so that the real game could get away.'

'We shan't know what actually happened till daylight,' Peyrade continued. 'The road is wet, and I've had it blocked at both ends by a couple of gendarmes. As soon as there's light enough to see we can tell by the footprints what people have passed that way.'

'Here are the prints of a horse-shoe,' said Corentin. 'Let's go to the stables.'

'How many horses have you here?' Peyrade asked Monsieur d'Hauteserre and Goulard as he returned to the drawing-room with Corentin.

'Come now, Mr Mayor, you know. Tell us,' Corentin shouted at this official as he saw him hesitating to answer.

'Well, there's the countess's mare, Gothard's pony and Monsieur d'Hauteserre's horse.'

'There's only one in the stable,' said Peyrade.

'Mademoiselle is out riding,' said Durieu.

'Does your ward often go out at night like this?' Peyrade asked Monsieur d'Hauteserre, with a suggestive leer.

'Very often,' the good man innocently replied. 'The mayor will bear witness to that.'

'Everybody knows what whims she has,' said Catherine. 'She was looking at the sky before going to bed, and it's my belief she was puzzled by the gleam of your bayonets in the distance. She wanted to know – so she told me as she went out – if yet another revolution had broken out.'

'When did she go out?' asked Peyrade.

'When she saw your guns.'

'Which way did she go?'

'I don't know.'

'Where's the other horse?' asked Corentin.

'The g–g–gendarmes t–t–took it away f–f–from me,' Gothard stuttered.

'But where were you going?' a gendarme asked him.

'I was f–f–following my m–m–mistress to the f–f–farm.'

The gendarme looked up at Corentin awaiting an order, but the boy's language seemed so false and yet so genuine, so utterly innocent and yet so crafty that the two Parisians exchanged a glance as if to repeat what Peyrade had said: 'They are no simpletons!'

Monsieur d'Hauteserre appeared not to have wit enough to understand the meaning of this glance. The mayor looked stupid. The mother, reduced to imbecility by maternal anxiety, was asking the agents idiotically naïve questions. All the servants had quite genuinely been startled out of their sleep. Faced with these small facts and sizing up these various characters, Corentin instantly recognized that his sole adversary was Mademoiselle de Cinq-Cygne. The police, however shrewd they may be, are up against innumerable disadvantages. Not only are they obliged to find out everything a conspirator knows: they must make innumerable conjectures before arriving at one single truth. A conspirator is continually on the defensive, whereas the police are only on the alert at certain times. If it were not for informers, nothing would be easier than to hatch conspiracies. One conspirator alone is more nimble-witted than the police, despite the immense resources at their disposal. Corentin and Peyrade, feeling as much mentally frustrated as they would have been physically by a door which they had expected to find open but would have staved in by simply making their men fling their weight against it, realized that someone or other was foreseeing and forestalling their every move.

'I'm sure,' the Arcis corporal whispered to them, 'that if the two Simeuses and the two d'Hauteserres spent the night here, they slept in the beds of the father, the mother, Mademoiselle de Cinq-Cygne, the chambermaid or the servants. Or else they wandered about the park, for there's not the slightest trace of their having been here.'

'But who can have warned them?' Corentin asked Peyrade. 'So far only the First Consul, Fouché, the Ministers, the Prefect of Police and Malin are in the know.'

'We'll leave some "sheep" round about,' Peyrade whispered to Corentin.

'You'll do all the better because Champagne is a sheep-rearing country,' said the curé, unable to repress a smile on overhearing the single word 'sheep', from which he guessed the rest.

'Heavens above!' thought Corentin, smiling back at the curé. 'There's only one intelligent man here. I might get something out of him; I'll have a try.'

'Gentlemen . . .' said the mayor, addressing the two agents, hoping that he still might give some proof of devotion to the First Consul.

'Citizens, you mean. The Republic still exists,' Corentin retorted at the curé with mockery in his eye.

'Citizens,' the mayor continued. 'Just as I was entering the drawing-room, and before I could open my mouth, Catherine rushed in to get hold of her mistress's whip, gloves and hat.'

A low murmur of horror was emitted from every breast except that of Gothard. All eyes, except those of the agents and the gendarmes, glared threateningly at the informer.

'Very good, Citizen mayor,' said Peyrade. 'That clears things up. Citizeness Cinq-Cygne must have been warned in good time,' he added, casting a glance of visible suspicion at Corentin.

'Corporal, handcuff this lad,' said Corentin to the gendarme, 'and take him to a separate room. Lock up the girl too,' he added, pointing to Catherine. Then he whispered to Peyrade: 'Have a good look round for papers. Search everywhere.

Leave no stone unturned . . . Monsieur l'Abbé,' he said confidentially to the curé. 'I have some important things to say to you.' And he took him out into the garden.

'Listen to me, Monsieur l'Abbé, you seem to me to have enough intelligence to be a bishop and (we shall not be overheard) you will follow my meaning. You are my only hope for saving two families who, out of stupidity, are rolling down into a pit from which there's no returning. The Simeuse and d'Hauteserre gentlemen have been betrayed by one of the infamous spies whom governments slip into every conspiracy so as to find out what it's about, how it's working and who belong to it. Don't confuse me with the wretched man who's with me: he's a policeman. But I have very honourable links with the Consular cabinet, and the last word lies with me. We don't want to destroy Messieurs de Simeuse. Malin would of course like to have them shot, but if they are still here and have no evil intentions, the First Consul wants to halt them on the brink of the precipice: he loves good soldiers. The agent who's with me is armed with full powers, but I know all about the plot. The agent is in with Malin, who no doubt has promised him protection, a post and perhaps money too, if he can find the Simeuses and deliver them up. The First Consul, a truly great man, gives no favour to covetous motives. – I'm not asking you if the two young men are here,' he said as he saw the gesture the curé gave, 'but there's only one way of saving them. You know of the law of 6 Floréal, Year X, which offers amnesty to *émigrés* still abroad provided they return to France before 1 Vendémiaire, Year XI, that is to say September of last year. But both the Simeuses and the d'Hauteserres, having held commissions in Condé's army, are excluded from this concession. Therefore their presence in France is a crime, and enough, in present circumstances, to implicate them in this heinous conspiracy. The First Consul detected the flaw in this exclusion, which creates irreconcilable opponents to his rule. He wants Messieurs de Simeuse to know that no proceedings will be taken against them on condition that they send him a petition stating that they are coming back to France intending to submit to the laws and promising to swear loyalty to the constitution. Understand that the document must be in his hands before their arrest and pre-dated by several days. I can take it to him. – I'm not asking you where they are,' he repeated at a new gesture of repudiation from the curé, 'but unfortunately we are bound to find them. There's a guard round the forest and both the Paris barriers and the frontiers are being watched. Take good heed! If these gentlemen are between this forest and Paris, they will be caught. If they turn back, poor souls, they will be arrested. The First Consul loves the old aristocracy and detests the Republicans: it's quite simple – if he wants to reign, liberty must be smothered. Let's keep this a secret between us. So look! I'll wait till tomorrow and keep my eyes closed. But beware of the agent. That accursed Provençal is an emissary of Satan. He takes his orders from Fouché, just as I take mine from the First Consul.'

'If the Simeuse gentlemen are here,' said the curé, 'I would give ten pints of my blood and one of my arms to save them; but even if Mademoiselle de Cinq-Cygne enjoys their confidence, I swear by my eternal salvation that she has kept it a dead secret and has not done me the honour of consulting me. As things stand I am glad she has been so discreet – if you can call it discretion. This evening, as on every other evening, we played boston until ten-thirty in the deepest silence: we saw nothing and heard nothing. Not even a child can pass through this lonely valley without everybody seeing and hearing him, and for the last fortnight no stranger has been here. Now Messieurs de Simeuse and d'Hauteserre are four persons – quite a troop! The worthy man and his wife have submitted to the Government and have made every imaginable effort to bring their sons back; they wrote again only the day before yesterday. And so I can say, sincerely and conscientiously, that only your descending upon us here has weakened my firm belief that they are still living in Germany. Between ourselves, there is no one here, except the young countess, who does not pay tribute to the outstanding qualities of Monsieur le Premier Consul.'

'He's a sly one!' thought Corentin. Then he replied out loud: 'If these young people get shot, they will have asked for it! I wash my hands of the affair.'

He had taken the Abbé Goujet to a strongly moonlit spot

and gave him a brusque stare as he uttered these fateful words. The priest showed great affliction, but it was that of a completely ignorant man who is taken by surprise.

'Understand this, Monsieur l'Abbé,' Corentin went on. 'Their title to the Gondreville estate makes them doubly guilty in the eyes of the lesser officials. In short, I should prefer them to be dealing directly with God Almighty rather than with His saints.'

'So there's a plot afoot?' the curé innocently asked.

'One so despicable, odious and cowardly, so little in tune with the generous spirit of the nation,' Corentin replied, 'that it will incur general opprobrium.'

'But Mademoiselle de Cinq-Cygne is incapable of cowardice,' the curé protested.

'Monsieur l'Abbé,' Corentin continued, 'mark my words. Speaking as one man to another, we have clear proofs of her complicity, though not yet enough to satisfy the law. She took to flight as soon as we came near ... And yet I had sent the mayor to you.'

'Yes, but for someone so keen on saving her, you followed rather closely on the mayor's heels.'

At this remark, the two men looked into each other's eyes; each of them had spoken his last word. Both of them were to be counted among those profound anatomists of thought for whom a single inflexion of the voice, a look or a word suffices for them to read people's minds, just as a Red Indian can detect the presence of an enemy from clues which are invisible to the eye of a European.

'I thought I might get something out of him and merely gave myself away,' thought Corentin.

'What a rogue!' the curé was saying to himself.

The old church clock was striking midnight when Corentin and the curé returned to the drawing-room. One could hear the doors of rooms and cupboards being opened and shut. The gendarmes were unmaking the beds. With the quick intelligence of a spy, Peyrade was searching and sounding everywhere. This ransacking excited both terror and indignation in the loyal-hearted servants, who were still standing about stock-still. Monsieur d'Hauteserre was exchanging sympathetic glances with his wife and Mademoiselle Goujet. Agonized curiosity was keeping everybody awake. Then Peyrade came downstairs into the drawing-room holding a casket of carved sandal-wood, which no doubt Admiral de Simeuse had formerly brought home from China. It was a handsome box, flat, and of the same size as a quarto volume.

Peyrade beckoned to Corentin and took him aside into the window-recess. 'I have it!' he said. 'The man Michu, who had enough money to pay Marion eight hundred thousand francs in gold for Gondreville, and who just now was stalking Malin with a gun, must be working for the Simeuses: his motive for threatening Marion and pointing his gun at Malin must be one and the same . . . It seemed to me that he was a man of ideas: in actual fact he had only one. He knows what's going on and must have come here to warn them.'

'Malin must have talked to his friend the notary about the conspiracy,' said Corentin, continuing the inferences made by his colleague, 'and Michu, lying in ambush, no doubt heard them talking about the Simeuses. In fact he only postponed his rifle-shot in order to forestall a mishap which to him would have been far more serious than the loss of Gondreville.'

'He had certainly recognized us for what we are,' said Peyrade. 'That's why it struck me that, for a peasant, he must be abnormally intelligent.'

'Oh, that merely proves that he was keeping his eyes open,' Corentin replied. 'But after all, my friend, let's not flatter ourselves: dirty work stinks to high heaven, and primitive-minded people smell it a mile off.'

'That only puts us in a stronger position,' said the Provençal.

'Fetch the Arcis corporal,' cried Corentin to a gendarme. 'Let's send someone to Michu's lodge,' he said to Peyrade.

'Our eavesdropper Violette is there,' said the Provençal.

'We went off without having any news from him,' said Corentin. 'We ought to have brought Sabatier with us. Two of us are not enough. – Corporal,' he said as he saw the gendarme come in, drawing him close between Peyrade and himself. 'Don't let yourself be put off the scent as the corporal from Troyes did, not long since. It looks as if Michu is in the plot. Go to the pavilion, keep your eyes open, and tell us what you see.'

'One of my men,' the gendarme replied, 'heard horses in the forest while we were arresting the young servants, and I have four stout fellows on the heels of anybody trying to hide there.' He went off, and the clatter of his galloping horse, on the pavement between the lawns, rapidly died away.

'That's it!' Corentin said to himself. 'Either they are moving towards Paris or going back towards Germany.' He sat down, drew a note-book from the pocket of his spencer, scribbled two orders in pencil, sealed them up and beckoned a gendarme towards him. 'Go to Troyes as fast as your horse can carry you, wake the Prefect, and tell him to get the semaphore working as soon as it gets light.'

The gendarme galloped away. Corentin's purpose and intentions were so clear that all the inhabitants of the château had their hearts in their mouths. This new anxiety intensified the torture they were suffering, for they all had their gaze fixed on the precious casket. The two agents, while they were talking together, were trying to fathom the thoughts behind those glowing eyes. As these stony-hearted men savoured the terror expressed on their victims' faces, they were stirred to a kind of cold fury. A police detective experiences all the emotions of the huntsman: in both cases all the powers of mind and body are called into play, but whereas the latter is only concerned with shooting a hare, a partridge or a buck, the former's task is to protect the State or the prince and so earn a generous reward. Thus the hunting of men outclasses hunting in the field by all the distance which separates man from the animals. Moreover, in playing his part, a spy has to rise to a level consonant with the grandeur and importance of the interests he is serving. And so, even though we have no experience of such activities, we may easily conceive that he is as impassioned in his quest as the huntsman is in pursuit of game. Therefore, the more light was cast on the situation, the more intent these two men grew; but they remained calm and cold of countenance and gaze, giving no inkling of their suspicions, ideas and plan of action. But anyone who could have observed the keen flair with which these two bloodhounds were scenting out unknown or hidden facts, anyone who could have interpreted the quiverings of canine agility which urged them to nose out the truth by a swift assessment of possibilities, would have had cause to shudder! How and why could these gifted men have sunk so low when they could have risen to such great heights? What flaw or imperfection, what evil passion brought them to such depths? Are men spies in the same way as other men are thinkers, writers, statesmen, painters or generals, being unable to do anything but spy in the same way as the others talk, write, govern, paint or fight? The inhabitants of the château had but one single longing in their hearts: would that a thunderbolt might fall on these infamous creatures! They were all athirst for vengeance, and would have risen in revolt but for the presence of the gendarmes.

'Who has the key of this coffer?' the cynical Peyrade demanded, questioning the assembly as much by the movement of his big red nose as by his speech.

Then he observed, not without a spasm of fear, that the gendarmes had gone. He and Corentin were alone. Corentin drew a small dagger from his pocket and started to dig into the slit under the lid. At that moment was heard, first on the road, then on the paving between the lawns, the startling clatter of a headlong gallop; but it was more startling still to hear the collapse and laboured breathing of a horse which fell flat and sprawling at the foot of the centre turret. All the spectators were thrown into a commotion like that produced by a peal of thunder when they heard the swish of Laurence's riding-habit and saw her coming in. The servants were quick to open a line for her to pass through. In spite of her headlong ride, she had been smarting from the pain which the divulgence of the conspiracy necessarily caused her: all her hopes were shattered! She had been galloping over the ruins of them, brooding over the necessity of submitting to the Consular government. And so, had it not been for the danger incurred by the four noblemen, which acted as a stimulant and helped her to conquer her fatigue and despair, she would have fallen asleep on her horse. She had almost ridden her mare to death in order to ward off death from her cousins. At the sight of this heroic girl, pale, with drawn features, her veil askew, her crop in her hand, standing on the threshold, her burning gaze taking in every detail of the scene, everyone realized, by the almost imperceptible twitch of Corentin's sour and troubled face, that the two real antagonists were now confronting each other. A terrible duel was about to begin.

*

Seeing the casket in Corentin's hands, the young countess raised her crop and leapt at him with such impetuosity and rapped him so violently on the knuckles that the casket fell to the floor. She seized it, hurled it straight into the fire and placed herself in front of the fire in a menacing attitude before the two agents had recovered from their surprise. Laurence's eyes were blazing with scorn; her pale forehead and disdainful lips were more insulting to the two men than the autocratic gesture with which she had struck at Corentin as if he were a venomous snake. The good d'Hauteserre was fired with chivalric valour; all the blood rushed to his face, and he regretted not having a sword. The servants trembled with joy first of all – the avenging thunderbolt they had evoked had blasted one of the spies. But the satisfaction they felt was forced back into the depth of their souls by a terrible fear: they could still hear the gendarmes coming and going in the attics.

A *spy* – this forcible substantive admits no shades of distinction between the many kinds of policemen, for the public has never consented to use specific terms for the diverse functions of those who have a hand in the devil's brew which all governments find necessary – a spy has this strange and splendid characteristic: he never loses his temper. He has the Christian humility of a priest; he expects to see contempt in other people's eyes and makes it a sort of barrier between himself and the pack of imbeciles who do not understand him. He is brazen-faced against insults and goes straight for his goal like an animal whose strong carapace is proof against anything but a cannon-ball. But, also like an animal, he is the more furious when anything gets through the armour he had thought to be impenetrable. The stroke of Laurence's whip on Corentin's knuckles, apart from the pain it caused, was the cannon-ball which pierces the carapace; coming from this magnificent and noble girl, this supremely contemptuous gesture humiliated him, not only in the eyes of the little gathering, but more so still in his own. The Provençal, Peyrade, rushed up to the fireplace; Laurence thrust him back with a kick, but he seized her foot, lifted it up and forced her, out of modesty, to fall back into the sofa in which she had been sleeping some hours before. It was like a farcical episode in a scene of terror, a contrast which frequently occurs in human experience. Peyrade scorched his hand in the attempt to seize the burning casket; but he did retrieve it, put it on the floor and sat down on it. These incidents happened in quick succession and in complete silence. Corentin, having now recovered from the pain of the blow, held Mademoiselle de Cinq-Cygne down by gripping her hands. 'Do not oblige me, *fair citizeness*, to use force against you,' he said with withering politeness. 'Will you promise to be reasonable?' he added in an insolent tone, picking up his dagger, but without making the mistake of threatening her with it.

'The secrets enclosed in this casket are no concern of the Government,' she replied with a tinge of melancholy in her air and accent. 'When you have read the letters in it, you will be ashamed, infamous as you are, to have read them. But are you still capable of shame?' she asked after a pause.

The curé threw a look at Laurence as if to say: 'In Heaven's name be calm!'

Peyrade stood up. The bottom of the casket, which had been in contact with the coals and was almost burnt through, left a brown singe on the carpet. The lid was already charred and the sides caved in. The grotesque Scaevola who had just sacrificed the seat of his apricot breeches to the policeman's deity – Fear – opened the two sides of the box as if it were a book and let three letters and two locks of hair slide out on to the table-cloth. He was about to smile across at Corentin when he noticed that the two locks were of different shades of white. Corentin left Mademoiselle de Cinq-Cygne in order to read the letter from which the hair had fallen.

Laurence also got up, stood by the two spies and said: 'Oh, read it aloud! That will be your punishment.' And as they were still running through it in silence, she herself read it out as follows:

'Dear Laurence,

'My husband and I heard how splendidly you behaved on the day of our arrest. We know that you love our darling twins, each of them, as much as we love them ourselves. That is why we are entrusting to you what will be at once a sad and a sacred relic for them. The executioner has just cut off our hair, for we are to die in a few seconds, and he has promised to commit to your care the only two tokens we can leave to our beloved orphans. So keep these remembrances of us and give them to them when better times come. We have left a last kiss on them with our blessing. Our last thoughts will be firstly for our sons, then for you, and lastly for God. Love them well.

BERTHE DE CINQ-CYGNE.
JEAN DE SIMEUSE.'

There were tears in every eye at the reading of this letter.

In a firm voicc, and with a petrifying look, Laurence said to the two agents: 'The public executioner showed more pity than you.'

Calmly, Corentin put the hair inside the letter and laid the letter on the table, placing a basket full of counters on it to prevent it being blown away. This coldness of heart in the midst of the general emotion was horrifying. Peyrade was opening the other two letters.

'Oh!' Laurence continued. 'These others are very much the same. You have heard their will read out: here is the sequel. Henceforth my heart will have no secrets for anyone, that's all.

'1794. Andernach, before the battle.

'Dear Laurence,

'I love you for life and I want you to be quite sure of it. But, in case I should be killed, let me tell you that my brother Paul-Marie loves you as much as I do. My only consolation in dying will be the certainty that one day you will be able to make my dear brother your husband without seeing me waste away with jealousy, as I assuredly should if, with both of us living, you preferred him to me. Yet after all I should consider this preference quite natural, for he is perhaps a better man than I.

MARIE-PAUL

'And here is the other,' she continued with a charming blush.

'Andernach, before the battle.

'My darling Laurence,

'I write this with a sad heart: but Marie-Paul is of too gay a character for you not to like him better than myself. Some day you will have to choose between us. Well, although I am passionately in love with you ...'

'You were corresponding with *émigrés*,' Peyrade interrupted, carefully holding the letters to the light in order to make sure there was nothing written in invisible ink between the lines.

'Yes,' Laurence replied, folding up the precious letters, now yellowed with age. 'But in virtue of what right do you thus violate my domicile, my personal liberty and all the domestic proprieties?'

'Ah indeed!' said Peyrade. 'By what right? That I must tell you, fair aristocrat,' he went on, drawing from his pocket an order issued by the Minister of Justice and countersigned by the Home Secretary. 'There you are, citizeness. The Ministers took it upon themselves to do that ... '

'We might ask you in turn,' Corentin whispered to her, 'by what right you harbour in your house men who propose to assassinate the First Consul. You have given me a rap over the knuckles, and some day that might provide me with an excuse for dispatching your noble cousins – and I came here to save them.'

By the mere curl of his lips and the look Laurence gave Corentin, the curé guessed what this cunning artist in treachery meant; he made a warning gesture to the countess which only Goulard perceived. Peyrade was lightly tapping the lid of the casket to find out if it consisted of two layers with a space between them.

'Oh, my God!' she said to Peyrade, snatching the lid from him. 'Don't break it. Look.'

She took a pin, pushed at the head of a figure carved on the lid, and the two layers, moved by a spring, came apart; in the hollow part were two miniatures of the Simeuse brothers in the uniform of Condé's army, two portraits which had been painted on ivory in Germany. Corentin, finding that he was facing an adversary worthy of all his wrath, beckoned Peyrade to a corner and conferred privately with him.

'How *could* you have thrown that in the fire?' the Abbé Goujet said to Laurence, looking towards the Marquise's letter and the locks of hair.

The girl's only reply was a significant shrug, by which the curé understood that she was sacrificing everything in order to keep the spies occupied and gain time; he raised his eyes to heaven in a gesture of admiration.

'I hear Gothard crying. Where did they arrest him?' she asked him in a voice loud enough to be overheard.

'I don't know,' the curé answered.

'Had he gone to the farm?'

'The farm!' Peyrade said to Corentin. 'Send some men there.'

'No,' replied Corentin. 'The girl certainly would not have entrusted her cousins' safety to a farmer. She's playing for time. Do what I told you, so that after making the mistake of coming here we can at least go away with some matters cleared up.'

He went and stood in front of the fireplace, lifted the long, tapering tails of his coat in order to warm himself and assumed the air, tone and manners of someone paying a call.

'Ladies, you may retire, and your servants too. Mr Mayor, your services are no longer required. The strict orders we have received do not allow us to act otherwise than we have acted; but once all the walls, which seem to me very thick, have been examined, we shall depart.'

The mayor took his leave and went out. Neither the curé nor Mademoiselle Goujet stirred an inch. The servants were too worried not to stay and see what was going to happen to their young mistress. Madame d'Hauteserre, who since Laurence's arrival had been studying her with the curiosity of a despairing mother, stood up, took her by the arm, led her into a corner and quietly asked her: 'Have you seen my sons?'

'Would I have let your children come under our roof without your knowing?' Laurence replied.

'Durieu,' she then said. 'See if it is possible to save my poor Stella. She's still breathing.'

'She must have had a long run,' Corentin remarked.

'Nearly forty miles in three hours,' she told the curé, who was gazing at her in stupefaction. 'I left at nine thirty, and got back well after one o'clock.' She looked at the clock: it was half-past three.

'And so,' said Corentin, 'you don't deny having made a forty-mile ride?'

'No,' she said. 'I admit that my cousins and Messieurs d'Hauteserre, in perfect innocence, were counting on not being excepted from the amnesty and were returning to Cinq-Cygne. And so, when I had reason to believe that the egregious Malin was trying to implicate them in some sort of treason, I went and told them to go back to Germany; and they will be there before the Troyes semaphore reports that they had crossed the frontier. If this is a crime, let me be punished for it.'

This reply, which Laurence had so carefully thought out and was so plausible in every detail, shook Corentin's convictions. She was looking at him out of the corner of her eye. At this critical moment, when every soul present was anxiously gazing at their two faces, and every eye was turning alternately from Corentin to Laurence and from Laurence to Corentin, the noise of a horse galloping back from the forest echoed along the road, through the gateway and along the drive. Desperate anxiety was depicted on every countenance.

Peyrade came in, his eyes gleaming with joy, rushed up to his colleague and said, loud enough for the countess to hear: 'We have nabbed Michu!' Laurence, whose cheeks were hectic with fatigue and the tension to which all her mental faculties were subjected, turned pale again and collapsed into an arm-chair, dumbfounded and almost swooning. Durieu's wife, Mademoiselle Goujet and Madame d'Hauteserre rushed up to her, for she was gasping for breath. She motioned to them to cut the frogs of her riding-habit.

'She's given herself away,' Corentin said to Peyrade. 'Her cousins are making for Paris. We must reverse our orders.'

They went out, leaving a gendarme on guard at the drawing-room door. The diabolic cunning of these two men had given them a deplorable advantage in this duel: they had tried one of their habitual tricks and caught Laurence in a trap.

At six o'clock in the morning, as day was breaking, the

two agents returned. They had explored the sunken road and ascertained that horses had passed along it to the forest. They were awaiting reports from the captain of gendarmerie, whose task it had been to reconnoitre the region. Leaving the encircled château under the surveillance of a corporal, they went to a Cinq-Cygne tavern for breakfast, though not before ordering the release of Gothard, who had not ceased to answer all questions with floods of tears, and Catherine, who had remained still and silent. They both went to the drawing-room and kissed Laurence's hands as she lay stretched out in her *bergère*. Durieu came to announce that Stella would survive but needed very careful treatment.

The mayor, anxious and curious, met Peyrade and Corentin in the village. He would not hear of senior officials breakfasting in a shabby tavern and took them home with him to his abbey, less than a mile away. As they walked along, Peyrade remarked that the Arcis corporal had sent no news of Michu and Violette.

'We have smart people to deal with,' said Corentin. 'They're one too many for us. No doubt the parson is taking a hand.'

Just as Madame Goulard was showing the two officials into a vast, unheated dining-room, the lieutenant of gendarmerie arrived, looking alarmed.

'We came upon the Arcis corporal's horse in the forest, riderless,' he told Peyrade.

'Lieutenant,' cried Corentin, 'hurry to Michu's pavilion and find out what's happening there. They have probably killed the corporal.'

This piece of news disturbed their breakfast with the mayor. They gulped down their food with the rapidity of huntsmen taking a snack during a halt and returned to the château in their basket-gig drawn by the post-horse, so that they could more swiftly move to any point where their presence might be required. When the two Parisians reappeared in the drawing-room to which they had brought so much confusion, fright, suffering and cruel anxiety, they found Laurence there in her dressing-gown, with d'Hauteserre and his wife, the Abbé Goujet and his sister sitting together in front of the fire, apparently quite calm.

'If they had really caught Michu,' Laurence had said to herself, 'they would have brought him in. I'm vexed to have lost my self-control and to have given some grounds for suspicion to those infamous men. But that can be remedied. – How long are we to remain your prisoners?' she asked the two agents with a free-and-easy, mocking air.

The spies gave each other a look which said: 'How can she know anything about our anxiety concerning Michu? No one from outside has entered the château. And yet she's jeering at us.'

'We shall not be bothering you much longer,' Corentin replied to Laurence. 'In three hours' time we shall be expressing our regrets at having disturbed your solitude.'

No one gave an answer. This contemptuous silence redoubled the rage inside Corentin, for the two intelligent people in this little group, Laurence and the curé, now knew what to make of him. Gothard and Catherine laid the table for lunch near the fire, and the curé and his sister partook of it. Neither mistress nor servants paid any attention to the spies, who were stalking about in the garden, the courtyard and along the road, though from time to time they returned to the drawing-room.

At two-thirty the lieutenant came back.

'I've found the corporal,' he told Corentin, 'lying full length on the road leading from the Cinq-Cygne lodge to the Bellache farm, with no other wound than a very bad bruise on his skull – probably resulting from a fall. He told me had been torn from his horse so rapidly and thrown backwards so violently that he can't explain how it was done. His feet came out of the stirrups, otherwise he'd have been killed, for the startled horse would have dragged him along in his flight. We have put him in the care of Michu and Violette.'

'What! Michu is in his lodge?' said Corentin with a side-glance at Laurence.

The countess gave a knowing smile, like a woman getting her own back.

'I found him in the act of completing a deal with Violette which they started on yesterday evening. They both looked drunk, but the surprising thing is that they were tippling all night long and still haven't come to terms.'

'Violette told you that?' exclaimed Corentin.

'Yes,' said the lieutenant.

'Ah! We ought to have done everything ourselves,' cried Peyrade with a glance at Corentin who was as doubtful as Peyrade himself of the lieutenant's intelligence. He nodded in reply to the older man's remark.

'What time did you get to Michu's lodge?' asked Corentin, noticing that Mademoiselle de Cinq-Cygne had glanced at the clock on the mantelpiece.

'About two o'clock,' said the lieutenant.

Laurence took one steady look at Monsieur and Madame d'Hauteserre, the Abbé and his sister, who felt as if they were under a mantle of azure. The joy of triumph was sparkling in her eyes, her colour came back, and her eyelids welled with tears. This girl, fortified against the greatest misfortunes, could weep only for pleasure. She was superb at this moment, especially in the curé's eyes: hitherto he had felt worried because she seemed so masculine in character, but now he realized how femininely tender-hearted she was, though her sensibility lay infinitely deep, like a treasure hidden under a block of granite. Just then a gendarme entered and asked if Michu's son, who had come from his father's house to talk to the gentlemen from Paris, should be let in. Corentin nodded assent. François Michu, a wily little terrier true to his breed, was waiting in the courtyard where Gothard, now released, was able to talk with him for a few seconds under the gendarme's nose. Little Michu discharged his errand by slipping something into Gothard's hand without the gendarme noticing. Gothard slid in behind François, went up to Mademoiselle de Cinq-Cygne and quietly handed her the two halves of her ring which she ardently kissed, for she understood that Michu, by thus restoring them, was telling her that the four nobles were safe.

'Papa wants to know what to do with the corporal. He's in a bad way.'

'What's wrong with him?'

'It's his head. He fell off his horse and gave it an awful bash. Bad luck for a policeman who knows how to ride a horse, but it must have tripped up. You could shove your fist in the hole in the back of his head. Poor man, he must have tumbled on to a nasty bit of rock. Policeman or not, he's hurt so much you can't help feeling sorry for him.'

The captain of gendarmes from Troyes rode into the courtyard, dismounted and beckoned to Corentin, who recognized him, ran to the window and opened it to save time.

'What is it?'

'They've been leading us on a wild-goose chase. Five horses have been found, ridden to death, their coats matted with sweat, right in the middle of the main forest avenue. I've set a guard over them to find out where they came from and who provided them. The forest is surrounded. No one inside it can get out of it.'

'What time do you think these horsemen entered the forest?'

'Half an hour after midday.'

'Not even a hare must leave the forest unseen,' Corentin whispered to him. 'I'll leave Peyrade with you and go and see that poor corporal. – Stay at the mayor's house,' he whispered to Peyrade. 'I'll send an able man to relieve you. We must make use of the local people. Look close at every face.' Then he turned to the company assembled and said '*Au revoir*' in an intimidating tone of voice.

The agents went out without receiving any salutations.

'What will Fouché say about a domiciliary visit which has yielded no results?' exclaimed Peyrade, as he helped Corentin into the gig.

'Oh! all isn't over yet,' Corentin said quietly. 'The four aristos must be somewhere in the forest.' He pointed to Laurence, who was looking at them through the small panes in the large windows of the drawing-room. 'I brought one woman to grief who got on the wrong side of me, and she was just as clever as this one.[7] If ever she gets in my way again I'll pay her out for striking me.'

'But the other one was a trollop,' said Peyrade. 'This one is in a very different position.'

'That makes no difference to me. All is fish that comes into

7. Marie de Verneuil, in *The Chouans*. Sent to Brittany by the Directory government to trap the Royalist leader, the Marquis of Montauran, she tried to thwart Corentin and was killed with the marquis.

my net!' said Corentin, making a sign to the driver to whip up the post-horse.

Ten minutes later the château of Cinq-Cygne was entirely and completely evacuated.

'How did they get rid of the corporal?' Laurence asked François Michu, whom she had made sit down and was feeding.

'My father and my mother told me it was a matter of life and death and that nobody was to get into our house. Well, I could tell from the sound of horses in the forest that those dirty gendarmes were about, and I wanted to keep them out of our house. So I got some thick ropes from our attic and tied them to trees at the end of each road. Then I stretched each rope across to be level with a horseman's chest and wound it round the opposite tree across the road on which I heard a horse galloping along. In this way the road was barred. The trick worked. The moon wasn't shining any more and the corporal came a cropper. But it didn't kill him. Gendarmes take some killing. Anyway, I did what I could.'

'You saved our lives!' said Laurence, giving François a kiss and leading him back to the gateway. And there, seeing no one about, she asked him in a whisper: 'Have they food?'

'I've just taken them a twelve-pound loaf and four bottles of wine. That will keep them quiet for a day or two.'

On returning to the drawing-room, Laurence saw that she was the object of mute interrogations from Monsieur and Madame d'Hauteserre, also from Mademoiselle and the Abbé Goujet, who were looking at her with as much admiration as anxiety.

'So you have seen them again?' cried Madame d'Hauteserre.

The countess put her finger to her lips with a smile, and went upstairs to bed. Having won the day, she was overwhelmed with fatigue.

*

The shortest way from Cinq-Cygne to Michu's pavilion was by the road leading from the village to the Bellache farm which came to an end at the *rond-point* where Michu had encountered the spies the previous day. And so the gendarme who was escorting Corentin followed this route, the one which the Arcis corporal had also taken. As they went along, the agent was trying to puzzle out by what device the corporal had been unsaddled. He blamed himself for having sent only one man to so important a point, and from this error he deduced an axiom for a sort of police code he was drawing up for his own use. 'Since they managed to shake off the gendarme,' he thought to himself, 'they also managed to put Violette out of action. It's obvious that the five dead horses carried Michu and the four conspirators back from the outskirts of Paris. – Has Michu a horse?' he asked the gendarme of the Arcis brigade.

'Yes, indeed,' the gendarme replied. 'A first-class pony, a race-horse from the stables of the former Marquis de Simeuse. He's all the better for being a fifteen-year-old. Michu can make him do fifty miles without him lathering at all. Oh! he looks after him well. He wouldn't sell him at any price.'

'What's the horse look like?'

'A brown coat verging on black; white spots above his hooves; lean and as lithe as an Arab.'

'So you've seen Arab horses?'

'I was drafted back from Egypt a year ago, and I have ridden Mameluke horses. I served in the cavalry for eleven years. I crossed the Rhine with General Steingal, then went to Italy, and I was with the First Consul in Egypt. So I'm due for a corporal's stripes.'

'When I get inside Michu's pavilion, go to the stable, and since you've been living with horses for eleven years you ought to be able to tell when a horse has had a long run.'

'Look. There's the place where our corporal was thrown off his horse,' said the gendarme, pointing to the spot where the track emerged into the circular clearing.

'You'll tell the captain to pick me up at the pavilion. We'll go to Troyes together from there.'

Corentin dismounted and spent a minute or two inspecting the ground. He studied two elm-trees facing each other, one of them standing up from the park wall, the other rising from the bank surrounding the *rond-point* intersected by the village by-road. Then he saw something no one had noticed: a uniform button lying in the dust, which he picked up. Entering the pavilion, he discovered Violette and Michu sitting at the kitchen table and still arguing. Violette stood up, saluted Corentin and offered him a drink.

'No, thank you,' the younger man said. 'I should like to see the corporal.' He guessed at a glance that Violette had been drunk for more than a dozen hours.

'My wife is looking after him upstairs,' said Michu.

'Well, corporal, how goes it with you?' asked Corentin after running upstairs and finding the gendarme lying on Madame Michu's bed with a compress round his head.

His hat, sabre and shoulder-belt were in a chair. Marthe, true to her womanly feelings, and for that matter knowing nothing of her son's exploit, was nursing the corporal in company with her mother.

'We are waiting for Monsieur Varlet, the doctor from Arcis,' said Madame Michu. 'Gaucher has gone to fetch him.'

'Leave us for a moment,' said Corentin, surprised at this spectacle, which clearly proved the innocence of the two women. 'Where were you hit?' he asked, looking at the uniform.

'In the chest,' the corporal replied.

'Let me see your equipment,' said Corentin.

On the yellow band edged with white piping which a recent law had given to the so-called National Gendarmerie, prescribing its uniform down to the last detail, was a badge fairly similar to the present-day country policeman's badge, on which the law had stipulated that the singular phrase *Respect for persons and property!* should be engraved. The rope used by François had necessarily hit against the cross-belts and deeply scored them. Corentin took up the coat and saw that a button was missing.

'At what time were you picked up?' Corentin asked.

'Just as dawn was breaking.'

'Were you carried up here straight away?' asked Corentin, noticing that the bed had not been rumpled.

'Yes.'

'Who carried you up?'

'The women and young Michu, who found me lying unconscious.'

'Right! They didn't go to bed,' Corentin said to himself. 'It was neither a bullet nor a blow from a cudgel which struck the corporal, for in order to hit him his attacker would have had to be on a level with him, and therefore on horseback. A length of wood? Impossible. An iron chain? It would have left marks. – What did you feel?' he said aloud to the corporal, coming forward to examine him.

'I was unhorsed so suddenly ...'

'Your skin is grazed under the chin.'

'I felt as if a rope were lashing my face ...'

'I've got it,' said Corentin. 'A rope was stretched between two trees to block your way.'

'That could well be,' said the corporal.

Corentin went downstairs to the living-room.

'Come on, you old twister,' Michu was saying to Violette, with one eye on the agent. 'Let's settle the matter. A hundred and twenty thousand francs all told, and my lands are yours. I shall invest the money and live on the interest.'

'I tell you, and it's the gospel truth, I've only got fifty thousand.'

'But you can pay me the rest in instalments! Look, we've been at it since yesterday and haven't finished the deal ... First-quality land!'

'The land's all right,' Violette replied.

'Wife, bring some wine!' cried Michu.

'Haven't you drunk enough?' Marthe's mother protested. 'You've had fourteen bottles since nine o'clock yesterday.'

'You've been here since nine o'clock this morning?' Corentin asked Violette.

'Excuse me, no. I haven't budged since nine o'clock last night, and I've got nowhere with him. The more drink he gives me, the more he asks for his property.'

'When you're haggling,' said Corentin, 'the more you lift your elbow, the more the price goes up.'

A dozen empty bottles in a row on the end of the table confirmed the statement about the previous night's proceedings. At this juncture the gendarme backoned Corentin outside and whispered, as they reached the doorstep: 'There's no horse in the stable.'

Corentin went in again. 'You must have sent your boy to the town on horseback,' he said. 'He should soon be back.'

'No, Monsieur,' said Marthe. 'He's walking.'

'Well then, what have you done with your horse?'

'He's on loan,' Michu curtly replied.

'Come here, you holy fraud,' said Corentin to the bailiff. 'I've a word or two for your ears alone.'

The two men went out.

'The carbine you were loading yesterday at four o'clock was intended for killing the Councillor of State. The notary Grévin saw you, though you can't be nabbed for that: malice aforethought, but few witnesses. You managed somehow or other to get Violette asleep, and your wife, your small boy and yourself spent the night out in order to warn Mademoiselle de Cinq-Cygne of our arrival and to save her cousins, whom you brought here – I still don't know where. Either your son or your wife very cleverly fetched the corporal off his horse. In short you got the better of us. You're a smart customer. But all is not over; the last word has not been spoken. Will you come to terms? Your masters will gain by it.'

'Come this way, we can talk without being overheard,' said Michu, leading the spy through the park to the pond.

When Corentin saw the sheet of water, he looked hard at Michu, who was no doubt reckoning on his strength to throw the man into the three-foot-deep water with seven feet of mud at the bottom. Michu in his turn gave him an equally fixed stare. It was absolutely like a cold and flabby boa constrictor squaring up to a red and tawny jaguar from Brazil.

'I'm not thirsty,' the elegant Corentin replied; he stood on the edge of the grass and put his hand in his side-pocket to feel for his little dagger.

'There can be no understanding between us,' Michu coldly replied.

'Be on your best behaviour, my good fellow. The Law will keep an eye on you.'

'If it doesn't see more clearly than you, all and sundry will be in danger,' the bailiff retorted.

'So you refuse?' said Corentin in an expressive tone of voice.

'I'd rather have my head cut off a hundred times – if a man's head could be cut off a hundred times – than strike a bargain with a scoundrel like you.'

Corentin looked Michu up and down, gave a last glance at the pavilion and the dog Couraut, who was barking at him. Then he sprang briskly on to the gig. He gave a few orders as he passed through Troyes and returned to Paris. All the brigades of gendarmes were given express and secret instructions.

During the months of December, January and February, active and continuous searches were made in every village large or small. There was eavesdropping in all the taverns. Corentin made three important discoveries. A horse similar to Michu's was found dead in the purlieus of Lagny. The five horses buried in the forest of Nodesme had been sold for five hundred francs each by farmers and millers to a man who, to judge by the description given of him, must have been Michu. When the law against Cadoudal's accomplices and those who harboured them was passed, Corentin confined his supervision to the forest of Nodesme. Then, when Moreau, the royalists and Pichegru were arrested, no more strange faces were seen in the neighbourhood. Michu then lost his post, the Arcis notary having delivered him a letter in which the Councillor of State, now a Senator, called on Grévin to settle accounts with his bailiff and dismiss him. In the space of three days Michu obtained his formal discharge and was now unemployed. To the great astonishment of all around, he went to live at Cinq-Cygne, where Laurence put him in charge of all the château demesne. By a stroke of fate, the day of his installation coincided with the execution of the Duc d'Enghien. Simultaneously throughout the whole of France the news came of that prince's arrest, trial, condemnation and execution: a terrible reprisal which was followed by the trial of Polignac, Rivière and Moreau.

2. *Corentin's Revenge*

WHILE waiting for the farmhouse to be built in which he was to live, Michu, nicknamed Judas, took up his abode in the servants' quarters over the stables, on the same side as the famous breach in the moat. He bought two horses, one for himself and one for his son, for they both joined Gothard in accompanying Mademoiselle de Cinq-Cygne on all her rides, undertaken of course in order to feed the four noblemen and to see that they had all they needed. François and Gothard, with the help of Couraut and the countess's dogs, went scouting round the site of the hiding-place and made sure there was no one in the vicinity. Laurence and Michu brought the food, which Marthe, her mother and Catherine prepared without the servants knowing, so as to keep it a close secret, for none of them doubted that there were spies in the village. Thus, as a measure of caution, this expedition never took place more than twice a week and always at different times, now by day, now by night. These precautions continued while Rivière, Polignac and Moreau were being tried. When the *Senatus-consultum* which proclaimed Napoleon emperor and conferred imperial status on the Bonaparte family was submitted to the vote of the French people, Monsieur d'Hauteserre signed his name on the register presented to him by Goulard. Finally the news came that the Pope was to come and crown Napoleon. From then on Mademoiselle de Cinq-Cygne no longer objected to an application being made by the two young d'Hauteserres and her cousins to have their names struck off the list of *émigrés* and regain their rights as citizens. The old man immediately hurried to Paris and went to see the former Marquis de Chargebœuf, who knew Monsieur de Talleyrand. This Minister, then in favour, forwarded the petition to Josephine, and she handed it over to her husband, who was being addressed as 'Your Majesty', 'Sire', and referred to as the Emperor before the result of the national vote was known. Monsieur de Chargebœuf, Monsieur d'Hauteserre and the Abbé Goujet, who also came to Paris, obtained an audience of

Talleyrand, and the latter promised his support. Napoleon had already pardoned the chief actors in the great conspiracy directed against him; but although the four noblemen were merely under suspicion, the Emperor, after a session of the Council of State, summoned the following people to his private cabinet: Senator Malin, Fouché, Talleyrand, Cambacérès, Lebrun, and Dubois the Prefect of Police.

'Gentlemen,' said the future Emperor, who was still wearing the uniform of First Consul, 'we have received from Messieurs de Simeuse and d'Hauteserre, officers in the Prince of Condé's army, a request for authorization to return to France.'

'They *are* in France,' said Fouché.

'But so are a thousand others whom I meet in Paris,' Talleyrand replied.

'I don't think', said Malin, 'that you have met those four here, for they are hiding in the forest of Nodesme and have made themselves quite at home there.'

He took care not to relate to the First Consul and Fouché the open-air conversation which had saved his life; but, basing his affirmations on reports made by Corentin, he convinced his hearers that the four nobles had taken part in the plot hatched by Rivière and Polignac, and that Michu had been their accomplice. The Prefect of Police confirmed the senator's assertions.

'And yet,' the Prefect went on to ask, 'how could the bailiff have known that the conspiracy had been divulged, at a time when the Emperor, the Council and myself were the only people who knew about it?' No one paid any attention to Dubois's remark.

'If they have been hiding in the forest for seven months without your finding them,' the Emperor said to Fouché, 'they have certainly atoned for their misdeeds.'

Malin was afraid that the Prefect of Police might get too near the heart of the matter. 'Your Majesty,' he said, 'the Simeuses are my enemies and therefore I feel I must emulate Your Majesty's generosity: I ask for the deletion of their names and constitute myself their advocate.'

Fouché looked fixedly at Malin and said, 'They will be less of a danger to you reinstated than they were as *émigrés*, for they will have taken the oath of fidelity to the laws and constitutions of the Empire.'

'In what way are they a threat to Monsieur le Sénateur?' asked Napoleon.

Talleyrand conversed in low tones for some time with the Emperor, and it seemed as if the application of the Simeuses and the d'Hauteserres was to be granted.

'Sire,' said Fouché, 'you may hear of those people yet again.'

Now Talleyrand, at the request of the Duc de Grandlieu, had just pledged the word of the four young men, on their honour as noblemen – a phrase which exerted some charm on Napoleon – that they would not engage in any enterprise against him and would make their submission unreservedly. 'Messieurs d'Hauteserre and Messieurs de Simeuse', he said, 'have no wish to bear arms against France after the recent events. They haven't much sympathy for the Imperial government and are the sort of persons Your Majesty will have to win over. But they will be content to live on French soil in obedience to the laws.' Then he showed the Emperor a letter he had received expressing these sentiments.

'So frank an avowal must be sincere,' said the Emperor to Lebrun and Cambacérès. 'Have you any further objections?' he asked Fouché.

'In Your Majesty's interests,' replied the future Minister of General Police, 'I ask to have the task of informing those gentlemen of the deletion of their names *once it has been definitely granted.*' He raised his voice at this last phrase.

'So be it,' said Napoleon, noting the expression of anxiety on Fouché's face.

This private deliberation broke off without the affair appearing to be decided; it resulted in a note of doubt subsisting in Napoleon's memory with regard to the four noblemen. Monsieur d'Hauteserre, confident of success, had written a letter in anticipation of good news. The inhabitants of Cinq-Cygne were therefore not astonished when, a few days later, Goulard came to tell Madame d'Hauteserre and Laurence that the four young men were to be sent to Troyes, where the Prefect would hand them the decree reinstating them in all their rights after they had taken the oath and promised adherence to the laws of the Empire. Laurence replied that she would have them informed.

'Then they are not here?' asked Goulard.

Madame d'Hauteserre looked anxiously at the girl, who left the mayor there and went out to consult Michu, who saw no reason why the *émigrés* should not be set free immediately. Laurence, Michu, his son and Gothard therefore rode off to the forest taking an extra horse, for the countess was to accompany the four noblemen to Troyes and return with them. The whole staff of servants, having heard the good news, assembled on the lawn to see the joyful cavalcade depart. The four young men emerged from their hiding-place, mounted their horses without being seen and, with Laurence, took the road to Troyes. Michu, with the help of Gothard and François, closed the entrance to the cellar and all three returned on foot. But on the way home Michu remembered he had left in the vault the cutlery and silver goblet his masters had used, and went back alone. On arriving at the edge of the pond, he heard voices in the cellar and made straight for the entrance through the brushwood.

'No doubt you're coming for your silver plate?' said Peyrade with a smile as he showed his huge nose through the foliage.

Without knowing why, since after all the young men were in safety, Michu felt a pain in every joint, so keenly was he affected by the kind of vague, indefinable apprehension which a future misfortune may foreshadow. Nevertheless he walked forward and found Corentin on the steps, holding a wax taper.

'We aren't vindictive,' he said to Michu. 'We could have nabbed your ex-aristos a week ago; but we knew they were off the list . . . You're a sharp fellow, and you've caused us too much trouble for us not at least to satisfy our curiosity.'

'I'd give a good deal', cried Michu, 'to know how and by whom we were betrayed.'

'If that puzzles you, my lad,' said Peyrade, smiling, 'take a look at your horses' shoes and you'll see that you gave yourselves away.'

'No ill-feeling,' said Corentin, beckoning to the captain of gendarmes to come with the horses.

'That miserable farrier from Paris who was once at Cinq-Cygne and shod horses so well in the English style, was on their side!' exclaimed Michu. 'All they had to do was to have our horses shod with calks and send a man disguised as a woodcutter or poacher to reconnoitre and follow the tracks of the horses when the ground was damp. Well, honours are even.'

Michu soon took comfort at the thought that discovery of the hiding-place could now do no harm since the noblemen were French citizens once again and had recovered their freedom. None the less all his presentiments were founded in reason. Both police officials and Jesuits have this one virtue: they never abandon either their friends or their enemies.

*

The worthy d'Hauteserre returned from Paris and was quite astonished not to have been the first person to bring the good news. Durieu was preparing the most succulent of dinners. The servants were dressing up, and everyone waited impatiently for the exiles. They arrived about four o'clock, feeling at once joyful and humiliated, for they were to be under police surveillance for two years, obliged to report every month at the Prefecture and enjoined to remain in the commune of Cinq-Cygne during those two years.

'I will send the register for you to sign,' the Prefect had said. 'Then, in a few months' time, you will apply to be released from these terms, which for that matter are imposed upon all Pichegru's accomplices. I will support your application.' These restrictions, though well merited, disconcerted the young people, but Laurence merely laughed.

'The Emperor of the French', she said, 'is an ill-bred man who is not yet in the habit of granting pardons.'

The noblemen found all the inhabitants of the château assembled at the gateway and, on the roadside, a fair crowd of villagers who had come along to see the young men whose adventures had made them the talk of the department. For a long time Madame d'Hauteserre held her sons in a close embrace, her face bathed in tears. She was unable to speak, and afterwards spent part of the evening in a daze, but very happy.

As soon as the Simeuses appeared and dismounted, there had been a general cry of surprise due to their astonishing resemblance. They were identical in looks, voice and manners. They each made the same gesture as they rose on their saddles, passed a leg over the horse's cruppers as they got down, and flung the reins aside with a similar motion. They were dressed exactly alike, and this also induced the spectators to take them for genuine Menechmi. They wore Souvorov boots shaped at the ankle, close-fitting white leather trousers, green hunting-jackets with metal buttons, black cravats and buckskin gloves. Both of these young men, then thirty-one years old, were, to quote an expression then current, 'charming cavaliers': of medium height but well-proportioned, with bright eyes fringed with long lashes and limpid like those of a child, black hair, fine forehead and olive-white complexion. Their speech, gentle as that of a woman, fell graciously from their red, well-moulded lips. Their manners, more elegant and polished than those of provincial noblemen, testified that a knowledge of men and things had provided them with that second education, more valuable than the first, which goes into the making of accomplished men. Thanks to Michu they had not lacked for money while they were abroad, had been able to travel and had been welcomed to foreign courts. The old gentleman and the Abbé thought them a little haughty, but this was perhaps the natural response of spirited persons to such a situation as theirs. They had the little touches of superiority resulting from careful breeding and were exceptionally adroit in all the exercises of the body. The only noticeable dissimilarity between them lay in their outlook. The younger brother charmed as much by his gaiety as the elder did by his melancholy, but this purely moral contrast could only be detected after long intimacy with them.

'Ah! my dear,' Michu whispered to Marthe, 'how could one fail to be devoted to these two young men?'

Marthe, who admired the twins both as woman and as mother, gave a pretty assenting nod and squeezed her husband's hand. The servants were allowed to embrace their new masters.

During the seven months of confinement which the young

men had brought upon themselves, they had several times committed the imprudence of taking a few much-needed outings, with Michu, his son and Gothard keeping a weather eye open. During these walks in the starlight or moonlight Laurence, reviewing both past and present in their life together, had come to realize the impossibility of choosing between the two brothers. Her heart was shared between the twins in a pure and equal love. She felt indeed as if she had two hearts. On their side, the two Pauls had not dared to talk to each other of their impending rivalry. Perhaps the three of them were leaving the matter to chance.

At this juncture Laurence's conduct was doubtless governed by her uncertainty of mind: after a moment of visible hesitation, she gave an arm to each of the brothers as they entered the drawing-room followed by Monsieur and Madame d'Hauteserre, who were clinging to their sons and questioning them. At this moment all the servants shouted: 'Long live the Cinq-Cygnes and the Simeuses!' Laurence, still standing between the two brothers, turned round and thanked them with a charming gesture.

When these nine persons arrived at the stage of observing one another – for in any family reunion, however intimate, a moment always comes after long absence when they all take stock of one another – at the first look which Adrien d'Hauteserre cast at Laurence, which caught the attention of both his mother and the Abbé Goujet, it became apparent to them that this young man was also in love with the countess. Adrien, the younger d'Hauteserre, was a man of gentle and affectionate disposition. He had remained adolescent in heart despite the catastrophes which had tested him as a man. In this respect, like many military men who remain pure in heart in the midst of continuous danger, he felt the attractive shyness of youth weighing upon him. Which means that he was entirely different from his brother, a man of rough demeanour, a mighty huntsman, a fearless soldier, full of resolution but material-minded and lacking nimbleness of wit as he lacked delicacy in matters of the heart. The one was all feeling, the other all action; yet both of them possessed to the same degree that sense of honour which means everything to men of noble birth. Dark, short, slim and spare, Adrien d'Hauteserre none the less gave an impression of great strength, whilst his brother, tall, fair-skinned and blond, gave an impression of inertia. Adrien, though highly-strung, possessed moral strength; Robert, though lymphatic of temperament, liked to make a show of purely physical strength. Such peculiarities are found within families, and it would be interesting to study the causes of them; but here it is only a question of explaining why Adrien was not likely to find a rival in his brother. Robert had a cousinly affection for Laurence and a nobleman's respect for a girl of his own caste. As far as feeling was concerned, the elder d'Hauteserre belonged to the category of men who consider woman as a dependant of the male, allowing her no rights but the physical one of maternity, looking for many perfections in her but giving her no credit for them. In their view, to allow woman influence in the social, the political and even the family sphere, is to turn society upside-down. Today we have moved so far away from this antiquated, primitive view-point that almost any woman, even those who do not lay claim to the disastrous freedom which the new sects promise them, might be shocked at it. But unfortunately this was the way Robert d'Hauteserre thought. Robert was a man of the Middle Ages, Adrien a man of the present day. But this divergence, instead of impeding affection between them, had on the contrary brought them closer together. From the first evening onwards these differences were grasped and appraised by the curé, Mademoiselle Goujet and Madame d'Hauteserre; and while they played their game of boston, they could already see difficulties ahead.

Laurence was twenty-three. After her solitary meditations and her anguish due to the failure of a great enterprise, she had become a woman once more, and felt a tremendous need for affection; she displayed all her qualities of mind and her winning personality. She revealed all the charms of a tender heart with the naïvety of a child of fifteen. During the last thirteen years she had been a woman only in suffering, and wanted to make up for lost time; so she showed herself as affectionate and sprightly as, hitherto, she had been high-minded and strong-willed. Consequently the four old people, the last to leave the drawing-room, were considerably disquieted by the changed demeanour of this attractive girl. What a force might passion become in a person of such character and such nobility! The two Simeuses were blindly and equally in love with the same woman. Which of them would Laurence choose? And would not the choice of one prove mortal to the other? As a countess in her own right, she would bring her husband a title, important privileges and an illustrious name. Perhaps, in view of these advantages, the Marquis de Simeuse would sacrifice himself and let Laurence marry his legal junior, who, thanks to the long-established laws of heredity, was poor and had no title. But could the younger Simeuse thus deprive his brother of the great bliss of having Laurence for his wife? Seen from a distance, this lovers' conflict had had few drawbacks; for that matter, so long as both brothers ran in danger of their lives, the hazard of battle might have cut the Gordian knot; but what would happen now they were both at hand? Now that Marie-Paul and Paul-Marie, both of them at an age when passion rages in all its violence, were to share their cousin's regard, her facial expressions, her attentions and conversation, would there not be manifestations of a jealousy which might have dire consequences? What would become of the twins' even tenor of life and mutual understanding? To these speculations, thrown out one by one by each of the older people in turn during the last hand of cards, Madame d'Hauteserre replied that she did not believe Laurence would marry either of her cousins. As the evening wore on, the elderly lady had experienced one of those inexplicable premonitions which are a secret between mothers and their Maker. As for Laurence, in her innermost heart she was not less alarmed at the prospect of close communication between her cousins and herself. The exciting drama of the conspiracy, the risks the two brothers had run and the misery of exile were giving place to a drama of which she had never dreamed. The noble-hearted girl felt herself unable to adopt the drastic expedient of refusing to marry either of the twins, for she was too honourable a woman to marry outside the family while still cherishing an irresistible passion at the bottom of her heart. To remain a spinster, to tax her cousins' patience by postponing her decision and eventually choosing the one who stayed faithful despite her apparent capriciousness, was a solution she envisaged but did not favour. As she fell asleep that night she told herself that the wisest thing would be to leave it to chance. For women in love chance takes the place of providence.

The next morning Michu departed for Paris and returned a few days later with four fine horses for his new masters. The hunting season was to open in six weeks' time, and the young countess had wisely thought that the distractions of this strenuous sport would provide relief from the embarrassment of intimate conversations inside the château. This produced an immediate and unforeseen result which surprised the witnesses of this strange romance and excited wonderment in them. Quite independently, the two brothers vied with each other in the tender care they gave to their cousin and this gave them an emotional satisfaction which at the time seemed sufficient. Their life with Laurence was as fraternal as the relationship between themselves. Nothing could be more natural: after such long absence, they felt the need to study their cousin, to get to know her well and to get her to know both of them well while leaving her the right to choose – and in this they were supported by their mutual affection, which made their separate lives one and the same life. Her love for them was no more able than maternal love to distinguish between the two brothers. In order to make sure of recognizing them, she was obliged to give them different cravats, a white one for the elder, a black one for the younger. Had it not been for this perfect resemblance, this identity in their way of life which confused everyone, such a situation would have seemed quite impossible. It can only be accounted for as a simple fact, unbelievable unless one had seen it; and when one does see such facts, they are more puzzling to explain than to believe. Laurence had only to speak, and her voice had the same resonance in these two equally loving and loyal hearts. Whatever ideas she might express, ingenious, amusing or profound, the glance she gave them was met by glances which followed her every movement, interpreted her every desire and smiled on her with an ever new expressiveness, gay in the one case, tenderly melancholic in the other. In any matter which concerned their lady, the two brothers felt and acted with a wonderful spontaneity which, in the Abbé Goujet's estimation, came near to the sublime. Thus, if something had to be fetched, if it was a question of one of the little attentions which men are so eager to pay to the woman they love, the elder brother would allow his junior the pleasure of paying it, while regarding Laurence with a look of tenderness mingled with pride. In his turn the younger brother would make a point of repaying the debt thus incurred. This magnanimous rivalry, prompted by a passion which often brings man to the jealous ferocity of an animal, confounded all the ideas of the old people as they studied it.

These little tributes often brought tears to the countess's eyes. One experience alone, one which may reach intensity in certain privileged beings, is analogous to the emotion she felt: that of listening to the perfect marriage of two fine voices (like those of Sontag and Malibran) in some harmonious duet or the blended strains of two instruments played by master performers, stealing into the soul like the impassioned sighing of one single heart. Sometimes the Abbé, when he saw the Marquis de Simeuse, reclining in an arm-chair, cast a glance of deep melancholy on his brother chatting and laughing with Laurence, believed him capable of a tremendous act of renunciation; but he soon discerned in his eye the gleam of unconquerable passion. Every time one of the twins found himself alone with Laurence, he might well believe that she loved him alone. When the Abbé questioned her about the state of her feelings, she would say: 'It seems to me that they are one and the same person.' On such occasions the priest recognized that she was totally devoid of coquetry. She genuinely did not believe she was beloved by two different men.

'But, my dear child,' Madame d'Hauteserre, whose son was pining away for love of Laurence, said to her one evening, 'you will have to make your choice all the same.'

'Let us enjoy our happiness,' she replied. 'God will save us from ourselves.'

Adrien d'Hauteserre concealed a devouring jealousy in the

depth of his heart but kept his tortures secret, knowing well that he had little hope. He contented himself with the bliss of just looking at this fascinating creature, who was in the full bloom of her beauty during the few months this contest lasted. In fact Laurence now thought of her looks and took such care of her personal appearance as women do when they are loved. She studied the fashions and more than once rushed off to Paris in order to enhance her beauty with the latest novelties in dress and adornment. And also, in order that her cousins might enjoy all the amenities of home life of which they had been so long deprived, and in spite of loud protests from her guardian, she turned her château into the most completely comfortable habitation in the whole of Champagne.

Robert d'Hauteserre understood nothing of this silent drama and had no inkling of his brother's love for Laurence. As for the girl, he loved to tease her for what he called her coquetry, making no difference between that odious defect and the natural desire to please; but he always showed the same incomprehension in all matters pertaining to sentiment, taste and culture. Consequently, whenever this figure from the Middle Ages took the stage, Laurence, without his realizing it, cast him for the role of simpleton: she amused her cousins by arguing with Robert and leading him on step by step until he floundered in the very bogs of stupidity and ignorance. She excelled in those mischievous pleasantries which are only completely successful when the victim is happily unaware of them. Yet Robert, coarse-grained though he was, never intervened during those halcyon days, the only happy period which the charming trio were to enjoy, with some blunt word which might have brought matters to a head between Laurence and the Simeuses. He was struck by the two brothers' sincerity. He no doubt divined how much Laurence, as a woman, might shrink from showing one of them signs of tenderness unshared by the other and likely to cause him pain; he also perceived how happy one of them was at kindness shown to the other even though he felt greatly afflicted at heart. This reticence on Robert's part throws much light on a situation which assuredly might have obtained privileged treatment in the ages of faith when the Sovereign Pontiff had the power to intervene and cut the Gordian knot of such rare phenomena,[1] which have so much in common with the most impenetrable mysteries. The Revolutionary upheaval had steeped their souls anew in the Catholic faith, and religious scruples thus made their crisis still more poignant, for nobility of character gives additional grandeur to grave situations. That is why neither Monsieur and Madame d'Hauteserre, nor the curé and his sister, expected the two brothers or Laurence to find any commonplace solution.

This drama, which was being played out in secret within the bosom of the family and silently watched by its members, took so rapid and yet so slow a course; it involved so many unexpected joys, minor conflicts, alternations of preference, reversals of hopes, cruel periods of waiting, deferred explanations and mute avowals, that Napoleon's coronation as Emperor passed unnoticed by the inhabitants of Cinq-Cygne. They sometimes called a truce to these impassioned exchanges and sought vigorous distraction in the pleasures of the chase, which by thoroughly tiring the body removes all opportunity for the mind to explore the perilous wasteland of reverie. Neither Laurence nor her cousins gave a thought to public affairs, for every day provided them with some exciting occupation.

'Truth to tell,' Mademoiselle Goujet said one evening, 'I just don't know which of them is the most in love.'

Adrien was alone in the drawing-room with the four card-players. He raised his eyes to heaven and turned pale. For the last few days he had lived only for the pleasure of seeing Laurence and hearing her talk.

'I think', said the curé, 'that the countess, being a woman, is the most far gone in love.'

A second or two later Laurence, the two brothers and Robert returned. The newspapers had come. England, seeing that internal conspiracies were ineffectual, was arming Europe against France. The Trafalgar disaster had upset one of the

1. i.e. by permitting polyandry? This curious notion seems to be based on the legend, possibly related to Balzac by Madame Hanska, of a Polish lord obtaining papal dispensation to keep two wives, a Christian and a Muslim one.

most extraordinary plans which human genius has ever conceived, one by which the Emperor would have paid for his election in France by destroying England as a world power. Now the camp at Boulogne had been struck. Napoleon, whose troops were inferior in number, was about to give battle to Europe on fields in which he had never yet appeared. The whole world was concerned with the outcome of this campaign.

'Oh! He'll come to grief this time,' said Robert as he finished reading the newspaper.

'He has all the forces of Austria and Russia to contend with,' said Marie-Paul.

'He has never campaigned in Germany,' Paul-Marie added.

'Who are you talking about?' asked Laurence.

'The Emperor,' the three noblemen replied.

Laurence gave her two suitors a look of unconcern which humiliated them but delighted Adrien. The spurned lover made a gesture of admiration, and the pride in his glance showed that *he* at any rate no longer thought about anyone but Laurence.

'You see,' the Abbé Goujet said quietly, 'Love has even made her forget her hatred for Napoleon.'

This was the first and last, the only reproach incurred by the two brothers; but at this moment they felt that their love was inferior to that of their cousin, who, two months later, only learnt of the astounding triumph of Austerlitz through a discussion the good d'Hauteserre had with his two sons. Still faithful to his plan, the old man wanted them to apply for military service: they would no doubt keep their rank and might still make a fine career in the army. But uncompromising royalism had won the day at Cinq-Cygne. The four noblemen and Laurence made fun of the prudent old man, who seemed to have a premonition of misfortunes to come. Prudence is perhaps not so much a virtue as the exercise of a *sense* of the mind, if it is possible to couple these two words; but no doubt the day will come when physiologists and philosophers will admit that the senses are to some extent a vehicle for the quick and penetrating action which proceeds from the mind.

*

After peace was signed between France and Austria in late February 1806, a relative of the Simeuses, one who had pulled strings for them when they were applying for rehabilitation, and who was later to give great proof of attachment to them, the former Marquis de Chargebœuf, whose estates extended from the Seine-et-Marne to the Aube departments, came from his country seat to Cinq-Cygne in that kind of barouche which at that time was mockingly called a *berlingot*. When they saw this shabby vehicle threading its way along the little drive, the inhabitants of the château, then at lunch, burst out laughing. But when Monsieur d'Hauteserre recognized the old man whose bare head was visible between the two leather curtains of the *berlingot*, he spoke his name, and they all rose from their chairs and went out to greet the head of the house of Chargebœuf.

'We shouldn't have let him forestall us,' said the Marquis de Simeuse. 'We ought to have gone and thanked him for helping us.'

A servant in peasant clothing, whose driving-seat was on a level with the body of the carriage, stuck his carter's whip into a crude leather holder and climbed down to help his master; but Adrien and the younger Simeuse were ahead of him, opened the door, which was hooked on to copper studs, and helped him down in spite of his expostulations. The marquis claimed that his yellow *berlingot* with its leather door was an excellent and commodious carriage. His servant, with Gothard's assistance, was already unharnessing the two good sturdy sleek-coated horses, which were no doubt used as much for farm-work as for travelling.

'You've come in this cold weather! Why, you're a doughty hero of the good old days!' said Laurence to her old kinsman, taking him by the arm and leading him off to the drawing-room.

'It's not for you to come and see an old fellow like me,' he said, thus addressing a subtle reproach to his young relatives.

'Why has he come?' Monsieur d'Hauteserre wondered.

Monsieur de Chargebœuf, a well preserved old man of seventy, with light-coloured breeches and spindly little legs encased in shadowed stockings, wore powder, a bag-wig, and pigeon-wings.[2] His hunting-coat of green cloth with gilt buttons was also adorned with gilt frogs. This accoutrement, still in fashion among old people, suited his type of face, which bore some resemblance to that of Frederick the Great. He never put on his three-cornered hat lest he should mar the effect of the half-moon traced on his cranium by a layer of powder. His right hand was resting on his bill-headed cane, and he held both cane and hat with a gesture worthy of Louis XIV. This fine old gentleman divested himself of his quilted silk topcoat and sank into an arm-chair, holding his cane and hat between his legs in a pose of which only the roués of Louis XV's court ever possessed the secret, one which left their hands free to toy with that ever precious trinket, the snuff-box. The marquis did indeed draw a valuable snuff-box from his waistcoat pocket, which was fastened with a flap embroidered in gilt arabesque. While preparing to take his pinch and offering snuff round with another charming gesture and affectionate glances, he noted the pleasure his visit was causing. Then he seemed to understand why the young *émigrés* had failed in their duty towards him. He appeared to be saying to himself: 'When one's busy courting, one doesn't pay calls.'

'You must stay with us for several days,' said Laurence.

'No, that's impossible,' he replied. 'Did not events keep us so far apart – for you have crossed greater distances than the geographical ones which separate us – you would know, dear child, that I have daughters, daughters-in law, grand-daughters and grandsons. They would be anxious if I didn't return this evening, and I have over forty miles to do.'

'You must have very good horses,' said the Marquis de Simeuse.

'Oh, I have only come from Troyes where I had business yesterday.'

After due inquiries about the family, the Marquise de Chargebœuf and quite unimportant matters in which politeness requires that one should take a lively interest, it became evident to Monsieur d'Hauteserre that Monsieur de

2. *bag-wig*: hair gathered into a pouch at the back of the head; *pigeon-wings*: hair falling over the temples at each side and cut to the shape of a pigeon's wing.

Chargebœuf had come in order to persuade his young kinsmen not to do anything imprudent. According to him, times had much changed, and no one could tell what future lay before the Emperor.

'Oh,' said Laurence, 'they'll make a god of him.'

The good old man spoke of concessions to be made. Monsieur d'Hauteserre, hearing him talk of the necessity for submission with much more assurance and authority than he himself used to express these views, looked at his sons almost with an air of supplication.

'Would *you* serve that man?' the Marquis de Simeuse asked the Marquis de Chargebœuf.

'Certainly, if my family interests demanded it.'

Finally the old man drew a picture, a vague one it is true, of dangers in the offing. When Laurence called on him to explain himself, he urged the four noblemen to give up hunting and remain quietly at home.

'You still look upon the Gondreville domains as your own,' he said to the Simeuses, 'and are thus fanning the embers of a terrible hatred. I see by your astonishment that you don't know that there is ill-will against you at Troyes, where people have not forgotten the courage you showed. They freely talk of the way you escaped the clutches of the Imperial General Police; some praise you for it, others regard you as the Emperor's enemies. A few hotheads express surprise at the clemency the Emperor showed you. But that's a small matter. You have outwitted men who thought they were more clever than you, and the rank and file never forgive. Sooner or later, the judicial authorities – in the Aube department justice emanates from your enemy Senator Malin, for he has posted his tools everywhere about, even among the law officials – will be very contented to find you involved in some sort of trouble. A peasant will pick a quarrel with you when you're on his land, you'll be carrying loaded guns, you're impetuous, and a disaster might happen. In a position like yours, in order not to be in the wrong you must be a hundred per cent in the right. I have my reasons for talking like this. The *arrondissement* you live in is under constant police supervision; they're keeping a commissary in that little hole, Arcis, for the express purpose of protecting the imperial Senator against attacks from you. He's afraid of you and he says so.'

'But he's slandering us!' cried the younger Simeuse.

'Yes, he's slandering you! I myself believe that. But what does the public believe? That's what matters. Michu aimed his gun at the Senator and the Senator hasn't forgotten. Since your return the countess has brought Michu here. And so many people, the greater part of the public, think Malin is in the right. You don't know in what a delicate situation *émigrés* stand in relation to those who have become owners of their property. The Prefect, an intelligent man, made some hints about you yesterday which worried me. In short, I wish you wouldn't stay here.'

This reply was received with profound stupefaction. Marie-Paul rang the bell loudly.

'Gothard,' he said when the lad came in, 'go and find Michu.'

The former bailiff of Gondreville did not keep them waiting.

'Michu, my friend,' said the Marquis de Simeuse, 'is it true you intended to kill Malin?'

'Yes, Monsieur le Marquis; and when he comes back I shall be on his trail again.'

'Do you know we are suspected of having set you on him, and that our cousin, by taking you on as her farmer, is accused of having been a party to your design?'

'Gracious Heaven!' cried Michu. 'I must be under a curse! Shall I never be able to rid you quietly of Malin?'

'No, my friend, no,' Paul-Marie replied. 'In fact you will have to leave the province and quit our service. We will look after you and help you to better yourself. Sell all you possess here, cash your bonds and we'll send you to Trieste, to one of our friends who has widespread connections and will give you very useful employment until things are better here for all of us.'

Tears came to Michu's eyes and he stood rooted to the floor in front of them.

'Were there any witnesses when you lay in ambush to fire on Malin?' asked the Marquis de Chargebœuf.

'Grévin the notary was talking to him, and it was he who prevented me from killing him. It was a lucky thing too.

Madame la Comtesse knows why,' said Michu, looking at his mistress.

'And Grévin is not the only one who knows about it?' said Monsieur de Chargebœuf, who seemed to be put out at this questioning of Michu, although it took place in private.

'Yes, the spy who came here some time ago to lay a trap for my masters knew about it too,' Michu replied.

Monsieur de Chargebœuf stood up as if he wished to make a tour of the gardens, saying: 'No doubt you've been developing Cinq-Cygne?' He then went out, followed by the two brothers and Laurence, who guessed why he had asked this question.

'You are frank and generous, but invariably imprudent,' the old man told them. 'It's natural enough that I should warn you about a public rumour *which of course is a slander*. But you are turning it into a truth for weak people like Monsieur and Madame d'Hauteserre, for their sons too. Oh! Young men! Young men! You ought to leave Michu here and go away yourselves! But at all events, if you stay in Champagne, write a note to the Senator about Michu. Tell him you have just learnt from me of the rumours circulating about your bailiff and that you have dismissed him.'

'We do that?' the two brothers exclaimed. 'Write to Malin, the man who assassinated our father and mother, the insolent man who despoiled us of our estates?'

'That's true enough, but he's one of the most prominent people at the Imperial court; and he rules the roost in the Aube department.'

'The man who voted for the death of Louis XVI in the event of Condé's army invading France, or, if not death, life imprisonment,' said the Comtesse de Cinq-Cygne.

'The man who probably recommended the execution of the Duc d'Enghien!' cried Paul-Marie.

'Well now!' the Marquis de Chargebœuf exclaimed. 'If you want to run through all his titles of nobility, here they are: the man who pulled Robespierre by the tail of his coat in order to bring him to the ground when he saw that those who were getting up to throw him down were in the majority; the man who would have had Bonaparte shot if 18 Brumaire had failed;

the man who would bring the Bourbons back if Napoleon were to totter on his throne; the man who will always be found at the side of the stronger to hand him a sword or pistol for finishing off an adversary he fears. All the more reason . . .'

'How low we are falling!' said Laurence.

'Children that you are!' said the old marquis, shepherding the three of them towards one of the lawns then covered with a sprinkling of snow. 'You're going to lose your tempers listening to a sensible man's advice. But I owe it to you, and this is what you should do: take as your go-between some simple old fellow – myself for example – and get him to ask Malin for a million francs in return for ratification of the sale of Gondreville . . . Have no fear, he would consent if it could be kept quiet. That would bring you, at present stock quotations, an income of a hundred thousand francs, and you could go off and buy some fine estate in another corner of France. You'd leave Monsieur d'Hauteserre in charge of Cinq-Cygne and you'd draw lots to find out which of you should marry the lovely heiress. But the talk of an old man in the ears of youth is like the talk of youth in the ears of old age: a meaningless babble!'

The gesture the old marquis gave indicated that he expected no reply. He re-entered the drawing-room, into which the Abbé Goujet and his sister had come during the colloquy. The idea of drawing lots for the hand of their cousin had revolted the two Simeuses, and Laurence felt some disgust at the unpalatable remedy her kinsman had suggested. Consequently, without ceasing to be polite, they were less gracious to the old man. The affection between them was bruised. Monsieur de Chargebœuf felt the chill, but many times threw compassionate glances at these three silly, charming creatures. The conversation turned to general topics, but he again urged the necessity of submitting to the course of events, and he praised Monsieur d'Hauteserre for insisting that his sons should take military service.

'Bonaparte', he said, 'is conferring dukedoms. He has set up Imperial fiefs and will be creating counts. Malin would like to be the Comte de Gondreville. It's an idea', he added with a glance at the Simeuse brothers, 'from which you could draw profit.'

'Or dishonour,' said Laurence.

As soon as the horses were harnessed, the marquis departed, with everybody there to see him off. Once installed in his carriage, he beckoned Laurence towards him, and she stood on the folding-steps with the lightness of a bird.

'You are no ordinary woman,' he whispered to her, 'and you ought to be able to understand. Malin has too much on his conscience to leave you in peace, and he will set some trap for you. At the very least be very careful about whatever action you take, even the slightest. In short, come to terms. That's my last word.'

The two brothers stood by their cousin in the middle of the grass, not moving a limb as they watched the *berlingot* pass through the gateway and roll away towards Troyes. Laurence had repeated the old man's parting words to them. Experience will always make the mistake of appearing in a 'berlingot', wearing shadowed stockings and a bag-wig. None of these youthful hearts had any conception of the changes that were coming about in France: they were quivering with indignation, honour was outraged and their blue blood was boiling in every vein.

'The head of the house of Chargebœuf!' said the Marquis de Simeuse. 'With its heraldic device: "Let the stronger man come!" *Adsit fortior!* One of the finest battle-cries.'

'He's come down to the second half of his name: the Ox!' [*bœuf*], said Laurence with a bitter smile.

'The age of Saint Louis is long past,' the younger Simeuse added.

'*We sing as we die!*' the countess exclaimed. 'The motto of the five sisters who founded our house shall always be mine!'

'Ours is: *Here I die!*' continued the elder Simeuse. 'And so we will not cry quarter, for we have only to think to realize that what our kinsman the Ox had to tell us was the result of careful chewing of the cud. A Malin to take the name of Gondreville!'

'And the castle also!' the younger brother exclaimed.

'Mansard designed it for noble habitation,' said Marie-Paul, 'and the common rabble will breed their young in it!'

'If that had to be, I would rather see Gondreville burnt down,' cried Mademoiselle de Cinq-Cygne.

A villager who had come to see a calf that Monsieur d'Hauteville was selling him happened to overhear this remark as he came out of the byres.

'Let's go in,' said Laurence with a smile. 'We've almost committed an indiscretion and proved the Ox to be right by reason of a calf. – My poor Michu,' she said on returning to the drawing-room, 'I had forgotten your little frolic, but we're not in the odour of sanctity in these parts, so don't get us into trouble. Have you any other little sins on your conscience?'

'Yes, the sin of not having killed the murderer of my old masters before rushing to the help of my young ones.'

'Michu!' the curé exclaimed.

'But I won't leave the province,' he went on, paying no attention to the curé's interjection, 'before knowing that you are safe. I've seen people I don't like prowling about. The last time we were out hunting in the forest the so-called keeper who took my place at Gondreville came across to me and asked me if we thought we were still at home there. "Well, my lad," I told him. "It's not easy in a month or two to get out of the habit of doing things we've done for a couple of centuries."'

'You shouldn't have said that, Michu,' the Marquis de Simeuse remarked. But he gave a smile of satisfaction.

'What was his answer?' asked Monsieur d'Hauteserre.

'He said he would tell the Senator about our pretensions.'

'Malin as Comte de Gondreville!' said the elder of the d'Hauteserre brothers. 'What a fancy-dress ball! Well, after all, they call Bonaparte "His Majesty".'

'And the Grand-Duke of Berg "His Highness",' said the curé.

'Who's he?' asked Paul-Marie.

'Murat, Napoleon's brother-in-law,' said Monsieur d'Hauteserre senior.

'Fine!' Mademoiselle de Cinq-Cygne interjected. 'And the Marquis de Beauharnais's widow, do they call her "Your Majesty"?'

'Yes, Mademoiselle,' said the curé.

'We ought to go to Paris and have a look at all that!' Laurence exclaimed.

'Alas, Mademoiselle,' said Michu. 'I went there to take François to his lycée, and I can tell you on oath that what they call the Imperial Guard is nothing to joke about. If the whole army's built on that model, all that may last longer than we shall.'

'They say there are noble families serving in it,' said Monsieur d'Hauteserre.

'And by the present laws,' the curé continued, 'your children will be forced to serve. The law no longer recognizes name or rank.'

'That man is doing us more harm with his court than the Revolution with its guillotine!' cried Laurence.

'He's prayed for in church,' said the curé.

These remarks, made in rapid succession, were like so many commentaries on the Marquis de Chargebœuf's sage words; but the young people were too loyal, too proud to accept a compromise. They also thought what defeated parties have thought in every age: the heyday of the victorious party would come to an end; the Emperor had only army support; sooner or later might would yield to right, and so on. Despite the advice given them, they were to fall into the pit dug for them, one which could have been avoided by people as prudent and tractable as the worthy d'Hauteserre. If men were frank with themselves they would perhaps recognize that never has misfortune befallen them without their receiving some warning, either patent or occult. Only after disaster has occurred have many of them realized the inner meaning of such premonitions, whether intuitive or rational.

'In any case, Madame la Comtesse knows that I can't leave the district without rendering my accounts,' said Michu to Mademoiselle de Cinq-Cygne. Her only reply was to give an understanding nod to her farmer, who took his departure.

*

Michu immediately sold his lands to Beauvisage, the farmer of Bellache, but had to wait for payment for about three weeks. One month, then, after the marquis's visit Laurence, who had told her two cousins about the fortune laid up for them, suggested that they should choose mid-Lent Sunday for recovering the million francs buried in the forest. Until then heavy falls of snow had prevented Michu from going and locating the hoard; but he preferred to carry out the operation in company with his masters. He was in a great hurry to leave the district, for he was afraid of his own impulses.

'Malin has suddenly arrived at Gondreville without anybody knowing why,' he told his mistress, 'and I should find it hard not to get Gondreville put up for sale as a result of the owner's decease. I feel a kind of guilt at not following my inspiration!'

'For what purpose can he be leaving Paris in mid-winter?'

'All Arcis is gossiping about it,' Michu replied. 'He's left his family in Paris and only has his manservant with him. Monsieur Grévin the notary, Madame Marion, wife of the Receiver-General of the Aube department and sister-in-law of Marion, Malin's cat's-paw, are staying with him.'

Laurence regarded mid-Lent Sunday as an excellent date, for it would enable her to get her servants out of the way. There were masquerades to draw peasants to the town, and no one would be out in the fields. But this choice of date was precisely that which favoured the designs of fate, as so often happens in affairs in which criminals become involved. Fate was to work things out just as skilfully as Mademoiselle de Cinq-Cygne made her calculations. Monsieur and Madame d'Hauteserre would have been so greatly perturbed if they had known that there were eleven hundred thousand gold francs in a lonely château on the borders of a forest that the younger d'Hauteserres themselves took the view that their parents should not be told. So the expedition was kept a close secret between Gothard, Michu, the four noblemen and Laurence. After much reckoning, it seemed feasible to put forty-eight thousand francs in a long sack on the crupper of each horse: three journeys would suffice. As a measure of prudence then, they agreed to send all the people whose curiosity might be dangerous to Troyes to take part in the mid-Lent merrymaking. Catherine, Marthe and Durieu, who could be relied upon, would guard the château. The servants very willingly accepted the holiday and set out before daybreak. Gothard and Michu groomed and saddled the horses very early. The party set off through the gardens of Cinq-Cygne and from there masters and servants reached the forest. Just as they were mounting, for the park gate was so low that each of them walked through the park leading his horse by the bridle, old Beauvisage, the Bellache farmer, happened to be passing.

'Let's go!' cried Gothard. 'Here's someone coming.'

'Oh!' said the honest farmer as he emerged. 'Good day, gentlemen. So you're off hunting in spite of the Prefect's orders. I won't make any fuss, but take care! You have friends, but you also have many enemies.'

'Oh!' said the sturdier of the two d'Hauteserres with a smile. 'Heaven grant that our hunt is successful and then you'll have your old masters back.'

These words, which in the upshot were to be given a quite different meaning, brought Robert a stern look from Laurence. The elder Simeuse believed that Malin would restore the Gondreville estate for a lump sum: the reckless young men were attempting to do the opposite of what the Marquis de Chargebœuf had advised them. That is what Robert, who shared their hopes, had been thinking of when he uttered this fateful remark.

'In any case, mum's the word, old chap!' Michu said to Beauvisage as he took the key of the gate and followed in the rear.

It was one of those fine days at the end of March when the air is crisp, the ground dry, the weather clear and the temperature at variance with the leafless trees. It was so mild that here and there the eye caught glimpses of verdure over the countryside.

'We are going to look for treasure, but you, cousin, are the real treasure of our house,' said Marie-Paul laughingly.

Laurence was riding in front with one of her cousins on either side of her. The two d'Hauteserres were following, and they in turn were followed by Michu. Gothard was riding ahead to reconnoitre.

'Since we are recovering our fortune, or at least a part of it, you should marry my brother,' said the younger Simeuse in a low voice. 'He adores you, and you'll be as rich as the nobility of our day ought to be.'

'No, let him have the whole fortune, and I'll marry you, for I'm rich enough for both of us,' she replied.

'Let that be so,' cried the Marquis de Simeuse. 'I'll leave you and look for a wife worthy to be your sister.'

'So you love me less than I thought,' Laurence continued, with an expression of jealousy on her face as she looked at him.

'No, I love both of you more than you love me,' said the marquis.

'Then you would sacrifice yourself?' asked Laurence of the elder Simeuse, and the look she gave him conveyed a momentary preference for him.

The marquis made no reply. His silence wrung a gesture of impatience from Laurence, and she retorted: 'Very well, if that happened I should be thinking of you all the time, and my husband would find that intolerable.'

'How could I live if you went away?' cried Paul-Marie, turning to his elder brother.

'When all's said and done,' said the marquis, 'you can't marry both of us.' And he added in the brusque tone of a heart-stricken man, 'It's time you made up your mind.'

He urged his horse on ahead so that the two d'Hauteserres should not hear. His brother and Laurence did likewise. When they had put a reasonable distance between themselves and the other three, Laurence tried to speak, but at first tears were the only language she could use.

'I'll go into a convent,' she said in the end.

'And let the Cinq-Cygne line die out?' said the younger Simeuse. 'And instead of there being only one unhappy man – by his own consent – you'll make two! No, that one of us who can only be your brother will resign himself. When we learnt that we were not as poor as we expected to be, we came to an understanding,' he said, with a look at the marquis. 'If I'm the chosen one, all our fortune goes to my brother. If I'm the unlucky one, he passes it over to me with the Simeuse title, for he will become a Cinq-Cygne. In either case the one who's unlucky will have a chance of establishing himself. And after all, if he feels he's dying of disappointed love, he'll join the army and get himself killed so as not to cast gloom on the household.'

'We are true knights of the Middle Ages, and worthy of our ancestors!' exclaimed the elder brother. 'Speak, Laurence.'

'We don't want to go on like this,' said the younger.

'Don't imagine, Laurence,' said the elder, 'that no pleasure comes from self-sacrifice.'

'My darlings,' she said, 'I'm incapable of deciding. I love you both as if you were one single person and as your mother loved you. God shall come to our help. I will not make the choice. We will leave it to chance, but I lay down one condition.'

'What condition?'

'The one of you that becomes my brother will stay near me until I permit him to leave me. I want to be the sole judge of the opportune moment for him to go away.'

'We agree,' the two brothers replied, without being able to fathom her thought.

'The first of you two whom Madame d'Hauteserre addresses this evening at table, after grace is said, shall be my husband. But neither of you will resort to any stratagem or induce her to ask him a question.'

'We will play fair,' said the younger brother. Each of the two kissed Laurence's hand. The certainty of a solution which each of them could hope would turn out in his favour made the twins inordinately gay.

'In any case, dear Laurence,' said the elder, 'you will be creating a count of Cinq-Cygne.'

'And it's head or tail as to which of us will cease to be a Simeuse,' said the younger.

'It looks as if Madame la Comtesse won't stay single much longer,' said Michu from behind the two d'Hauteserres. 'My masters are very merry. If my lady makes her choice, I'm not going away, I want to be at the wedding!'

Neither of the d'Hauteserres replied. Suddenly a magpie flew off between them, and Michu, who was superstitious like all primitive beings, felt as if he were hearing a funeral bell toll. So then the day began gaily for the lovers, for lovers rarely notice a magpie when they are together in the woods. Michu used his sketch-plan to identify the sites. Each of the noblemen was armed with a pick. The coins were found; the part of the forest in which they were hidden was deserted and remote from any track or habitation; and so the gold-laden convoy met no one. That was unfortunate, for when the convoy came from Cinq-Cygne to fetch the last two hundred thousand francs, emboldened by success, it took a more direct route than the one it had followed on the preceding journeys. This road passed by an eminence which looked out over the Gondreville park.

'There's a fire!' said Laurence, noticing a column of flame and smoke.

'It's some bonfire or other,' Michu replied.

Laurence, who knew every path in the forest, left the convoy and spurred on to the Cinq-Cygne pavilion where Michu had formerly lived. Although it was empty and locked up, the gate was open, and traces of the passage of several horses struck Laurence's gaze. The column of smoke was rising from a meadow in the English park and she supposed that weeds were being burnt there.

'Ah! You're in this too, Mademoiselle,' cried Violette, galloping out of the park on his nag and stopping in front of Laurence. 'But it's just a carnival joke, isn't it? They won't kill him?'

'Kill whom?'

'Your cousins aren't planning his death?'

'Whose death?'

'The senator's.'

'You're crazy, Violette!'

'Well then, what are you doing here?' he asked.

At the thought that her cousins might be in danger, the intrepid horsewoman spurred her horse and arrived at the hiding-place just as the sacks were being filled.

'Hurry up! I don't know what's happening, but we must get back to Cinq-Cygne.'

While the noblemen had been transporting the fortune which the old marquis had saved up for them, a strange scene was being enacted at the château of Gondreville. At two in the afternoon, the senator and his friend Grévin were playing chess in front of the fire in the grand salon on the ground floor. Madame Grévin and Madame Marion were chatting on a sofa at the chimney corner. All the château servants had gone to see an interesting masquerade which had long been announced in the Arcis *arrondissement*. The family of the keeper who had replaced Michu in the Cinq-Cygne pavilion had gone there too. Only the senator's man-servant and Violette had stayed on the premises. The gate-keeper, two gardeners and their wives were still at their posts; but their lodge stood at the entrance to the courtyards at the end of the avenue leading from Arcis, and the distance between this pavilion and the château was too great even for a rifle-shot to be heard. Besides, these servants were standing on the doorstep and looking towards Arcis, a mile and a quarter away, in the hope of seeing the masquerade come their way. Violette was in a spacious anteroom, waiting to be received by the Senator and Grévin in order to discuss the renewal of his lease. Suddenly five men in masks and gauntlets who in figure, manner and gait resembled the d'Hauteserres, the Simeuses and Michu, pounced upon the man-servant and Violette, gagged them with scarves and tied them to chairs in a room in the servants' quarters. Despite the swiftness of the assault, the operation was not carried out without some shouting from the man-servant and Violette. Their calls were heard in the salon, and the two women were sure it was a cry of alarm.

'Listen!' said Madame Grévin. 'It's thieves.'

'Oh no! It's the revellers giving voice,' said Grévin. 'We're going to have the maskers in the château.'

This discussion gave the five unknown intruders time to shut the doors opening on to the main courtyard and lock up the man-servant and Violette. Madame Grévin, a very obstinate woman, was intent on finding out what the noise was about. She got up and came against the five masked men, who dealt with her as they had with Violette and the man-servant. Then they burst into the salon, where the two strongest of them seized hold of the Comte de Gondreville, gagged him and dragged him away through the park while the two others gagged Madame Marion and the notary and bound each of them to an arm-chair. It did not take them more than half an hour to carry out this assault. The three unknown men were soon rejoined by the two who had abducted the senator, and they ransacked the château from cellar to attic. They opened every cupboard and wardrobe without having to pick the locks. They pounded all the walls to see if they were hollow; in short they remained in possession of the château until five o'clock in the evening. By then the man-servant had used his teeth to loosen the ropes tied round Violette's hands. Freed from his gag, Violette began to shout for help. Hearing his shouts, the five intruders returned to the garden, jumped on their horses, which were very like the Cinq-Cygne horses, and made off, but not too swiftly for Violette to catch a glimpse of them. After untying the man-servant, who untied the women and the notary, Violette mounted his pony and set off in pursuit of the malefactors. When he got to the pavilion, he was as stupefied to see the gate wide open as to see Mademoiselle de Cinq-Cygne, apparently standing sentinel.

The countess had disappeared by the time Violette was rejoined by Grévin on horseback, accompanied by the Gondreville rural policeman whom the gate-keeper had supplied with a horse from the château stables. The latter's wife had gone off to inform the Arcis police.

*

Violette immediately told Grévin about his encounter with Laurence and the flight of that audacious girl, whose deep and resolute character they well knew.

'She was keeping watch,' said Violette.

'Could it possibly be the Cinq-Cygne set who did the job?' cried Grévin.

'Why!' Violette replied. 'Didn't you recognize that burly fellow Michu? He was the man who jumped on me. I could tell it was his grip all right. And sure enough the five horses were from Cinq-Cygne.'

Seeing the horses' shoe-prints on the sandy clearing and in the park, the notary left the constable on watch at the gate to make sure that these important prints should not be obliterated, and he sent Violette for the stipendiary magistrate at Arcis[3] so that he could take note of them. Then he promptly returned to the Gondreville salon, where the lieutenant and sub-lieutenant of the Imperial gendarmerie arrived with four men and a corporal. This lieutenant was, as we might suspect, the former corporal whose head François Michu had broken two years before, and to whom Corentin had revealed the identity of his mischievous adversary. This man, Giguet by name, whose brother was a soldier and was to become one of the best colonels of artillery, was commendable for his proficiency as an officer of gendarmerie. Later on he was put in command of the Aube squadron. The sub-lieutenant, a man called Welff, was the man who had escorted Corentin to the pavilion and from there to Troyes. As they had gone their way, the Parisian had fully informed the veteran from Egypt about what he called Laurence's piece of trickery. These two officers therefore had good motives for their hostility to the inhabitants of Cinq-Cygne. Malin and Grévin, working for their reciprocal interests, had both had a hand in drawing up the legal code dated 'Brumaire Year IV' (November 1796) which the so-called National Convention had compiled and the Directory promulgated. And so Grévin, completely conversant with this new legislation, was able to proceed with terrible dispatch in this affair, but he did so with a presumption amounting to certainty that Michu, the d'Hauteserres and the Simeuse brothers were the guilty parties. In our days no one, except a few old magistrates, remembers the organization of the judicial procedure which at that precise moment Napoleon was superseding in favour of his Penal and Civil Codes and the institution of the magisterial system which is now operative in France.

The Code of November 1796 made the director of the Departmental Jury responsible in the first instance for investigating the 'delict' committed at Gondreville. We may observe by the way that the National Convention had deleted the word

3. The French term for this is *juge de paix*, not be be confused with our unpaid justices of the peace. The *juge de paix* could also act as a *juge d'instruction*, a magistrate who investigates charges and decides whether there is a case or not. This man, Pigoult, acts mostly in the latter capacity.

‘crime’ from its judicial vocabulary. It only acknowledged ‘delicts’ involving fines, imprisonment, loss of civil rights and ‘retributive penalties’. Death was a retributive penalty, although it was intended that it should be abolished in peacetime and replaced by penal servitude for twenty-four years. Thus the National Convention reckoned that twenty-four years’ penal servitude was equivalent to the death penalty – so what should we say of the present penal code which inflicts penal servitude for life? The judicial system which was then being worked out by Napoleon’s Council of State was doing away with the jury directors, who indeed were invested with enormous powers. In regard to prosecution for delicts and committal for trial, a jury director was to some extent both police magistrate, public attorney, examining magistrate and court judge. But his procedure and the charge he drew up were subject to the visa of a commissary of the executive power and the verdict of eight jurymen, to whom he laid bare the facts resulting from his investigation; they heard witnesses and accused, and brought in a preliminary verdict which in England is known as a ‘true bill’. A director’s task was to exert so much influence on his jurymen, whom he summoned to his chambers, that they were obliged to co-operate with him. They constituted what the English call a grand jury. There was also another jury which sat at the criminal tribunal, and it was their business to try the accused. To differentiate them from the grand jury, they were known as the court, or, as we should say, the petty jury. The criminal tribunal, on which Napoleon had just conferred the title of Criminal Court, consisted of a chairman, four judges, the public prosecutor and a government commissary. Nevertheless, from 1799 to 1806, there were so-called Special Courts which in certain departments sat in judgement without juries on specific kinds of crime: they were composed of judges drawn from the Civil Tribunal which acted as a Special Court. This rivalry between special and criminal justice gave rise to questions of competence on which the Appeal Tribunal gave its ruling. If the department of the Aube had had its Special Court, no doubt an assault committed on the person of a senator of the Empire would have been referred to it. But this quiet department was exempt from this exceptional jurisdiction. Therefore Grévin sent the sub-lieutenant to the jury director at Troyes. The veteran from Egypt rode there at full speed and returned to Gondreville bringing the all-powerful magistrate back with him post-haste.

The jury director of Troyes had occupied a minor judicial post before the Revolution, had been a salaried secretary to one of the National Convention committees, and was a friend of Malin, to whom he owed his post. This magistrate, Lechesneau by name, a man well trained in the established routine of criminal justice, had, like Grévin, given valuable assistance to Malin in his judicial work on the Convention. In return Malin had recommended him to Cambacérès, who had appointed him attorney-general in Italy. Unhappily for his career, Lechesneau had illicit relations with a great lady of Turin, and Napoleon was obliged to discharge him in order to stave off proceedings brought against him by the lady's husband in regard to the abstraction of an adulterine child. Lechesneau, being greatly indebted to Malin, and divining the importance of such a criminal assault, had brought along the captain of gendarmerie and a picket of twelve men.

Before leaving Troyes, naturally he had conferred with the prefect who, since night had fallen, was unable to use the semaphore. A dispatch-rider was sent to Paris to inform the Minister of General Police, the Chief Justice and the Emperor of this unheard-of crime. In the Gondreville salon Lechesneau found Madame Marin, Madame Grévin, Violette, the senator's man-servant and the examining magistrate with his clerk. A thorough search of the château had already been made. The magistrate, with Grévin's assistance, was painstakingly collecting the basic facts for his report. He was struck straight away by the deep-laid nature of the plot, revealed by the choice of day and time – late enough in the afternoon to prevent an immediate search for clues and evidence. At this season, at half-past five, it had been almost dark before Violette was able to go off in pursuit of the delinquents; and night-time often spells impunity for malefactors. And to have chosen a day of public rejoicing, when all and sundry would be out watching the masquerade at Arcis and when the senator was likely to be alone in his house, was certainly the best way of securing the absence of witnesses.

'Let us do justice to the perspicacity of the agents sent by the prefecture of police,' said Lechesneau. 'They have repeatedly put us on guard against the nobles of Cinq-Cygne and warned us that sooner or later they would be up to some mischief.'

Assured of the activity of the prefect of the Aube, who sent dispatch-riders to all the prefectures in the districts surrounding Troyes so that the five masked men and the senator could be tracked down, Lechesneau began to lay the basis for his investigation, a task which was rapidly carried out with two such experienced lawyers as Grévin and the magistrate putting their heads together. The latter, Pigoult by name, formerly chief clerk in the solicitor's office where Malin and Grévin had studied pettifoggery in Paris, was three months later to be appointed president of the Arcis tribunal. With regard to Michu, Lechesneau was aware of the threats he had previously made to Marion and the ambush from which the senator had escaped in his park. These two facts, the one a consequence of the other, were taken to be the prelude to the crime just committed, and suspicion pointed the more clearly to the former bailiff as the leader of the malefactors because Grévin, his wife, Violette and Madame Marion claimed to have recognized a man exactly like Michu among the five masked gangsters. The colour of his hair and side-whiskers and his stocky build made any disguise practically futile. And besides, who other than Michu would have had a key to open the gate at Cinq-Cygne? The present keeper and his wife, questioned on their return from Arcis, stated that they had locked both gates. And the gates themselves, which the magistrate inspected with the aid of his clerk and the village policeman, showed no signs of having been broken open.

'When we threw him out of his job,' said Grévin, 'he must have kept duplicate keys of the château. And he was certainly planning some desperate *coup*, for he sold his property in a space of three weeks and collected the money in my office the day before yesterday.'

'They must have put the whole thing on his shoulders,'

cried Lechesneau, impressed by this circumstance. 'He has been their tool.'

Who better than the Simeuses and the d'Hauteserres could have known their way about the château? Not one of the assailants had faltered in his searches; they had gone about their business with a certainty which proved that the gang knew what they were after and above all knew where to find it. None of the closets they had ransacked had been forced open, therefore the criminals must have had the keys. And strange to say they had not stolen the slightest article, so that theft was out of the question. Finally Violette, recognizing the horses as coming from the Cinq-Cygne stables, had found the countess on guard, he averred, in front of the keeper's lodge. From this assemblage of facts and depositions there resulted, even for the least prejudiced investigators, presumption of guilt in the case of the Simeuses, the d'Hauteserres and Michu which was likely to harden into certainty in the mind of a jury director. What then were they intending to do with the future Comte de Gondreville? Did they intend to force him to cede his property, for the purchase of which Michu had announced, as early as 1799, that he had the necessary capital? But at this point the aspect of things changed completely.

The learned criminal jurist asked himself what could have been the purpose of the busy searches carried out in the château. Had it been a mere question of revenge the delinquents could have killed Malin out of hand. Perhaps indeed the senator was already dead and buried. Nevertheless to have kidnapped him suggested that they intended to keep him prisoner. But why this imprisonment after the ransacking of the château? They were certainly mad if they thought that the abduction of an Imperial dignitary could long remain a secret! The crime would be so swiftly noised abroad that any profit accruing from it would be cancelled out.

Pigoult's reply to these objections was that judicial investigations could never divine all the motives of wrongdoers. In all criminal cases, he said, there existed areas of darkness between judge and delinquent, impenetrable to both: there were unplumbed depths in the human conscience to which light could never penetrate save through the guilty party's confession.

Grévin and Lechesneau nodded assent to this argument, but went on trying to peer through the darkness and clear the matter up.

'And to think that the Emperor pardoned them!' said Pigoult to Grévin and Madame Marion. 'They were struck off the list, even though they had joined the conspiracy hatched against him!'

Without further delay Lechesneau dispatched all his gendarmes to scour the forest and valley of Cinq-Cygne, sending the magistrate with Giguet and thus constituting him, according to the terms of the Code, his auxiliary officer of judicial police. He instructed him to go round the commune of Cinq-Cygne collecting data for the investigation and to proceed with the necessary interrogations. In order to speed matters up, he rapidly dictated and signed an order for Michu's arrest, since there seemed to be clear grounds for charging him. Once the gendarmes and the magistrate had departed, Lechesneau resumed the important task of issuing warrants for the arrest of the Simeuses and the d'Hauteserres. According to the Code, these writs had to include all the charges brought against the delinquents. Giguet and the magistrate made so swiftly for Cinq-Cygne that they met the château servants on their way back from Troyes. They were arrested and brought before the mayor for questioning. Each one of them, unaware of the importance of the replies they gave, naïvely stated that, on the previous evening, they had been given leave to spend the whole day in Troyes. Cross-examined by the magistrate, each of them also replied that Mademoiselle had offered them this holiday without their having thought of asking for it. These statements seemed so grave to the magistrate that he sent the Egyptian veteran to Gondreville to request Monsieur Lechesneau himself to proceed with the arrest of the Cinq-Cygne noblemen so that the two operations could be simultaneous, for he was about to move to Michu's farm in order to lay hands on the alleged leader of the gang. These new data seemed so conclusive that Lechesneau left immediately for Cinq-Cygne, enjoining Grévin to see to it that the horses' shoe-prints in the park were carefully preserved. The jury director knew what pleasure would be felt at Troyes if he took proceedings against ex-nobles, enemies of the people, now enemies of the Emperor. In such a disposition of mind, a magistrate readily accepts simple presumption for clear proof. Nevertheless, as he went from Gondreville to Cinq-Cygne in the senator's own carriage, Lechesneau, who would certainly have made a great magistrate but for the passion which had caused his disgrace thanks to the Emperor's access of prudery, bethought him that the audacity of the young men and Michu was a piece of madness, and little in keeping with Mademoiselle de Cinq-Cygne's turn of mind. His own belief was that they had other intentions than to extort cession of Gondreville from the senator. In every walk of life, even that of a magistrate, there exists what one must call a professional conscience. Lechesneau's perplexity of mind resulted from the conscientiousness which all men bring to the fulfilment of duties they find congenial – scientists to their researches, artists to their craft and judges to their judicial functions. That is perhaps why judges offer a better guarantee to accused persons than jurymen do. A magistrate puts his faith only in the laws of reasoning, whereas a juryman lets himself be carried away by waves of emotion.

The jury director put several questions to himself, hoping that satisfactory answers would emerge from the fact of the delinquents' arrest. Although Troyes was already buzzing with the news of Malin's abduction, it was still unknown at Arcis at eight o'clock, for everyone was at supper when the gendarmes and the examining magistrate were sent for. Nor was it known at Cinq-Cygne. Here both valley and château were surrounded for the second time: but this time in the name of the law and not merely as a police measure. Accommodations are possible with the police, but often impossible with legal officials.

*

Laurence had only had to tell Marthe, Catherine and the Durieu couple to stay in the château and neither go nor look outside, to be sure of their strict obedience. On each trip the horses had been stationed in the sunken road opposite the breach and from that point Robert and Michu, the most stalwart members of the troop, had been able to transport the sacks secretly through the breach into a cellar underneath the stairs of the tower known as Mademoiselle's tower. Having arrived at the château about five-thirty, the five men instantly set about stowing the gold away. Laurence and the d'Hauteserres thought it advisable to wall up the cellar. Michu undertook this task with the help of Gothard, who hurried to the farm to fetch several bags of plaster left over from the building operations, and Marthe went with him in order to hand over the bags to him in secret. The farm built for Michu stood on the high ground from which he had formerly espied the gendarmes, and the sunken road led to it. Michu was very hungry and worked so quickly that by seven-thirty he had finished his task. He was returning at a brisk pace in order to prevent Gothard from bringing one final bag of plaster which he had thought he would need. The Cinq-Cygne constable, the magistrate, his clerk and three gendarmes were already on watch around the farm; they kept out of sight and, when they heard him coming, allowed him to go in.

Michu met Gothard with a bag on his shoulder and shouted from a distance: 'It's finished, my boy. Take the bag back and have dinner with us.'

His brow wet with sweat, his clothes dirty with plaster and the muddy stone rubble taken from the breach, Michu stepped joyfully into the kitchen of the farm. Marthe and her mother were serving the soup while they waited for him.

Just as Michu was turning on the kitchen tap to wash his hands, the examining magistrate presented himself, accompanied by his clerk and the village constable.

'What might you be wanting with us, Monsieur Pigoult?' asked Michu.

'In the name of the Emperor and the law, I arrest you!' said the magistrate.

Then the three gendarmes arrived, dragging Gothard along. On seeing the braided hats, Marthe and her mother exchanged a look of terror.

'Nonsense! What for?' asked Michu, sitting down to table and saying to his wife, 'Serve up. I'm dying of hunger.'

'You know what for as well as we do,' said the magistrate,

beckoning to the clerk to begin taking notes after showing the farmer the warrant for his arrest.

'Why now, Gothard,' said Michu, 'you look quite bowled over. Are you going to dine or not? Let them go on writing their rubbish.'

'You acknowledge the state your clothes are in?' said the magistrate. 'Nor can you deny the words you spoke to Gothard in your courtyard.'

Michu, served by his wife, who was stupefied at his calmness, was eating with the avidity of a famished and innocent man; he made no answer. Gothard was so terribly frightened that he had no appetite for food.

'Come now,' the policeman whispered to Michu. 'What have you done with the senator? From what the lawyers say, you are liable to the death penalty.'

'God in Heaven!' Marthe cried out. She had overheard the last few words and fell flat as if struck by a thunderbolt.

'Violette must have played some dirty trick on us!' cried Michu as he recalled what Laurence had told him.

'Ah! So you know that Violette recognized you!' said the magistrate.

Michu bit his lips and decided to keep his mouth shut. Gothard followed suit. The magistrate, seeing the uselessness of his efforts to make him talk, knowing moreover of Michu's reputation for perversity in the neighbourhood, ordered the gendarmes to handcuff both of them and take them away to the château of Cinq-Cygne; then he set off there himself in order to rejoin the jury director.

The four noblemen and Laurence were too hungry and too eager for dinner to delay it by changing their clothes. They came in, she in her riding-habit and they in their white deerskin breeches, top-boots and green jackets, and found Monsieur and Madame d'Hauteserre in the drawing-room, both of them very worried. The old man had observed their comings and goings, and even more their lack of confidence in himself, for Laurence had not been able to dispose of him as she had of her servants. And so, on one occasion when one of his sons had evaded his questions by slipping away, he had gone to his wife and said: 'I'm afraid Laurence is getting us into trouble again.'

'What sort of hunting have you been doing today?' Madame d'Hauteserre asked Laurence.

'Oh!' she replied with a laugh. 'One of these days you'll learn what piece of roguery your sons have taken part in today!'

Though spoken jestingly, these words made the old lady tremble. Catherine announced that dinner was ready. Laurence gave her arm to Monsieur d'Hauteserre and smiled at the mischievous trick she was playing on her cousins by obliging one of them to offer an arm to the old lady who, by their agreement, was to settle their fate.

The Marquis de Simeuse escorted Madame d'Hauteserre to the dinner table. And then the situation became so solemn that, once grace was said, Laurence and both of the cousins felt their hearts thumping violently. Madame d'Hauteserre, who was serving, was struck by the anxiety written on the faces of the two Simeuses and the change of expression on Laurence's normally placid countenance.

'Has something out of the ordinary happened today?' she asked, looking at all three of them.

'Which of us are you talking to?' said Laurence.

'All of you,' the old lady replied.

'Well anyway, Mother,' said Robert, 'I'm ravenously hungry, and there's nothing extraordinary about that.'

Madame d'Hauteserre, still troubled in mind, offered the Marquis de Simeuse a plate of food which she had meant for the younger brother.

'I'm like your mother,' she said, addressing the marquis, 'I always get you two mixed up in spite of your different cravats. I thought I was serving your brother.'

'You are serving him better than you think,' said the younger brother, turning pale. 'You have made him Comte de Cinq-Cygne.'

The poor young man, usually so gay, became sad for ever; but he had the strength to smile at Laurence and stifle his deadly grief. In an instant the suitor was lost in the brother.

'What! Has the countess made her choice?' cried the old lady.

'No,' said Laurence. 'We left it to chance, and you were to be its instrument.'

She recounted the agreement made that morning. The elder Simeuse, noting the increasing pallor on his brother's face, felt more and more impelled as the meal went on to cry out: 'You marry her! I will go away and die!' Then, as dessert was being served, the inhabitants of the château heard someone knocking at the dining-room window on the garden side. The elder d'Hauteserre went to open it and let in the curé, who had torn his knee-breeches on the trellis as he climbed over the park walls.

'You must fly! You are going to be arrested!'

'Why?'

'I don't yet know, but proceedings are being taken against you.'

These words were greeted with general laughter. 'We haven't committed any crime,' the young men exclaimed.

'Whether you have or not,' said the curé, 'get on your horses and make for the frontier. There you'll be in a position to prove your innocence. A conviction *in absentia* can be quashed, but not a conviction after full trial, obtained by appealing to popular passions and built up on prejudice. Remember what President de Harley said: "If I were accused of stealing the towers of Notre-Dame I'd make myself scarce straight away."'

'But is not taking flight an admission of guilt?' asked the Marquis de Simeuse.

'Don't run away,' said Laurence.

'Always the same high-minded idiocy!' said the curé, in despair. 'If I had the power of Almighty God I would carry you off myself. But if they find me here, in this state, they'll turn this strange visit against both you and myself. I'm clearing off the way I came. Think! You still have time. The officers of the law didn't think of the presbytery party wall, but you're hemmed in on all other sides.'

The clatter of horses' hooves and the rattle of the gendarmes' sabres filled the courtyard and reached the dining-room a few seconds after the departure of the unhappy curé, whose advice was no more heeded than that of the Marquis de Chargebœuf had been.

'The life we lead in common', the younger Simeuse said in

a melancholy voice to Laurence, 'is an abnormality; so is the love we bear one another and the love you have for us. Perhaps it's because twins are an exception in nature that all those whose life-stories have come down to us have been unfortunate. As for us, see how inexorably destiny pursues us. Your decision was fated to be postponed.'

Laurence was in a daze. She heard a buzz of words of sinister meaning for her, uttered by the jury director. 'In the name of the Emperor and the law, I arrest Messieurs Paul-Marie and Marie-Paul Simeuse, Adrien and Robert d'Hauteserre. These gentlemen', he added, pointing out to his companions the traces of mud on the clothes of the prisoners, 'will not deny having spent part of the day on horseback.'

'Of what are they accused?' Mademoiselle de Cinq-Cygne haughtily asked.

'Are you not arresting Mademoiselle?' asked Giguet.

'I shall leave her free on bail, pending a further examination of the charges to be brought against her.'

Goulard offered to go bail for the countess, asking no more than her word of honour that she would not escape. She withered the former stud-groom of the house of Simeuse with an extremely haughty look which made him her enemy for life; and tears filled her eyes, the tears of rage which tell of an inferno of suffering. The four noblemen exchanged a terrible glance and stood stockstill. Monsieur and Madame d'Hauteserre, fearing that the four young men and Laurence had deceived them, were in a state of utter bewilderment. Glued to their chairs, these parents, seeing their children torn from them after having so much feared for their safety and after recovering them, were watching with blind eyes and listening with deaf ears.

'Do I have to ask you to go bail for me, Monsieur d'Hauteserre?' Laurence cried out to her former guardian: he was awakened from his stupor by this cry, as shrill and startling for him as the trumpet of doomsday. The old man wiped away the tears which had come to his eyes, took the situation in and said in a weak voice to his kinswoman: 'Forgive me, Countess, you know I belong to you body and soul.'

Lechesneau, initially impressed by the tranquillity of the

supposed culprits as they ate, returned to his earlier feelings about their guilt when he saw the bewilderment of the older couple and Laurence's perplexed demeanour as she tried to guess what snare had been laid for her.

'Gentlemen,' he said politely, 'you are too well-bred to offer ineffectual resistance. Follow me, all four of you, to the stables, where we must remove your horses' shoes in your presence, since they will be important pieces of evidence at your trial and may perhaps prove either your innocence or your guilt. Please come too, Mademoiselle . . . '

The Cinq-Cygne blacksmith and his assistant had been required by Lechesneau to come in their capacity as experts. While this was going on in the stables, the examining magistrate brought in Gothard and Michu. It took some time to remove the shoes from each horse, collect them and label them so that they could be compared with the prints left in the park by the horses ridden by the authors of the crime. Nevertheless Lechesneau, when he was informed that Pigoult had arrived, left the accused men with the gendarmes and went to the dining-room to dictate his report, while Pigoult pointed out the state of Michu's clothing and gave him details about the arrest.

'They must have killed the senator and walled up his body,' Pigoult said to Lechesneau by way of conclusion.

'I now fear that is so,' the magistrate replied. 'Where did you take the plaster to?' he asked Gothard.

Gothard started to weep.

'He's frightened of beaks,' said Michu, whose eyes were blazing like those of a lion caught in a net.

All the servants of the house who had been detained at the mayor's office then arrived and crowded into the anteroom where Catherine and the Durieu couple, in tears, told them the significance of the answers they had given. To every question put by the jury director and the examining magistrate, Gothard replied with sobs; in the end he wept himself into what looked like a fit of convulsions. This alarmed them, and they left him alone. The little rascal, seeing that they were no longer watching him, looked across at Michu and smiled, and Michu gave him a wink of approval.

Lechesneau left the magistrate and went to question the experts.

'Monsieur,' said Madame d'Hauteserre at last, addressing Pigoult, 'can you explain these arrests?'

'These gentlemen are accused of having kidnapped the senator by main force and hidden him away – for we do not suppose they have murdered him, in spite of appearances.'

'And what penalty would the authors of such a crime incur?' the old man asked.

'Well, since the laws which the present Code has not superseded are still in force, the death penalty,' the magistrate continued.

'The death penalty!' cried Madame d'Hauteserre. Then she fainted.

At this moment the curé came in with his sister, who summoned Catherine and Madame Durieu.

'But we haven't even clapped eyes on your blasted senator,' cried Michu.

'Madame Marion, Madame Grévin, Monsieur Grévin, the senator's man-servant and Violette can't say the same about you,' Pigoult replied with the sour smile of a magistrate who has made up his mind.

'I just can't understand,' said Michu. Pigoult's retort had dumbfounded him and he now began to believe that he and his masters were being entangled in some plot laid against them.

Just now everyone returned from the stables. Laurence rushed up to Madame d'Hauteserre, who only regained consciousness in order to tell her: 'It's a matter of the death penalty.'

'The death penalty! . . .' Laurence repeated, looking at the four noblemen.

The phrase spread terror all around, and Giguet, taking a leaf out of Corentin's book, seized his opportunity. He drew the Marquis de Simeuse into a corner of the room and said: 'There's still time to come to an arrangement. Maybe this is only a bit of fun. You're army men, dammit: soldiers understand one another. What have you done with the senator? If you've killed him the fat's in the fire. But if you've only put him away, give him up. You can see that your dodge hasn't come off. I'm sure the jury director and the senator will get together and hush the matter up.'

'We haven't the slightest idea what you're talking about,' said the marquis.

'If that's the line you're taking, you're asking for trouble,' said the lieutenant.

'My dear cousin,' said the marquis. 'We are going to prison. But don't worry. We'll be back in a few hours. All this is a misunderstanding which will be cleared up.'

'I hope so for your sake, gentlemen,' said the magistrate, making a sign to Giguet to take the four noblemen, Gothard and Michu away. 'Don't take them to Troyes,' he said to the lieutenant. 'Keep them in the police station at Arcis. They must attend tomorrow when their horses' shoes are checked with the shoe prints left in the park.'

Lechesneau and Pigoult only left the château after questioning Catherine, the d'Hauteserre parents and Laurence. The Durieu couple, Catherine and Marthe declared that they had only seen their masters at lunch-time; Monsieur d'Hauteserre declared that he had seen them at three o'clock. When at last, at midnight, Laurence found herself alone with Monsieur and Madame d'Hauteserre, the Abbé Goujet and his sister, and without the four young men who for eighteen months had been the life and soul of the place, her love and her joy, she maintained a long silence which no one ventured to break. Never was affliction more profound or complete. At last a sigh was heard, and they looked round. Marthe had been left to herself in a corner. She stood up and said: 'Death, Madame! They are innocent, but they'll be killed.'

'What have you been up to?' the curé asked Laurence. She left the room without answering. She simply had to be alone to recover her strength, beset as she was with this unforeseen disaster.

3. A Political Trial in Imperial Times

AFTER a time-lapse of thirty-four years, during which three great revolutions have taken place, old people alone can remember today the incredible stir created in Europe by the abduction of a senator of the French Empire. No legal trials, except that of Trumeau, the grocer in the Place Saint-Michel, that of widow Morin during the Empire, those of Fualdès and Castaing during the Restoration, those of Madame Lafarge and Fieschi during the present regime, aroused so much interest and curiosity as the trial of the young people accused of kidnapping Malin. Such an attack on a member of his Senate excited wrath in the Emperor, who was informed almost simultaneously of the perpetration of the crime, the negative result of the inquiries and the arrest of the supposed delinquents. The forest was searched in its length and breadth, the Aube and surrounding departments were scoured from end to end, but not the slightest trace was found of the passage or whereabouts of the Comte de Gondreville. The Chief Justice, who had received information from the Minister of Police, was summoned by Napoleon and explained to him Malin's position in relation to the Simeuses. The Emperor, who then had graver preoccupations, looked to previous facts for a solution to the affair.

'These young men are demented,' he said. 'A legal expert like Malin is bound to go back on agreements extorted by violence. Keep those nobles under surveillance in order to learn on what terms they will release the Comte de Gondreville.' He ordered that this affair should be dealt with very promptly: he regarded it as an attack on his institutions, a critical case of resistance to the effects brought about by the Revolution, a challenge to the great issue of national property and an obstacle to the fusion of parties which was the constant goal of his home policy. To sum up, he thought that these young people who had promised to live peacefully were trying to fool him. 'Fouché's prophecy has come true,' he exclaimed, recalling the remark which the man who was now his Minister of Police had let slip two years before and which had been prompted merely by the report Corentin had made about Laurence.

Living as we do with a constitutional government under which no one takes any interest in a body politic which is blind, dumb, ungrateful and cold, we can scarcely imagine what zeal one word from the Emperor could infuse into his political or administrative machinery. His dynamic will seemed to communicate itself to things as well as persons. Once he had had his say on the matter, the Emperor, whom the Coalition of 1806 had taken by surprise, forgot about it. He was thinking of new battles to be fought and was concerned with massing his regiments in order to deal a telling blow at the heart of the Prussian monarchy. But his desire to see justice done promptly was powerfully furthered by the uncertainty of status affecting all the magistrates of the Empire. At this moment Cambacérès, in his capacity as Arch-Chancellor, and Régnier as Chief Justice were busy setting up the courts of first instance, the Imperial Courts and the Court of Appeal. They were debating the question of magisterial and administrative costumes, on which Napoleon rightly laid such great store. They were revising the personnel and trying to salvage remnants from the *parlements* of the Old Regime. Naturally therefore, the magistrates of the Aube department believed that a display of zeal in the affair of the Comte de Gondreville's abduction would be an excellent recommendation for them. Hence it was that Napoleon's surmises were accepted as certitudes by both time-servers and the populace.

Peace still reigned on the continent, and France was unanimous in its admiration of the Emperor: he encouraged self-interest and flattered personal vanities; this cajolery extended to things and even memories. So then everybody looked on the Gondreville crime as an attack on the public weal, and the unfortunate noblemen, though innocent, were covered with public opprobrium. The rest of the nobility, few in number and confined to their estates, might well deplore the affair among themselves, but not one of them dared open his mouth. How indeed could they run counter to the current of public opinion? The whole department raked up the memory of the eleven people shot dead in 1792 through the shutters of the Cinq-Cygne mansion, and the blame for this was heaped on the heads of the accused. It was feared that the emboldened *émigrés* would abstain from no kind of violence against those who had bought their property, in order to pave the way for its restitution by making this sort of protest against an iniquitous spoliation. The young nobles were therefore denounced as brigands, thieves, assassins; and having Michu as their accomplice was particularly fatal to them. He or his father-in-law had been responsible for all the executions in the department during the Terror, and absurd tales were told about him. The exasperation felt was the more keen because almost all the civil servants in the Aube owed their posts to Malin. No one was generous enough to raise a voice in opposition to general opinion. In short the unhappy young men had no legal means of combating prejudice because, by submitting the case for the prosecution and the verdict to jurymen, the Code of November 1796 had failed to allow accused persons the tremendous safeguard of appeal in cases of legitimate doubt.

Two days after the arrest, masters and servants in the château of Cinq-Cygne were summoned to appear before the grand jury. Cinq-Cygne was left in the care of the farmer, under the supervision of the Abbé Goujet and his sister, who settled in there. Mademoiselle de Cinq-Cygne, Monsieur and Madame d'Hauteserre took up their abode in the little house owned by Durieu in one of the long, broad suburbs which sprawl around Troyes. Laurence was dismayed when the fury of the masses, the malignity of the middle-class citizens and the hostility of officialdom were brought to her attention by several little occurrences such as always happen to the relatives of people implicated in criminal proceedings in the provincial town where the trial is held. Instead of encouraging and compassionate words they overhear conversations envenomed by the most appalling spitefulness; they meet with manifestations of hatred instead of acts of strict politeness or the reserve demanded by decorum; above all they find themselves ostracized, a painful experience for ordinary folk, one whose effects are more swiftly felt because misfortune excites suspicion.

Laurence had recovered all her strength, was counting on innocence coming to light, and despised the crowd too much to take fright at the disapproving silence with which she was received. She bolstered up the courage of the d'Hauteserre parents, keeping in mind the judicial battle which, judging by the rapidity of the proceedings, must soon be fought in the criminal court. But she was about to receive an unexpected blow which lowered her courage.

In the midst of this disaster, and thanks to the outbreak of popular fury, at the moment when this afflicted family felt as if it were living in the wilderness, one man suddenly acquired grandeur in Laurence's eyes and displayed all his fineness of character. The day after the 'true bill', sanctioned by the formula *There are grounds for proceeding* written by the foreman of the jury at the foot of the document, was forwarded to the public prosecutor and the warrant for arrest was converted into an order for committal, the Marquis de Chargebœuf came courageously along in his antiquated barouche to the help of his young kinswoman. Foreseeing that the case would be promptly tried, this head of a great family had hastened to Paris, and from there he had brought one of the shrewdest and most honest of old-time attorneys, Bordin, who for ten years had acted as solicitor for the nobility in Paris, before the celebrated Derville succeeded him. This worthy attorney immediately decided to brief the grandson of a former president of the *parlement* of Normandy, who was aiming at judicial office and had studied the law under Bordin's tutorship. This young advocate, to use a designation which had been abolished but which the Emperor was about to revive, was, in fact, appointed Deputy Attorney-General in Paris after the present case was ended, and became one of our most celebrated magistrates. This Monsieur de Granville accepted the brief for the defence as an opportunity for making a brilliant start in his career. During that period advocates were replaced by unofficial counsels for the defence. Thus there was no restriction on the right to defend; any citizen could plead the cause of innocence; none the less accused persons entrusted their defence to former advocates. The old marquis, startled at the ravage which grief had wrought in Laurence, showed admirable good taste and tact. He did not remind her of the advice he had wasted on her, but presented Bordin as an oracle whose instructions were to be obeyed to the letter and the young Granville as a defending counsel in whom she could place entire confidence.

Laurence offered her hand to the old marquis and clasped his with an impulsiveness which won him over.

'You were right,' she said.

'Will you take my advice now?' he asked.

Both the young countess and Monsieur and Madame d'Hauteserre gave a gesture of assent.

'Very good. Come to my house, which is in the town centre near the law-courts. You and your advocates will be much better off there than here, where you are all crowded together and much too far from the field of battle. You would have to cross the town every day.'

Laurence accepted, and the old man took her and Madame d'Hauteserre into his house, where the defending lawyers and the denizens of Cinq-Cygne stayed for the duration of the trial. After dinner, behind closed doors, Bordin asked Laurence for an exact account of the circumstances of the affair, begging her not to omit any detail, even though the marquis had told Bordin and the young counsel some of the preliminary facts during their journey from Paris to Troyes. As for the young barrister, he could not prevent being divided between admiration for Mademoiselle de Cinq-Cygne and the attention he had to pay to the elementary data of the case.

'And that is all?' asked Bordin after Laurence had recounted such events of the drama as this story has so far related.

'Yes,' she replied.

The deepest silence reigned for some moments in the drawing-room of the Chargebœuf residence where this scene was taking place – one of the gravest, also one of the rarest that can happen in life. Every legal case is judged by the barristers before it comes to the magistrates, just as the death of a patient is foreseen by his doctors, in advance of the fight which the latter will put up against nature and the former against the law. Laurence, the d'Hauteserre parents and the marquis had their eyes fixed on the swarthy, weather-beaten and deeply pock-marked face of the old attorney who was about to pronounce sentence of life or death. Monsieur d'Hauteserre wiped beads of sweat from his brow. Laurence gazed at the young advocate and saw that his face was downcast.

'Well, my dear Bordin?' said the marquis, offering him his snuff-box, from which the attorney absent-mindedly took a pinch.

Bordin rubbed the calves of his legs, which were sheathed in coarse, black silk stockings, for he was in black cloth knee-breeches and was wearing a coat which was similar in cut to the so-called French-style coat. He gave his clients a shrewd but apprehensive glance which chilled them.

'Do you want me to analyse all that and speak my mind?' he asked.

'Of course we do, Monsieur,' said Laurence.

'All your innocent acts give scope for charges against you,' the practised old lawyer then told her. 'We cannot get your kinsmen acquitted; we can only work for a lighter penalty. The fact that you ordered Michu to sell his property will be taken as the clearest proof of your criminal intentions with regard to the senator. You sent your servants to Troyes on purpose, in order to be alone; that is a fact, and it will tell against you. The terrible remark which the elder d'Hauteserre made to Beauvisage will condemn you out of hand. You yourself made another remark in your courtyard which proved long in advance your ill-will against Gondreville. And you yourself were on the watch at the gate at the time when the crime was being committed; the reason why they are not prosecuting you is that they don't want to bring the factor of personal animosity into the affair.'

'There's no case for the defence,' said Monsieur de Granville.

'So much the more is that so,' continued Bordin, 'because we cannot now reveal the truth. Michu, Messieurs de Simeuse and Messieurs d'Hauteserre must be content merely to claim that they spent part of the day with you in the forest and came back to Cinq-Cygne for lunch. But what witnesses have we to confirm the fact that you were all at Cinq-Cygne at three o'clock while the attack was being made? Marthe, the wife of one of the accused; the Durieu couple and Catherine, people in your service; Monsieur and Madame, the parents of two of the accused. Such witness is invalid: the law does not allow them to testify against you, and common-sense rejects them as witnesses for the defence. If you were so ill-advised as to say you had gone to the forest to dig up eleven hundred thousand francs in gold, you would be sending all the accused to the galleys as robbers. Everybody, the public prosecutor, the judges and jury and audience, the whole of France would believe you had stolen this gold from Gondreville and that you kidnapped the senator in order to bring off your *coup*. Taking the charge as it is at the moment, the affair lacks clarity: but if you admitted the simple truth, all would seem crystal-clear: the jury would take any obscurity as explicable in terms of theft, for today 'royalist' is a synonym for 'brigand'. The case as it stands at present suggests an act of vengeance which is plausible considering the political situation. The accused are liable to the death penalty, but not everyone considers that a disgrace; whereas if the abstraction of specie, which will never be looked on as legitimate, is mixed up with it, you will lose the benefit of the interest which attaches to people condemned to death when their crime has extenuating circumstances. At the outset, when you could have shown where the money was hidden and produced the plan of the forest, your metal containers and the gold, in order to justify the use you made of your time, it would have been possible to exculpate yourselves in the presence of impartial magistrates. But as things stand, you must say nothing. Heaven send that none of the accused have compromised their case: we shall have to see what use we can make of the answers they gave when they were being questioned.'

Laurence wrung her hands in despair and raised her eyes to heaven despondently, for she now saw how deep was the abyss into which her cousins had fallen. The marquis and the young counsel agreed with Bordin's devastating analysis. The worthy d'Hauteserre was in tears.

'Why didn't they listen to the Abbé Goujet when he tried to persuade them to run away?' said Madame d'Hauteserre in exasperation.

'Ah!' cried the former public attorney. 'If you could have got them to escape and didn't do so, you have as good as killed them. Absconding from justice gains time and, given time, innocent people may get matters cleared up. This affair seems to me the most tangled I've ever met with in my lifetime, and I've had many such to sort out.'

'It's inexplicable to everyone, and even to us,' said Monsieur de Granville. 'If the accused are innocent, the *coup* was engineered by other people. It's not by magic that five persons turned up in this locality, provided themselves with horses shod like those of the accused, got themselves up to look like them and threw Malin into a pit, with the express purpose of destroying Michu, the d'Hauteserres and the Simeuses. These unknown men, the real criminals, had some motive or other for putting themselves in the shoes of these five innocent men. In order to track them down and find them we should need – the Government itself would need – as many policemen, as many eyes as there are villages for fifty miles round.'

'That would be impossible,' said Bordin. 'It's no use thinking of it. Never, since human societies invented justice, have they found a means of allowing wrongly accused people a power equal to that which a magistrate wields in the pursuit of crime. Justice is not bilateral. Defending lawyers, who have neither spies nor police, have not the public resources at their disposal in favour of their clients. The only resource of innocence is argument, and argument, though it may impress the judges, is often powerless against the narrow minds of jurymen. You have the whole countryside against you. The eight grand jurors who brought in a true bill were owners of national property. Among the petty jurors will be people who, like the others, are purchasers or vendors of national property, or else government clerks. In short, we shall have a jury of Malins. And so you must build up a complete case for the defence, stick to it, and perish in your innocence. You will be found guilty. We shall put in an appeal and drag it out as long as we can. If in the meantime I am able to collect evidence in your favour, you will be able to ask for a reprieve. That is my analysis of the affair and my opinion. If we won (at law everything is possible), it would be a miracle; but your counsel, among all those I know, is the most capable of performing this miracle, and I shall help him.'

'The senator must hold the key to this enigma,' Monsieur de Granville then said, 'for a man always knows who bears a grudge against him and why. This is the picture: he leaves Paris at the end of winter, comes to Gondreville, with no retinue, shuts himself up with his notary and practically delivers himself over to five men who seize hold of him.'

'Assuredly', said Bordin, 'his behaviour has been, to say the least, as extraordinary as that of our clients. But, with the whole of the district against us, how can we, the accused, become the accusers? We should need goodwill and help from the Government, and far stronger evidence than in an ordinary situation. I detect malice aforethought, of the subtlest kind, in our unknown adversaries, who knew how things stood between Michu, Messieurs de Simeuse and Malin. They said nothing and stole nothing: there's caution for you! The masks they wore disguised something more than common malefactors. But what's the use of saying such things to the kind of jurymen we shall get?'

This insight into private affairs, which raises certain barristers and magistrates to such great heights, astonished and confounded Laurence; her heart sank as she listened to this inexorable logic.

'Out of one hundred criminal affairs,' said Bordin, 'there aren't ten which the courts delve into in all their ramifications, and in quite a third of such cases they don't know what lies underneath. Your case is one of those which prove unintelligible both to accused and to accusers, to both judges and public. As for our Sovereign Lord, he has other fish to fry beside coming to the rescue of Messieurs de Simeuse, even if they hadn't schemed to overthrow him. But who on earth has it in for Malin? And what did they want of him?'

As Bordin and Monsieur de Granville scanned each other, they looked as if they doubted Laurence's veracity. The pain this caused her was one of the most excruciating of all those she had suffered in this affair, and she cast a look at the two lawyers which stifled any suspicions they may have felt.

The next day the case for the defence was formally

committed to them and they were allowed to interview the accused. Bordin informed the family that the six accused, to use a professional term, 'had comported themselves with dignity and decorum.'

'Monsieur de Granville will defend Michu,' said Bordin.

'Michu?' exclaimed Monsieur de Chargebœuf, astonished at this change-over.

'Yes. He's the central figure, and there lies the danger,' the old attorney retorted.

'If he's in the most exposed position, that seems right to me!' cried Laurence.

'We can see a loop-hole or two,' said Monsieur de Granville, 'and we're going to look well into them. If we are able to get an acquittal, it will be because Monsieur d'Hauteserre told Michu to repair one of the gate-posts in the sunken road and because a wolf had been seen in the valley. Everything depends on the arguments brought before the court, and they will turn on small details which you will see will become tremendously important.'

Laurence fell into that state of moral dejection which is bound to mortify the soul of all active and thinking people once the futility of action and thought is made clear to them. It was no longer a question of overturning a man or a regime with the aid of devoted adherents and fanatical ideals wrapped in the veils of mystery: she saw that the whole of society was in arms against her cousins and herself. One cannot, single-handed, take a prison by assault or set prisoners free in the teeth of a hostile populace and under the eyes of a police force alerted by the alleged audacity of the accused. And so when the young counsel, alarmed by the apathy of this noble and courageous creature, who looked even more apathetic than she really was, attempted to revive her courage, she replied: 'I can't talk. I can only suffer and wait.' The accent and gesture of this reply, and the look she gave as she made it, imparted to it a sublimity which in a wider sphere of action would have earned it celebrity. A few instants later the ingenuous d'Hauteserre was saying to the Marquis de Chargebœuf: 'What trouble I have taken for the sake of my unhappy children! I have already provided them with nearly eight thousand francs' income from State bonds. If they had been willing to serve in the army they would have reached high rank and could have made advantageous marriages today. All my plans have miscarried.'

His wife said, 'How *can* you think of their financial interests when their lives and honour are at stake?'

'Monsieur d'Hauteserre thinks of everything,' said the marquis.

*

While the inhabitants of Cinq-Cygne were waiting for the trial to begin and unsuccessfully applying for permission to see the prisoners, an event of the gravest importance was happening in dead secrecy at the château. Marthe had returned to Cinq-Cygne immediately after giving testimony before the grand jury, and her evidence was of so little import that she was not summoned to appear before the criminal court. Being a person of extreme sensitivity, the poor woman used to sit on her chair in the drawing-room, where she kept Mademoiselle Goujet company, in a state of pitiable stupefaction. To her, as also to the curé and all those who did not know how the accused had spent their time on the fateful day, their innocence appeared to be doubtful. There were moments when Marthe believed that Michu, her masters and Laurence really had committed some act of vengeance against the senator. The unhappy woman was sufficiently aware of Michu's loyalty to realize that of all the accused he was the most in danger, whether because of his antecedents or because of the part he might have played in the execution of this design. The Abbé Goujet, his sister and Marthe were lost in the conjectures to which this notion gave rise; they turned them over so much in their minds that they had perforce to adopt some viewpoint or other. The absolute doubt postulated by Descartes can no more obtain in human thinking than a vacuum in nature, and the intellectual operation by which this doubt might be reached would be, like the effect of a pneumatic machine, exceptional and anomalous. In any matter whatsoever one has to believe something. Now Marthe was so afraid the accused men were guilty that her fear amounted to a belief. This state of mind proved fatal to her. Five days after the arrest, just as she was about to retire, at approximately ten o'clock at night, she was summoned to the courtyard by her mother, who had walked over from the farm.

'A workman from Troyes wants to speak to you on behalf of Michu and is waiting for you on the sunken road,' she told Marthe.

They both went through the breach to take a short cut. The night was dark and so was the road, and Marthe was unable to see anything more than the bulk of a man's body standing out in the blackness.

'Speak to me, Madame, so that I may be sure you really are Madame Michu,' the man said in an anxious tone of voice.

'Certainly I am Madame Michu. What do you want of me?'

'Good,' said the unknown person. 'Give me your hand, and have no fear of me. I have come', he added, leaning towards her and speaking quietly, 'to bring you a note from Michu. I am one of the prison warders, and if my superior officers noticed my absence we should all be lost. Trust in me. In time past it was your good father who got me my post, and that's why Michu counted on me.'

He handed Marthe a letter and vanished into the forest without waiting for a reply. A shudder passed through Marthe at the thought that she was no doubt going to learn the secret of the affair. She ran to the farm with her mother and shut herself up in her room to read the following letter:

My dear Marthe,

You can count on the discretion of the man who is bringing you this letter. He can't read or write. He was one of the staunchest republicans in Babœuf's conspiracy; your father often used him, and he regards the senator as a renegade. Now, my dear wife: we have shut the senator up in the vault where we formerly hid our masters. The wretched man has only five days' rations, and as it is in our interest for him to stay alive, as soon as you have read this note, take him enough food for at least five days more. No doubt the forest is being watched, so take as many precautions as we did for our young masters. Don't say a single word to Malin, don't talk to him at all and put on one of our masks, which you will find on one of the cellar steps. If you don't want to endanger our lives you'll keep absolute silence about the secret I'm forced to confide to you. Don't say a word to Mademoiselle de Cinq-Cygne – she might lose her nerve. Have no fears about me. We are certain things will come out all right, and when the time comes Malin will be our saviour. And lastly, as soon as you've read this letter, needless to say burn it: if anyone else read a single line of it, it would cost me my head.

All my love,

MICHU

The existence of the vault under the hillock in the middle of the forest was known only to Marthe, her son, Michu, the four noblemen and Laurence – at least Marthe naturally thought so, since her husband had not mentioned to her his encounter with Peyrade and Corentin. Thus the letter, which moreover appeared to have been written and signed by Michu, could only have come from him. Assuredly, if Marthe had immediately consulted her mistress and her two legal advisers who knew that the accused were innocent, the wily attorney would have begun to see through the perfidious schemes in which his clients were entangled; but Marthe, with typically feminine impulsiveness, convinced that her previous suspicions were now clearly established, threw the letter in the fire. However, inspired by a strange glimmer of prudence, she withdrew the blank side of the letter from the flames, tore off the first five lines, whose tenor could not compromise anyone, and stitched them inside the lower hem of her dress. Then, alarmed at knowing that the immured man had not eaten for twenty-four hours, she decided to take him wine, bread and meat that very night. Neither her curiosity nor her humane feelings allowed her to put it off till the following day. She heated her oven and with her mother's help made a hare and duck pie, a rice cake, roasted two chickens, took three bottles of wine and herself baked two round loaves. About half past two in the morning she set out for the forest with a basketful of food, accompanied by Couraut, who on all these expeditions scouted round with admirable intelligence. He could scent strangers far and wide, and whenever he detected their presence would come back to his mistress with a quiet growl, gaze at her and point his muzzle in the direction where danger lay.

Marthe arrived at the pond at about three in the morning and left Couraut there to keep guard. After working for half an hour to clear the entrance, she approached the door of the vault with a dark lantern, covering her face with the mask which she had indeed found on one of the stone steps. The senator's confinement seemed to have been premeditated a long time in advance. A hole one foot square, which Marthe had not seen on previous occasions, had been crudely cut out of the top of the iron door enclosing the vault; but to prevent Malin from dislodging the cross-bar with the patience that all prisoners have at their command, it had been secured with a padlock. The senator, who had got up from his bed of moss, heaved a sigh on perceiving a masked face, for he guessed that he was not yet to be released. He scrutinized Marthe in so far as the flickering light of the lantern allowed him to do so, and recognized her by her clothes, feminine curves and movements. When she passed him the pie through the hole, he let it fall and seized hold of her hands and with surprising nimbleness tried to pull from her fingers two rings, her wedding-ring and another little ring which Mademoiselle de Cinq-Cygne had given her.

'You won't deny that it is you, my dear Madame Michu,' he said.

As soon as she felt the senator's fingers fumbling at her, Marthe clenched her fist and gave him a vigorous blow in the chest. Then, without a word, she went out, cut a fairly strong stick and passed the rest of the provisions to the senator on the end of it.

'What do they want of me?' he asked.

Marthe slipped away without answering. As she was returning home at about five o'clock, at the edge of the pond Couraut warned her of the presence of an intruder. She turned back and made for the pavilion in which she had lived for so long. But when she entered the avenue she was spotted from far off by the Gondreville country policeman; she decided to walk straight up to him.

'You're about very early, Madame Michu,' he said as he approached her.

'We are in such a fix', she replied, 'that I'm obliged to do a servant's work. I'm going to Bellache to fetch some grain.'

'So you haven't any at Cinq-Cygne?' he asked.

Marthe made no reply. She went on and when she arrived

at the Bellache farm she asked Beauvisage for a small quantity of seed-corn, telling him that Monsieur d'Hauteserre had recommended her to get it from him so that he could try out a new kind. When Marthe had left, the Gondreville constable came to the farm to find out what Marthe had gone there for. Six days later Marthe, now more cautious, took the food supply at midnight in order not to be caught by the police, who were so evidently watching the forest. After taking the senator food for a third time, she was seized with a kind of terror on hearing the curé read out the cross-examination which the accused had undergone in open court, for by now the hearings had begun. She took the Abbé aside and, after making him swear to keep what she was about to tell him as secret as if she were making her confession, she showed him the fragment of the letter received from Michu, told him what it had contained and let him into the secret of the place where the senator was imprisoned. The curé immediately asked Marthe if she had other letters from her husband so that he could compare the handwriting. She went home to fetch them, but there she found a subpoena to appear before the court as a witness. Back at the château, she learnt that the Abbé and his sister had also been summonsed at the request of the accused. So they were obliged to proceed instantly to Troyes. Thus all the characters in this drama, and even those who so to speak had only a walking-on part to play, were assembled on the stage on which the destiny of the two families was at stake.

*

There are few localities in France where justice borrows from concrete things the prestige with which it should always be accompanied. Next to religion and monarchy, is not this the most important part of the social machinery? Everywhere, even in Paris, the shabbiness of the buildings, the awkward lay-out of the premises, the paucity of decoration – and yet France is the vainest and the most theatrical nation of our days in respect to public monuments – reduce the efficacity of this formidable authority. In almost every town the arrangement is the same. At the far end of a long square hall you see a desk covered in green baize, standing on a dais behind which the judges are seated in very ordinary arm-chairs. On the left is the public prosecutor's seat and, on the same side, along the wall, a long tribune with chairs for the jurymen. Facing the jury there stretches another tribune with a bench for the accused and the police who guard them. The clerk of the court sits below the platform at the table on which the incriminating evidence is laid out. Before the Imperial judicial system was instituted, the government commissary and the jury director each had a seat and a table, one on the right and the other on the left of the magisterial bench. Two ushers flit to and fro in the space left open in front of the court for the witnesses to come forth. The lawyers for the defence stand underneath the prisoners' bench. A wooden balustrade runs between the two tribunes towards the other end of the court-room, forming an enclosure fitted with benches for witnesses who have been heard and for privileged spectators. Then, opposite the tribunal, above the entrance door, there is always a shabby gallery reserved for officials and ladies residing in the department, selected by the presiding judge, who is responsible for court arrangements. The unprivileged public remains standing in the space between the entrance door and the balustrade. This, the normal lay-out of French tribunals and present-day courts of assize, was also that of the criminal court of Troyes.

In April 1806, neither the four judges and chairman comprising the court, nor the public prosecutor, nor the jury director, nor the government commissary, nor the ushers, nor counsel for the defence, no one in fact except the gendarmes, wore official robes or any other distinctive mark to relieve the bareness of the furnishings and the Lenten faces of all and sundry. There was no crucifix for the edification either of judges or of accused. Everything was dismal and commonplace. Pomp and circumstance, so necessary to the social interest, perhaps gave some consolation to the criminal. The avid throng of spectators was what it has been and will be on all similar occasions so long as manners and customs remain unreformed and France has not realized that the admission of the public to trials is no guarantee of real publicity, and that hearings in open court themselves constitute so extreme a penalty that if the legislator had had any suspicion of this he would not have inflicted it. Conventional morality is often more cruel than the law. It is merely human prejudice, whereas the law is the expression of a nation's reason. Yet conventional morality, though often unreasonable, prevails over justice.

There were crowds milling around the law-courts. As at all sensational trials, the chairman of the bench was obliged to place pickets of soldiers on guard at the doors. The audience standing behind the balustrade was so tightly packed that they could scarcely breathe. Monsieur de Granville, who was defending Michu, Bordin, counsel for the Simeuses, and an advocate from Troyes who was pleading for the d'Hauteserres and Gothard, the least seriously implicated of the six accused, were at their posts before the session opened, and confidence was written on their faces. Just as a doctor conceals his apprehensions from his patient, so an advocate always displays a hopeful countenance to his clients. This is one of those rare cases when falsehood becomes a virtue.

When the accused were brought in, sympathetic murmurs were raised at the sight of the four young men, who, after three weeks' detention spent in anxiety, had become somewhat pallid. The perfect resemblance between the twins excited the greatest interest. Perhaps everyone felt that nature ought to accord special protection to one of its rarest phenomena, and all the onlookers felt tempted to make up for the neglect that destiny had shown them. Their simple and noble demeanour, free from the slightest tint of shame but also free from bravado, moved many of the women. The four noblemen and Gothard were wearing the same clothes they had worn at the time of their arrest; but Michu, whose clothes formed part of the incriminating evidence, had put on his best garments – a blue frock-coat, a brown velvet waistcoat in Robespierre style and a white neck-cloth. The unfortunate man paid the penalty for his unprepossessing looks. When he cast his amber eyes with their clear and penetrating glance round the assembly, they all responded with a murmur of horror. They were inclined to see the finger of God in his appearance on the prisoners' bench to which his father-in-law had brought so many victims. But this truly great-hearted man looked at his masters with a touch of irony in his smile. He seemed to be saying to them: 'I'm doing you harm!' These five accused men exchanged affectionate smiles with their counsel. Gothard was still playing the idiot.

After defending counsel, primed in this matter by the Marquis de Chargebœuf, who courageously sat next to Bordin and Monsieur de Granville, had sagaciously exercised the right of challenge, once the jury was empanelled and the charge read, the accused were separated so that each might be examined. They all answered with remarkable consistency: after a morning ride in the forest they had returned to Cinq-Cygne for lunch at one o'clock; after the meal, from three to half past five, they had been in the forest again. Such was the basic statement made by the accused, and any variations followed from the special position of each one. When the chairman asked Messieurs de Simeuse to explain why they had gone out so early, one after the other declared that, ever since their return home, they had been thinking of buying back Gondreville and that, with a view to bargaining with Malin, who had arrived the evening before, they had gone out with Michu and their cousin to survey the forest in order to decide what price they would offer. While they were doing that, Messieurs d'Hauteserre, their cousin and Gothard had gone off to hunt a wolf which the peasants had caught sight of. If the jury director had examined their horses' shoe-prints in the forest as carefully as those of the horses which had crossed the Gondreville park, there would have been proof that they had been riding in parts very far from the château.

The questions put to Messieurs d'Hauteserre confirmed the statements of Messieurs de Simeuse, and their answers were consistent with what they had told the examining magistrate. The need to justify their excursions had prompted each one of them to put it down to hunting. They too alleged that, several days before, peasants had reported that a wolf was roaming in the forest.

However, the public prosecutor called attention to discrepancies between the original questioning, when the d'Hauteserres had said that all of them had been out hunting together, and their statement in court, namely that they and

Laurence had gone out hunting while the Simeuses were valuing the forest. Monsieur de Granville pointed out that since the delict had not been committed until between two o'clock and half past five, the prisoners' explanations of how they had spent the day ought to be accepted. To this the public prosecutor replied that the accused had a motive for concealing the preparations they had made for kidnapping the senator.

The skill with which the defence was being conducted then became apparent to everybody. Judges, jurors and public soon realized that the case was going to be hotly contested. Bordin and Monsieur de Granville appeared to have foreseen every eventuality. An innocent man has to give a clear and plausible account of his actions, and so it is the task of the defence to present a plausible tale in opposition to the less plausible one put forward by the prosecution. To a defending counsel who believes in his client's innocence, the case for the prosecution is merely a fiction. The cross-examination of the four noblemen put things in a fairly favourable light for them. So far all was going well. But Michu's cross-examination took a more serious turn, and the fight was now on. It then became clear why Monsieur de Granville had preferred to undertake the defence of the servant rather than that of the masters.

Michu admitted his threats against Marion, but denied they were as violent as was made out. He had not lain in ambush for Malin, he maintained, but was simply making his rounds in the park: the senator and Grévin might well have taken fright on seeing the muzzle of his rifle and imagined it was aimed at them although he had no hostile intention whatsoever. He remarked that, in the evening twilight, a man who is not in the habit of hunting may believe a firearm is pointing at him even when it is being carried on the shoulder. To explain the state of his clothes at the time of his arrest, he said he had stumbled into the breach while returning home. 'It not being light enough for me to see as I was climbing across,' he said, 'I somehow or other slithered down with the loose stones over which I was walking as I climbed up from the sunken road.' As for the plaster which Gothard had brought him, he gave the same reply as at all previous questionings: he had used it to bed in one of the gate-posts in the sunken road.

The public prosecutor and the chairman of the bench asked him to explain how at one and the same time he had managed to be in the breach and on top of the sunken road bedding in the gate-post, particularly since the examining magistrate, the gendarmes and the rural constable had declared they had heard him approaching from down below. Michu replied that Monsieur d'Hauteserre had scolded him for not having carried out this small repair, which he was anxious to see completed because of the difficulties he might have with the communal council concerning the road. So Michu had gone to tell Monsieur d'Hauteserre that the gate-post was made good again.

It was a fact that Monsieur d'Hauteserre had put up a gate at the top of the sunken road to prevent the commune from taking it over. Michu had made a pretext of this on seeing how much stress was laid on the state of his clothes and the plaster, which he could not deny having used. If in a law-court truth often looks like fiction, fiction also looks very much like truth. Both prosecution and defence laid great emphasis on this matter, and both the doubts entertained by the prosecution and the efforts put forth by defending counsel made a crucial point of it.

When he was put into the witness-box, Gothard, no doubt primed by Monsieur de Granville, admitted that Michu had asked him to get some bags of plaster – on previous occasions he had always started weeping when questioned.

'Why did neither you nor Gothard take the examining magistrate to see the gate straight away?' the public prosecutor asked Michu.

'I never imagined', said Michu, 'that we were going to be accused of a capital offence.'

All the accused except Gothard were taken out. Now that Gothard was alone, the chairman adjured him to tell the truth in his own interest, now that he had ceased pretending to be an idiot. None of the jurors believed that he was an imbecile. By refusing to speak in court, he might incur grave penalties, whereas if he spoke the truth the case against him would probably be dismissed. Gothard stood there blubbering and swaying, then at last he said that Michu had asked him to fetch him several bags of plaster; but each time he had met him in front of the farm. He was asked how many bags.

'Three,' he replied.

Michu was recalled, and an argument ensued between him and Gothard as to whether it was three including the one he was bringing him at the moment of the arrest, which reduced the bags used to two, or three in addition to the last. Michu won the argument in the end. The jurymen were satisfied that only two bags had been used, but they seemed to have made up their minds about what it was for. Bordin and Monsieur de Granville deemed it necessary to give them a surfeit of plaster and to tire them out so much that their wits became fuddled. The drift of Granville's conclusions was that experts should be called in to inspect the condition of the gate. 'The jury director', he said, 'contented himself with visiting the spot, not so much in order to make a truly expert inspection as to catch Michu out. In our opinion he failed in his duty, and this omission ought to count in our favour.'

The court did in fact send experts to check that one of the gate-posts had recently been cemented up. On his side, the public prosecutor tried to win his point before the verification was made. 'Is it likely', he asked Michu, 'that you would have chosen a time when the light was going, from half past five to half past six, to plaster up the post all by yourself?'

'Monsieur d'Hauteserre had told me off!'

'But,' said the public prosecutor, 'if you used the plaster on the gate, you must have used a trowel and mortar-board. Now if you went straight away to tell Monsieur d'Hauteserre that you had carried out his orders, you cannot possibly explain why Gothard was bringing you more plaster. You had to pass by your farm, and therefore you must have left your tools there and told Gothard you had finished.'

This crushing argument produced a terrible silence in court.

'Come, own up,' the public prosecutor continued. 'It was not a post you were burying.'

'So you think it was the senator!' said Michu with a profoundly sarcastic air.

Monsieur de Granville formally requested the public prosecutor to explain himself on this count. Michu was accused of abduction and illegal restraint, not of murder. Nothing, he said, could be more grave than this interpolation. The Code of November 1796 forbade a public prosecutor to introduce any new count into the proceedings; these proceedings would be null and void if he did not keep within the terms of the indictment.

The public prosecutor replied that Michu, the leading spirit in the attack on Malin, who in his masters' interests had taken all responsibility on his shoulders, might well have needed to seal up the entrance to the still undiscovered spot where the senator was languishing in captivity.

Hard-pressed with questions, harassed in his confrontation with Gothard, manoeuvred into contradicting himself, Michu banged his fist hard on the rail of the prisoners' bench and said: 'I had no part in the senator's abduction. My belief is simply that he has been shut up by his enemies. But if he reappears, you'll see that the plaster had nothing to do with it.'

'Good!' said his counsel, addressing the public prosecutor. 'You have done more for my client's case than anything I could have said.'

The hearing was adjourned on this bold allegation, which surprised the jurymen and gave the advantage to the defence. Accordingly the advocates of the town and Bordin enthusiastically congratulated the young counsel. The public prosecutor, disconcerted at Granville's assertion, feared he had fallen into a trap; he had in fact walked into one which the defence had very cleverly set for him, and Gothard had played his part admirably. The wits of the town said that the affair had been plastered up, that the public prosecutor had mixed his mortar badly and that the Simeuses had had a coat of white-wash. In France everything is a matter for jesting, and pleasantry reigns supreme. People jest on the scaffold, on the battlefield, at the barricades, and no doubt some Frenchman will make the grand assizes of the Last Judgement an excuse for a joke.

Next day the witnesses for the prosecution were heard: Madame Marion, Madame Grévin, Grévin himself, the senator's man-servant and Violette, whose testimony can readily be imagined in view of what had taken place. All of them more or less identified the five accused: hesitantly in the case of the four noblemen, but with certainty as regards Michu. Beauvisage repeated Robert d'Hauteserre's indiscreet remark. The peasant who had come to buy a calf repeated what Mademoiselle de Cinq-Cygne had said. The experts were heard, and confirmed their report on the comparison of the shoe-prints with those of the four noblemen's horses: the prosecution maintained that they were absolutely identical. This piece of evidence was naturally a subject for heated argument between Monsieur de Granville and the public prosecutor. Counsel for the defence harried the Cinq-Cygne blacksmith and succeeded in establishing that similar horse-shoes had been sold some days beforehand to individuals unknown in the district. The smith declared, moreover, that he used that kind of shoe not only for the horses of the château but also for many others in the canton. Finally it turned out, for a wonder, that the horse which Michu regularly rode had been shod at Troyes, and no prints of these shoes were found among those discovered in the park.

'Michu's double was unaware of this circumstance,' said Monsieur de Granville with a glance towards the jury, 'and the prosecution has not established that any of the château horses were used.'

He also demolished Violette's testimony regarding the resemblance between the horses, which he had seen only from behind and from afar! But in spite of counsel's incredible efforts, the mass of positive evidence bore heavily on Michu. The public prosecutor, judges and jurymen all felt, as the defence had foreseen, that the guilt of the servant involved that of the masters. Bordin had accurately divined where the crux of the matter lay when he assigned Monsieur de Granville to Michu as counsel; but by doing so the defence was showing its weak spot. Accordingly, everything to do with the former bailiff of Gondreville was of vital interest. Michu's bearing for that matter was superb. In these cross-examinations he displayed all the sagacity with which nature had endowed him, and the public had only to look at him to acknowledge his superiority. But the astonishing thing was that, by virtue of this, it appeared more obvious that he was the author of the crime. The witnesses for the defence, who are always taken less seriously by judge and jury – and by the law itself – seemed merely to be discharging their task, and were listened to for form's sake. For one thing, neither Marthe, nor Monsieur nor Madame d'Hauteserre was required to take the oath; Catherine and the Durieu couple, in their capacity as family servants, were similarly exempted. Monsieur d'Hauteserre did in fact testify that he had ordered Michu to replace the fallen post. The declaration of the experts who at that juncture read out their reports confirmed the old gentleman's testimony, but they also vindicated the jury director by declaring that they were unable to determine at what period the work had been carried out: it might have been done, not twenty days, but many weeks ago. Mademoiselle de Cinq-Cygne's appearance excited the liveliest curiosity, but when she saw her cousins in the dock after over three weeks' separation, she was seized with such violent emotion that she looked like a guilty person.

She felt a terrible yearning to be standing beside the twins and, as she said later, she had to summon up all her strength to repress the furious impulse which urged her to assassinate the public prosecutor so that she might share the criminality which everybody was attributing to them. She related quite simply how, as she was returning to Cinq-Cygne, seeing smoke rising in the park, she had thought there must be a fire somewhere. For a long time she had thought the smoke came from a bonfire.

'However,' she said, 'I later remembered a detail which I now bring to the attention of the court. In the frogs of my riding-habit and the folds of my collar I found fragments like those of burnt paper carried along by the wind.'

'Was there a lot of smoke?' asked Bordin.

'Yes,' she replied. 'I thought there must be a house on fire.'

'This may change the whole look of the case,' said Bordin. 'I request the court to order an immediate inspection of the locality where the fire took place.' The chairman ordered this inquiry.

Grévin, recalled by the defence, and questioned about this occurrence, declared he knew nothing about it. But between Bordin and Grévin there was an exchange of glances which gave them mutual enlightenment.

'That's the nub of the case,' the old attorney said to himself.

'They're getting round to it!' the notary thought.

But each of these sly foxes believed that the inquiry was useless. Bordin told himself that Grévin would be as silent as the grave, and Grévin congratulated himself on having had all traces of the fire removed. To settle this point, a side-issue as regards the proceedings, and apparently trivial, but a capital one for the vindication which history owes to the young men, Pigoult and the experts assigned to inspect the park declared they had not found any spots showing traces of a fire. Bordin cited two farm-hands who testified that, at the keeper's orders, they had ploughed up a portion of a meadow in which the grass was scorched; but they had not noticed what substance the ashes came from. The keeper in question, recalled by the defence, said that as he was passing by the château to go and see the masquerade at Arcis, he had received orders from the senator to plough up the part of the meadow which the senator had noticed that morning while taking a walk.

'Had weeds or papers been burnt there?'

'I saw no signs of papers having been burnt there,' the keeper replied.

'In any case,' the defence contended, 'even if weeds were burnt there, someone must have carted them there and set fire to them.'

The testimony of the Cinq-Cygne curé and Mademoiselle Goujet created a favourable impression. While taking a walk in the forest after vespers they had seen the noblemen and Michu leaving the château on horseback and making for the forest. The Abbé Goujet's status and rectitude lent weight to his words.

The speech of the public prosecutor, who felt sure of a verdict of guilty, was typical of all such indictments. The accused were incorrigible enemies of France, its institutions and laws. They were athirst for disorder. Even though they had been implicated in attempts against the life of the Emperor and had belonged to Condé's army, that magnanimous sovereign had struck them off the list of *émigrés*. And this was the return they made for his clemency! In short, he gave vent to all the oratorical declamations which have been repeated since then in the name of the Bourbons against the Bonapartists and are repeated today against Republicans and Legitimists in the name of the younger dynasty. Commonplaces like this, which might have some meaning under stable forms of government, will at least seem farcical once historical research has found them to be typical of ministerial utterances at all periods. One can say of them what was said in earlier periods of disturbance: 'The inn-sign has changed, but it's still the same wine!' The public prosecutor, who for that matter became one of the most distinguished Attorney-Generals of the Empire, attributed the crime in question to the resolution taken by the returned *émigrés* to protest against the confiscation of their estates. He made the audience really tremble at the thought of the senator's situation. Then he accumulated proofs, half-proofs and probabilities with a certain amount of talent, stimulated by the certainty that his zeal would reap its reward, and finally he sat down and waited for the defence to return his fire.

Monsieur de Granville was never to plead any criminal cause after this one, but he made his name by it.

'Where is the *corpus delicti*? Where is the senator?' he asked. 'You accuse the defendants of having taken him prisoner and even immured him with stone and plaster. In that case, they alone know where he is, and as they have been kept in prison for twenty-three days he must have died of starvation. And so they are murderers: and yet you have not accused them of murder. But if he is still alive they must have accomplices: if they had accomplices and the senator were still alive, would they not have produced him? The purpose which you attribute to them having failed, would they gratuitously render their crime more heinous? They could, by repenting, obtain pardon for an act of vengeance which has failed: would they therefore persist in keeping in captivity a man from whom they can obtain nothing? Is it not absurd? Take away your plaster,' he said to the public prosecutor. 'It has missed its effect, for either the defendants are criminal imbeciles – that you do not believe – or innocent victims of circumstances which neither they nor you can explain! You ought rather to inquire about the mass of documents which were burnt in the senator's grounds: this would show that far graver interests than those of the defendants are involved and reveal the motives for the abduction.' Granville went into these hypotheses with marvellous dexterity. He emphasized the moral integrity of the witnesses for the defence, keenly religious people who believed in an after-life and the wrath to come. Here he reached the heights of eloquence and the audience was deeply moved. 'What!' he exclaimed. 'These wicked people go on calmly eating their dinners when their cousin informs them of the senator's abduction! When the officer of gendarmes suggests a means for making their peace, they refuse to give the senator up and pretend complete ignorance!' He then gave hints of some underground intrigue the key to which was in the hands of Time, which one day would reveal the injustice of the charge. Once embarked on this theme, he had the audacity, ingenuity and adroitness to imagine himself as one of the jurymen. He supposed himself deliberating with the other jurymen; he showed how unhappy he would be later if, after voting for the cruel verdict of 'Guilty!', the error came to light. He gave such a graphic picture of the remorse he would feel and so forcibly recalled to himself the doubts raised in his mind by the speech for the defence, that he left the jurymen in a horrible state of uncertainty.

Juries had not yet become blasé about this sort of allocution, which then had the charm of novelty: this jury was shaken. After Monsieur de Granville's impassioned speech, they had to listen to the specious subtleties of the public prosecutor, who multiplied the points at issue, brought out all the mysterious aspects of the case and proved it to be unfathomable. His policy was to appeal to the jurymen's reasoning powers, whereas the defending counsel's address had been aimed at their hearts and imagination. In short, Granville's tone of grave conviction had so hypnotized the jury that the public prosecutor could see the whole structure of his argument collapsing. This was so obvious that the advocate of Messieurs d'Hauteserre and Gothard left their case to the discretion of the jurymen, believing they would throw out the charge. The public prosecutor requested that the hearing should be adjourned so that he might make a reply the following day. Bordin could read acquittal in the jurymen's eyes if they considered their verdict immediately after these two speeches, and he objected, both on legal and on factual grounds, to his innocent clients having to suffer yet another night of anxiety. He did so in vain, for the court went into deliberation. 'My view is', said the chairman, 'that the public interest has a claim equal to that of the accused. The court would be violating all notions of equity if such a request, when made by the defence, were refused; it must therefore be granted to the prosecution.'

'Life has its up and downs,' said Bordin, looking at his clients. 'You might have been acquitted this evening; to-morrow you may be found guilty.'

'In any case,' said the elder Simeuse, 'we have nothing but admiration for you.'

Mademoiselle de Cinq-Cygne had tears in her eyes. After the doubts expressed by the counsel for the defence, she could scarcely believe things had gone so well. She was congratulated, and everyone came to assure her that her cousins would be acquitted. But unfortunately a dramatic turn of events was in the offing: one as sensational, sinister and unforeseen as any that has ever reversed the trend of a criminal trial.

*

At five in the morning, the day after Monsieur de Granville made his speech for the defence, Senator Malin was found on the highroad leading to Troyes, having been freed from his fetters by unknown liberators as he slept. Knowing nothing of the trial, unaware that his name was echoing throughout Europe, he was happy to be breathing fresh air once more. The man on whom the whole drama hinged was as stupefied by what he was told as the people who found him had been at seeing him. He was given a lift in a farmer's trap and quickly arrived at the Prefecture in Troyes. The prefect immediately informed the jury director, the government commissary and the public prosecutor, who, acting on the account given by the Comte de Gondreville, sent the police to Durieu's house to fetch Marthe from her bed while the jury director was drawing up and issuing a warrant for her arrest. Mademoiselle de Cinq-Cygne, who was only free on bail, was snatched from one of the rare moments of sleep vouchsafed to her in the midst of her continual anguish, and was taken to the Prefecture for questioning. An order to keep the accused men from any kind of communication, even with their counsel, was sent to the governor of the prison. At ten o'clock the assembled crowd was informed that the hearing was postponed until the afternoon.

This change of time, coinciding with the news of the senator's liberation, the arrest of Marthe and Mademoiselle de Cinq-Cygne and the severance of communication with the accused, brought terror to the Chargebœuf household. The whole town, the sightseers who had come to Troyes to attend the trial, the press reporters and indeed the whole population were agog with excitement. About ten o'clock the Abbé Goujet came to see Monsieur and Madame d'Hauteserre and the defence lawyers. They were breakfasting – in so far as one can take breakfast in such circumstances. The curé took Bordin and Monsieur de Granville and told them what Marthe had confided to him and gave them the fragment of the letter she had received. The two defending counsel exchanged a glance, after which Bordin said to the curé: 'Not a word about it! It looks as if all is lost; but at least let's put a bold front on it.'

Marthe was not equal to standing up to the jury director and the public prosecutor together. Moreover there was abundant proof against her. At the Senator's suggestion, Lechesneau had had a search made for the under-crust of the last loaf Marthe had brought to him, which he had left in the cellar; also the empty bottles and other objects. During his long hours of captivity Malin had made conjectures about his situation and looked for clues which might put him on the track of his enemies; and naturally he communicated his observations to the magistrate. Michu's newly built farmhouse, he said, necessarily had a new oven, and the tiles and bricks on which dough was laid must have a certain pattern of pointing. It would therefore be possible to prove that his bread had been baked in that oven if one took the impression of the floor, whose scorings would correspond to those on the crust. Also the bottles sealed with green wax would no doubt tally with the bottles in Michu's cellar. These subtle suggestions induced the examining magistrate to visit the farm, taking Marthe with him, and his inspection produced the results which the senator had foreseen. Marthe herself, taken in by the apparent kindness shown her by Lechesneau, the public prosecutor and the government commissary in persuading her that only a full confession could save her husband's life in the face of such damning proof, admitted that the place where the senator had been concealed was known only to Michu, the Simeuses and the d'Hauteserres, and that on three different nights she had taken food to the senator. Laurence, questioned on this matter of the vault, was forced to admit that Michu had discovered it and shown it to her, long before the abduction, as a refuge where the four noblemen could hide from the police.

As soon as the questioning was over, jury and counsel were informed of the resumption of the hearing. At three o'clock the chairman opened the session and announced that the case was to be retried in the light of new evidence. He produced three bottles of wine and asked Michu if he acknowledged that they belonged to him, pointing out that the wax caps on two empty bottles were identical with that of a full bottle taken that morning from the farm by the magistrate in his wife's presence. Michu denied that they belonged to him, but these new exhibits were inspected by the jurymen. to whom the chairman explained that the empty bottles had just been found in the place where the senator had been held captive. Each of the accused was questioned about the vault under the monastery ruins. Witnesses both for prosecution and defence were recalled, and cross-examination established that the hiding-place had been discovered by Michu and was known only to him, his wife, Laurence and the four noblemen. One may imagine the effect produced on court and jurymen when the public prosecutor announced that this cellar, known only to the accused and two of the witnesses, had served as a prison for the senator. Marthe was brought in. Her appearance caused the liveliest emotion among both audience and the accused. Monsieur de Granville rose to object to a wife being called to testify against her husband. The public prosecutor contended that, by her own admission, Marthe was an accomplice in the crime; she could not be required to take the oath as a witness, but had to be heard merely in the interests of truth. 'Moreover,' said the chairman, 'we only have to give a reading of the statement she made to the jury director.' He ordered the clerk of the court to read out the report drawn up that morning.

'Do you confirm this statement?' the chairman asked.

Michu looked across at his wife, and Marthe, realizing the mistake she had made, fell down in a dead faint. It is no exaggeration to say that the accused in the dock and counsel for the defence were thunderstruck.

'I never wrote to my wife from prison, nor do I know any of the warders,' said Michu.

Bordin handed him the fragment of the letter, and Michu needed only to cast one glance at it. 'My handwriting has been forged,' he declared.

'Denial is your last resource,' said the public prosecutor.

The Senator was then brought in and put through the usual formalities. His entry caused a sensation. Malin, who was addressed as Comte de Gondreville without regard for the feelings of the former owners of this fine property, at the chairman's invitation scrutinized the accused with the greatest attention and for a long time. He recognized that the clothes worn by his kidnappers were very like those of the noblemen; but he declared that his senses were so confused at the moment of his abduction that he could not positively identify them as the guilty persons.

'I will go further,' he said. 'I am convinced that these four gentlemen had nothing to do with it. The hands which blindfolded me in the forest were rough ones. And so' – Malin looked across at Michu – 'I am more inclined to believe that my former bailiff undertook the task. But I beg the gentlemen of the jury to weigh my testimony very carefully. My suspicions in this respect are very slight and I have not the least certainty, for the following reason: the two men who seized hold of me put me on horseback behind the man who had blindfolded me, who had red hair like Michu. However singular one thing that I noticed may be, I must speak of it, for it is the basis of a conviction I have which is favourable to the accused, and I ask him not to take offence at it. Having been tied to the back of an unknown man, I could not help noticing how he smelt, even though the journey did not last long. Now I did not recognize Michu's particular odour. However, I am certain that the person who on three occasions brought me food was Marthe, Michu's wife. The first time she came I recognized her by a ring given her by Mademoiselle de Cinq-Cygne which she had not thought of taking off. The court and the gentlemen of the jury will take note of the discrepancies between these different facts: I myself cannot yet explain them.'

Malin's testimony was received with favourable murmurs and unanimous approbation. Bordin asked permission of the court to put a few questions to this important witness.

'Monsieur le Sénateur, do you then believe that your imprisonment was determined by other causes than the motives imputed to the accused by the indictment?'

'Certainly I do!' said the senator. 'But I don't know what the real motives were, for I declare that, during my twenty days of captivity, I saw no one.'

'Do you believe', the public prosecutor interpolated, 'that at your Gondreville château there might have been such information, deeds or documents as might have made it necessary for Messieurs de Simeuse to search it?'

'I do not think so,' said Malin. 'Even had it been so, I do not believe these gentlemen were capable of taking possession of them by violence. They only had to ask me for them, and I would have handed them over.'

'Monsieur le Sénateur,' Granville broke in abruptly, 'did you not have some papers burnt in your park?'

The senator looked at Grévin. After exchanging a sharp glance with the notary – Bordin noticed it – he replied in the negative. When the public prosecutor asked him for information about the ambush to which he had nearly fallen victim in the park and whether he had not been mistaken about the position of the rifle, the senator replied that Michu had been watching them from a tree. This reply, which tallied with Grévin's testimony, made a lively impression. The noblemen had remained impassive while their enemy was being cross-examined and was overpowering them with his generosity. Laurence was suffering the most terrible anguish, and from time to time the Marquis de Chargebœuf took her by the arm to hold her back. The Comte de Gondreville withdrew after bowing to the four noblemen: they did not return his bow. A small matter; but it incensed the jurymen.

'They're done for,' Bordin whispered to the marquis.

'Yes, alas! And, as always, through pride,' Monsieur de Chargebœuf replied.

'Gentlemen,' said the public prosecutor, rising and looking towards the jurymen. 'Our task has become only too easy.'

He explained the use of the two bags of plaster by the need to fix the iron pin to hold the padlock securing the bar which fastened the cellar door, a description of which had been given in the report made by Pigoult that morning. It was not difficult for him to prove that only the accused men knew of the existence of the vault. He exposed the false statements made by the defence and pulverized all its arguments in the light of the new evidence, which had arrived so miraculously. In 1806 people were still too near the 'Supreme Being' of 1793[1] to talk of divine justice, and so he spared the jury any allusion to the intervention of Heaven. To conclude, he said that the police would keep on the look-out for the unknown accomplices who had freed the senator; and he sat down to await the verdict with confidence.

The jurymen believed there was a mystery behind all this; but they were all persuaded that it came from the accused themselves and that they were keeping silent for the sake of some very important private interest.

Monsieur de Granville stood up. That some plot had been hatched was now clear to him; but he seemed overwhelmed, less on account of the new evidence produced than because the jurymen were manifestly convinced. His speech for the defence was perhaps even better than that of the previous day and its logic more pressing. But he felt his warmth repelled by the coldness of the jury. He could see that his eloquence was wasted: a horrible, chilling situation! He contended that the senator's liberation, carried out as it were by magic and most

1. The very aloof and remote deity invented by the Revolutionaries.

certainly not through the agency of any of the accused, nor by Marthe, corroborated his earlier arguments. Yesterday, he said, the accused had been practically certain of acquittal; and if, as the prosecution supposed, it lay in their power to keep the senator captive or have him released, they would not have freed him until after judgement was pronounced. He tried to convey to the jury that only enemies lurking in the background could have dealt them this blow.

Strange to say, Monsieur de Granville aroused qualms of conscience only in the public prosecutor and the judges, for the jurymen were only listening out of a sense of duty. The public itself, usually so sympathetic to accused persons, was convinced of their guilt. Feelings create an atmosphere. In a court of justice the feelings of the crowd bear heavily on judge and jury, and conversely. Sensing this attitude of mind, one which can be recognized or felt, counsel for the defence, in his peroration, rose to a kind of feverish exaltation born of his conviction.

'In the name of the accused, I pardon you in advance for a fatal error that nothing will dissipate!' he cried. 'We all are the playthings of some unknown and Machiavellian power. Marthe Michu is the victim of an odious deception, and the community will only realize it when irreparable harm has been done.'

Bordin based his demand for acquittal on the senator's testimony.

The chairman summed up with so much the more impartiality because, visibly, the jurymen had made up their minds. He even dipped the scales in favour of the accused by dwelling on the senator's testimony, but this gracious act did not compromise the success of the indictment. That night, at eleven o'clock, after the foreman of the jury had given his verdict on the various charges, the court condemned Michu to the penalty of death, the Simeuse brothers to twenty-four years and the two d'Hauteserres to ten years of penal servitude. Gothard was acquitted. The whole court-room was agog to see what face the five men would put on it at the supreme moment when, brought in unshackled before the court, they heard their condemnation. The four noblemen looked across at Laurence. She looked back at them with dry eyes, but they had the flame of martyrdom in them.

'She would be weeping if we had been acquitted,' said the younger Simeuse to his brother.

Never did accused persons confront an iniquitous condemnation with greater serenity or more dignity of bearing than these five victims of a nefarious plot.

'You have received our forgiveness through our counsel!' said the elder Simeuse, addressing the court.

Madame d'Hauteserre fell ill and stayed in bed for three months in Monsieur de Chargebœuf's house. Her husband returned peacefully to Cinq-Cygne but, consumed with an old man's grief unrelieved by any of the distractions of youth, he often had fits of absent-mindedness which made it clear to the curé that this unhappy father's life had been suspended on the morrow of the fatal sentence. Marthe was not brought to trial, for she died in prison, three weeks after her husband's condemnation, commending her son to Laurence, in whose arms she expired. Once the judgement became known, political events of the greatest importance blotted out the memory of the trial, and it ceased to be talked about. Human society is like the ocean: it resumes its normal level and rhythm after a cataclysm, and obliterates all traces of it by the ebb and flow of its voracious interests.

Without her steadfastness and the certainty of her cousins' innocence Laurence would have succumbed, but she gave fresh proofs of her strength of character and astonished Monsieur de Granville and Bordin by the apparent serenity with which noble minds respond to great calamities. She nursed and tended Madame d'Hauteserre and spent two hours in the prison every day. She vowed that she would marry one of her cousins even if they were in the galleys.

'The galleys!' said Bordin. 'But, Mademoiselle, let's think only of asking the Emperor for a pardon.'

'Pardon! ... And from Bonaparte!' Laurence exclaimed with horror.

The worthy old attorney's spectacles sprang from his nose; he grasped them before they fell, and gazed at the girl who now had so much of the woman in her. Every aspect of her character became clear to him. He took the Marquis de Chargebœuf by the arm and said: 'Monsieur le Marquis, let us hurry off to Paris to save them without her help.'

*

The appeal lodged by the Simeuses, the d'Hauteserres and Michu was the first case which came before the Supreme Court of Appeal, and so its decision was fortunately delayed by the ceremonies attending its inauguration. Towards the end of September, after three hearings taken up with counsels' speeches and a summing-up by the Attorney-General, Merlin, the appeal was dismissed. The Imperial Court of Paris was now in being, Monsieur de Granville had been appointed Assistant Attorney-General on it, and as the Aube department was within the jurisdiction of this court, he was able to pull some strings inside the Ministry of Justice in favour of the condemned men; he importuned his patron Cambacérès. The morning after the judgement, Bordin and Monsieur de Chargebœuf went to his house in the Marais quarter and found that he was away on honeymoon, for in the meantime he had got married. Despite all the changes which had come about in the life of the former barrister, Monsieur de Chargebœuf clearly saw, by the affliction he showed, that the young deputy attorney-general was still loyal to his clients. Certain barristers, artists in their profession, treat their cases as they would their mistresses. This is rare, so do not count on it. As soon as his former clients were alone with him in his office, Monsieur de Granville said to the marquis: 'I didn't wait for you to come to me. I have used up all my credit already. Don't try to save Michu or you won't get the Simeuses reprieved. They must have at least one victim.'

'Good heavens!' said Bordin, showing the young magistrate the three petitions for reprieve. 'Can I take it upon myself to suppress the petition of your former client? To burn this paper would amount to cutting his head off.'

He presented him with Michu's signed petition. Granville took it and scanned it.

'We cannot suppress it. But realize this: if you ask for everything you'll get nothing.'

'Have we time to consult Michu?' asked Bordin.

'Yes. The order for execution is a matter for the Attorney-General's department, and we can give you a few days. We put people to death,' he added with a tone of bitterness, 'but we are sticklers for form, especially in Paris.' Monsieur de Chargebœuf had already obtained particulars from the Chief Justice's department which lent tremendous weight to Monsieur de Granville's dispirited comment.

'Michu is innocent. I know it. I repeat it,' the magistrate continued. 'But what can one man do against the rest of the world? And consider that today I have only a silent part to play. I have to erect the scaffold on which my former client is to be decapitated.'

Monsieur de Chargebœuf knew Laurence well enough to be sure that she would never consent to save her cousins at Michu's expense. So he tried a last expedient. He had asked for an audience with the Minister for Foreign Affairs, to see if a way of escape could be found in high diplomatic circles. He took Bordin with him, for the latter knew the Minister and had done him some services. The two old men found Talleyrand absorbed in the contemplation of his fire, his legs stretched out, his head resting on his hand, his elbow on the table, and a newspaper on the floor. The Minister had just been reading the decision of the Court of Appeal.

'Please sit down, Monsieur le Marquis,' he said. 'You too, Bordin,' he added, motioning him to a seat opposite him at the table, 'and write as follows:

'Sire,

'Four innocent nobles, found guilty by a jury, have just learnt that their sentence is confirmed by your Court of Appeal.

'There is now no other resort for them than that your Imperial Majesty should pardon them. They only ask this of your august clemency in order to have the opportunity of meeting a useful death by fighting under your command, and respectfully sign themselves the obedient servants of your Imperial and Royal Majesty . . .'

'Only a prince like you could be so obliging,' said the Marquis de Chargebœuf, taking from Bordin's hands the precious draft of the petition to be signed by the four noblemen, in support of which he was counting on marginal signatures from august persons.

'Your kinsmen's lives, Monsieur le Marquis,' said Prince Talleyrand, 'depend on the chances of war. Try to reach the Emperor the day after a victory and they will be saved.' He took a pen, himself wrote a confidential letter to the Emperor, one of about ten lines to Marshal Duroc, then rang a bell, asked his secretary for a diplomatic passport, and quietly asked the old attorney: 'What is your serious opinion about this trial?'

'Do you not know then, Your Excellency, who it is that has caught us in such a snare?'

'I have some idea, but I have reasons for wishing to make sure,' the prince replied. 'Return to Troyes, bring the Comtesse de Cinq-Cygne to me, here, tomorrow, at this time, but secretly; come through Madame de Talleyrand's apartments – I will forewarn her of your visit. If Mademoiselle de Cinq-Cygne, whom I shall post in a position to see the man who will be standing in front of me, recognizes him for the one who came to her château at the time of the Polignac and Rivière conspiracy, let her make no gesture and utter no word, whatever I say, and whatever be his reply. Also, think only of saving Messieurs de Simeuse: don't put yourself to the trouble of trying to save that rogue of a gamekeeper.'

'A splendid man, Your Excellency!' Bordin exclaimed.

'What enthusiasm! And coming from you, Bordin! The man must be worth his salt.' Then he added, changing his tone: 'Our sovereign is prodigiously touchy, Monsieur le Marquis. He's about to dismiss me so that he can commit follies without anyone to gainsay him. He's a great soldier capable of altering the laws of time and space; but he can't change men, even though he would like to remould them for his own use. And now, don't forget that there is only one person who can obtain pardon for your kinsmen: Mademoiselle de Cinq-Cygne.'

The marquis set off alone for Troyes and told Laurence how things stood. Laurence obtained permission from the Imperial Attorney-General to see Michu; the marquis went with her to the prison gates and waited for her. She came out weeping copiously.

'The poor man', she said, 'tried to get down on his knees to implore me not to worry about him, without remembering that his feet were shackled! Yes, marquis, I shall plead his cause. Yes, I will go and lick the Emperor's boots. And if I fail, well, I will see to it that this man lives for ever in the memory of our family. Put in his petition for reprieve to gain time. I want to have his portrait painted. Let us go.'

The next day, when the Minister for Foreign Affairs learnt by an agreed signal that Laurence was at her post, he rang, his usher came and received the order to admit Monsieur Corentin.

'My friend,' said Talleyrand, 'you're a clever fellow, and I have a use for you.'

'Excellency . . .'

'Listen. Serving Fouché, you'll make money, but you'll never rise to honour or a respectable position. But if you continue to serve me as you have just done at Berlin, you'll gain consideration . . .'

'Your Excellency is most kind.'

'You showed genius in your latest bit of business at Gondreville.'

'To what does Your Excellency refer?' asked Corentin, without showing either too much coldness or too much surprise.

'Monsieur,' the Minister dryly answered, 'you'll get nowhere. You're too afraid of . . .'

'Of what, Your Excellency?'

'Of death!' said the Minister in his fine, deep but hollow voice. 'Farewell, my friend.'

'That's the man,' said the Marquis de Chargebœuf as he came in. 'But we've nearly killed the countess. She's suffocating!'

'He's the only man capable of playing such tricks,' the Minister replied. 'Monsieur,' he went on, 'there's some risk of your not succeeding. Pretend to be taking the road to Strasbourg. I will send you duplicate passports in blank. Choose yourselves doubles, make skilful changes of route and particularly of vehicle, let your doubles get halted at Strasbourg instead of yourselves, make for Prussia via Switzerland and Bavaria. Say nothing and be careful. You have the police against you, and you've no idea what that means!'

Mademoiselle de Cinq-Cygne offered Robert Lefebvre, already at that time a famous painter, a large sum to persuade him to come to Troyes to do Michu's portrait, and Monsieur de Granville promised him every facility. Monsieur de Chargebœuf departed in his old *berlingot* with Laurence and a manservant who spoke German. But, before reaching Nancy, he joined up with Gothard and Mademoiselle Goujet, who had gone ahead of him in an excellent barouche, and they exchanged carriages. The Minister had been right. At Strasbourg the General Commissary of Police refused to visa their passports, having received peremptory orders not to do so. Even while this was happening Laurence and the marquis were leaving France via Besançon with their diplomatic passports. Laurence crossed through Switzerland in the early days of October without vouchsafing the slightest attention to its magnificent landscapes. She sat in the back of the barouche in the benumbed state of a criminal awaiting the moment of execution. In such a state one only sees nature through swirling mists, and even the most commonplace objects assume fantastic guise. The thought 'If I don't succeed they'll take their own lives' was hammering at her mind in the same way as the executioner's bar in former times beat down on the limbs of a man being broken on the wheel. She was feeling more and more depressed and her energy was oozing away as she awaited the cruel, decisive and brief moment when she would find herself face to face with the man who held the fate of the four noblemen in his hands. She had made up her mind not to fight against her dejection in order not to make a useless expense of energy. Incapable of understanding this husbanding of spiritual strength in its various outer manifestations – for during such crucial waiting periods certain superior minds can even abandon themselves to surprising gaiety – the marquis feared that he might not be able to bring Laurence alive to this encounter: one of grave import for them alone, but one which assuredly went far beyond the ordinary scope of private life. Laurence felt that to humble herself before the man she hated and scorned involved the death of all her noble sentiments.

'When that's over,' she said, 'the Laurence who survives will bear no resemblance to the Laurence about to perish.'

Nevertheless it was very difficult for the two travellers not to take notice of the activity of men and things around them once they arrived in Prussia. The Jena campaign had begun. Laurence and the marquis saw the magnificent divisions of the French army spreading out and parading as if they were at the Tuileries. Amid this deployment of military splendour, which only biblical language and metaphor could describe, the man whose spirit was animating these masses assumed gigantic proportions in Laurence's imagination. Soon victorious cries resounded in her ears. The Imperial armies had just scored two signal advantages. The Prussian Crown Prince had been killed the day before the two travellers arrived at Saalfeld in their effort to catch up with Napoleon, who was moving at lightning speed. At last, on 13 October, a date of ill omen, Mademoiselle de Cinq-Cygne was moving along a river bank in the midst of battalions of the Grande-Armée, seeing nothing but confusion, being shuffled backwards and forwards from village to village, from division to division, terrified at travelling alone with an old man, and tossed about on an ocean of a hundred and fifty thousand men who were aiming their rifles at a hundred and fifty thousand others. Tired of seeing nothing but this river above the hedges of a muddy road that she was following over a hill, she asked a soldier what it was called.

'It's the Saale,' he said, pointing to the Prussian army grouped in great masses on the other side of the stream.

Night was coming on. Laurence saw fires flare up and weapons gleaming. The old marquis, with the intrepidity of a knight-at-arms, was himself driving the carriage, drawn by two good horses bought the day before, while his manservant sat beside him. The old man knew that he would find neither postilion nor horses once he arrived on the battlefield. Suddenly this adventurous barouche, which aroused astonishment in all the soldiers, was halted by a gendarme of military police who swooped down on the marquis shouting: 'Who are you? Where are you going? What are you after?'

'The Emperor,' said the Marquis de Chargebœuf. 'I have an important ministerial dispatch for Grand-Marshal Duroc.'

'Well, you can't stay here,' said the gendarme. None the less,

Mademoiselle de Cinq-Cygne and the marquis had no choice but to remain where they were because night was near.

'Where are we?' she asked, stopping two officers whom she saw coming, their uniform hidden under cloth great-coats.

'You are in front of the vanguard of the French army, Madame,' one of the officers replied. 'You cannot even remain here, for if the enemy made a movement and an artillery action began you would be taken between two fires.'

'Indeed!' she said with an indifferent air.

At this exclamation the other officer said: 'How does this woman happen to be here?'

'We are waiting', she answered, 'for a gendarme who has gone to get in touch with Monsieur Duroc, on whose support we are relying in order to speak to the Emperor.'

'Speak to the Emperor?' said the first of the officers. 'Can you think of such a thing on the evening before a decisive battle?'

'Ah! You are right,' she cried. 'I must only talk to him the day after tomorrow. Victory will soften his heart.'

The two officers took up their position twenty paces away and brought their horses to a halt. Thereupon the barouche was surrounded by a squadron of generals, marshals and staff officers, all of them in very brilliant array. They respected the carriage for the precise reason that it had got so far.

'God save us!' said the marquis to Mademoiselle de Cinq-Cygne. 'I fear we have been talking to the Emperor.'

'The Emperor?' said a colonel-general. 'But there he is!'

And then Laurence perceived, a few paces away, alone in the foreground, the officer who had exclaimed: 'How does this woman happen to be here?' One of the two officers, the Emperor in fact, wearing his famous great-coat over a green uniform, was astride a richly caparisoned horse. He was looking through field-glasses at the Prussian army on the other bank of the Saale. Laurence then understood why the barouche had not been moved on and why the Emperor's escort had not interfered with it. A convulsive terror ran through her: the time had come! Then she heard in the background the noise of masses of armed men rapidly taking up their positions on the plateau. The batteries seemed to have their own special language, thunder came from the gun-carriages and the cannons were spitting out fire.

'Marshal Lannes with his entire corps will take up his position in front, Marshal Lefebvre and the Guards will occupy the summit,' said the other officer, who was Major-General Berthier.

The Emperor dismounted. Roustan, his famous mameluke, rushed forward to hold his horse. Laurence was dizzy with astonishment: all this seemed so incredibly simple.

'I shall spend the night on this plateau,' said the Emperor.

Just then Grand-Marshal Duroc, whom the gendarme had at last found, came to the Marquis de Chargebœuf and asked why he had come there. The marquis replied that a letter from the Minister of Foreign Affairs would explain how urgent it was for Mademoiselle de Cinq-Cygne and himself to have audience with the Emperor.

'His Majesty will no doubt dine in his bivouac,' Duroc said as he took the letter, 'and once I have seen what all this is about I will tell you if the interview is possible. – Corporal,' he said to the gendarme, 'accompany this carriage and bring it up to the hut behind the line.'

Monsieur de Chargebœuf followed the gendarme and halted his carriage behind a miserable cottage built of wood and clay, surrounded by a few fruit trees and guarded by pickets of infantry and cavalry.

There assuredly the majesty of war shone forth in all its splendour. From the top of this hill the lines of both armies could be seen in the moonlight. After an hour's wait, disturbed by the constant coming and going of aides-de-camp, Duroc came for Mademoiselle de Cinq-Cygne and the Marquis de Chargebœuf and took them into the cottage, whose floor was of beaten earth like that of our threshing-floors. In front of a table from which food had been cleared and a smoky fire of green wood, Napoleon was sitting on a roughly-fashioned chair. His mud-spattered boots bore witness to his cross-country rides. He had removed his celebrated great coat, and his famous green uniform with the sash of the *cordon rouge* across it, brought into relief by the lower part of his white kerseymere breeches and waistcoat, admirably showed off his pale, stern face, that of a Caesar. He had his hand on an unfolded map on his knees. Berthier was standing erect in the dazzling uniform of the Imperial Vice-Constable. Constant, his valet, was offering the Emperor his coffee on a tray.

'What do you want?' he asked with feigned bluntness, looking right through Laurence with his eagle glance. 'So you're no longer afraid of talking to me before the battle? What is the matter in hand?'

'Sire,' she said, fixing her no less steady look on him, 'I am Mademoiselle de Cinq-Cygne.'

'And so?' he replied testily, thinking that he saw defiance in her look.

'Do you not understand? I am the Countess of Cinq-Cygne, and I am asking you for a pardon,' she said, falling to her knees and holding out the petition drawn up by Talleyrand, with the signatures of the Empress, Cambacérès and Malin added.

The Emperor graciously lifted the supplicant to her feet, giving her a sharp glance and saying: 'Will you be sensible henceforward? Do you realize what the French Empire is to be? . . .'

'Ah! At this moment I realize what the Emperor is,' she said, vanquished by the kindly tone with which the Man of Destiny had uttered these words, which made her feel that the pardon would be forthcoming.

'Are they innocent?' asked the Emperor.

'All of them,' she enthusiastically replied.

'All of them? No, the gamekeeper is a dangerous man. He would kill my senator without consulting you . . .'

'Oh Sire!' she said. 'If you had a friend who had sacrificed himself for you, would you leave him in the lurch? Would you not . . .'

'You are a woman,' he said with a tinge of mockery.

'And you a man of iron!' she retorted with a passionate harshness which pleased him.

'This man has been found guilty in a court of law.'

'But he is innocent.'

'Child that you are!' he said. He took Mademoiselle de Cinq-Cygne by the hand and led her out on to the plateau.

'See there!' he said with that eloquence peculiar to him which turned cowards into heroes. 'Here are three hundred thousand men, and they too are innocent! Well, tomorrow thirty thousand of them will be dead, will have died for their country! Among the Prussians is perhaps some outstanding mathematician, a man of vision, a genius who will be cut down. We on our side shall certainly lose some unknown great men. In fact, I may see my best friend struck down! Shall I accuse God? No, I shall keep silent. Learn, Mademoiselle,' he added as he took her back to the hut, 'that one must be ready to die for the laws of one's own country as men here will die for its glory.'

'Go. Return to France,' he said with a glance at the marquis. 'My orders will follow you.'

Laurence believed that Michu's penalty was going to be commuted, and in an outburst of gratitude she curtsied and kissed the Emperor's hand.

'You are Monsieur de Chargebœuf,' he then said, turning to the marquis.

'Yes, Sire.'

'Have you any children?'

'Many children.'

'Why should you not give me one of your grandchildren? I would make him one of my pages.'

'Ah! There's the sub-lieutenant coming out!' thought Laurence. 'He wants payment for the reprieve.'

The marquis bowed without replying. Then, opportunely, General Rapp burst into the hut.

'Sire, the cavalry of the Guard and that of the Grand-Duke of Berg will not be able to rejoin us before midday tomorrow.'

'No matter,' said Napoleon, turning towards Berthier. 'We too have our hours of reprieve. Let's take advantage of them.'

At a wave of his hand, the marquis and Laurence withdrew and stepped into their carriage. The corporal set them on their route and escorted them to a village where they spent the night. The next day, the two of them left the battle area amid the roar of eight hundred cannons, which went on booming for ten hours, and on their way home they learnt of the astounding victory of Jena. Eight days later they entered the suburbs of Troyes. An order from the Chief Justice, transmitted to the Imperial attorney at the Troyes court of first instance, enjoined that the four noblemen should be released on bail pending the Emperor's decision; but at the same time the public prosecutor's department issued the order for Michu's execution. These two orders arrived that very morning. Laurence then went to the jail at two o'clock in her travelling clothes. She obtained leave to remain with Michu, who was going through the dismal ceremony called 'the condemned man's toilet'. The good Abbé Goujet, who had asked leave to accompany him to the scaffold, had just given absolution to Michu, who was lamenting having to die while still uncertain of his masters' fate. Consequently, when Laurence appeared, he gave a cry of joy.

'I can die now,' he said.

'They are pardoned, on what conditions I don't know,' she answered. 'But they certainly are pardoned, and I did my very best for you, my friend, although advised not to. I thought I had saved you, but the Emperor deceived me by the graciousness he showed as a sovereign.'

'Heaven had decreed', said Michu, 'that the watch-dog should be executed in the same spot as his old master.'

The last hour passed by quickly. As he left for the scaffold, Michu did not venture to ask any other favour than to kiss Mademoiselle de Cinq-Cygne's hand; but she tendered him her cheeks and let herself be chastely embraced by the noble victim. He refused to get on the tumbril.

'Innocent people should go on foot!' he said.

He would not allow the Abbé Goujet to take his arm, but marched up to the scaffold with dignity and resolution. When the moment came to lie down on the plank, he said to the headsman, as he asked him to turn down his coat collar which came up to his neck, 'My coat belongs to you. Try and not cut it.'

The four noblemen scarcely had time to see Mademoiselle de Cinq-Cygne again. An orderly of the general commanding the military division brought them commissions as sub-lieutentants in the same cavalry regiment, with orders to go immediately to the corps headquarters at Bayonne. After heart-rending farewells, for they all had presentiments of the future, Mademoiselle de Cinq-Cygne returned to her deserted château.

The twins died together under the Emperor's eyes, at Sommo-Sierra, each defending the other, both of them now being squadron-leaders. Their last words were: 'Laurence, *cy meurs*!'

The elder d'Hauteserre died a colonel in the attack on the redoubt of Moscow, and his brother took his place.

Adrien, promoted brigadier-general at the battle of Dresden, was gravely wounded in it and was allowed to return to be nursed at Cinq-Cygne. In an attempt to save the only survivor of the four noblemen she had had around her for a brief space, the countess, by then thirty-two, married him; but she could only offer him a broken heart. He accepted: men in love either have no doubts at all or doubts about everything.

Laurence welcomed the Restoration without enthusiasm. Nevertheless she had no cause for complaint. Her husband was made a peer of France with the title of Marquis de Cinq-Cygne, became a lieutenant-general in 1816 and obtained the blue ribbon as a reward for the services he had rendered.

Michu's son, whom Laurence cared for as if he were her own child, became an advocate in 1817. After two years as counsel, he was appointed assistant justice at the court of Alençon and then became public attorney at the Arcis tribunal in 1827. Laurence had seen to the investment of Michu's capital, and when the young man attained his majority she handed him securities yielding twelve thousand francs per annum. She later got him married to a rich heiress, Mademoiselle Girel of Troyes. The Marquis de Cinq-Cygne died in 1829, with Laurence, his father, his mother and his loving children around him. At the time of his death, no one had yet penetrated the secret of the senator's abduction. Louis XVIII did not refuse to repair the wrong done in this affair, but he did not disclose the cause of the catastrophe to the Marquise de Cinq-Cygne, who consequently believed that he had had a part in it.

Conclusion

THE late Marquis de Cinq-Cygne had applied his savings and those of his parents to the acquisition of a splendid town-house in the rue du Faubourg du Roule, included in the considerable estate in tail which he instituted for the maintenance of his peerage. The sordid economy practised by the marquis, his father and mother, which often distressed Laurence, was thus explained. And so, after this purchase was made, the marquise, who lived on her estate, saving up for her children, the more willingly spent her winters in Paris because her daughter Berthe and her son Paul were reaching an age when their education required the resources which Paris could offer. Madame de Cinq-Cygne did not go much into society. Her husband could not be ignorant of the womanly regrets which dwelt in her heart, but he treated her with the most delicate thoughtfulness and died without having loved any other woman. His nobility of heart had for some time remained unappreciated, but in more recent years the generous daughter of the Cinq-Cygnes had fully returned his love, and in the long run he was completely happy. Laurence lived above all for family joys. No woman in Paris has been more cherished by her friends, or more respected.

To visit her house is an honour. Kind, indulgent, intelligent, but above all uncomplicated, she is much liked by people of discernment, who find her attractive despite the impress of grief revealed in her attitude. Everyone seems to feel protective towards this woman so strong in character, and this secret feeling of protectiveness perhaps explains why people are drawn to her as a friend. She had much sorrow in her youth, but the evening of her life is beautiful and serene. Her sufferings are known, and no one has ever needed to ask who was the original of the portrait by Robert Lefebvre which, since Michu's death, has been the principal ornament in her salon, even though it recalls sad memories. Her face has the maturity of fruits that have been slow to ripen; the tribulation written on her forehead has given place to a kind of religious pride.

At the moment when the marquise began to keep house in Paris, her income, increased by the act of indemnity,[1] then amounted to two hundred thousand francs a year from her State bonds, without counting her husband's emoluments. She had inherited the eleven hundred thousand francs left her by the Simeuses. From then on she spent a hundred thousand francs a year and put the rest aside in order to provide a dowry for Berthe. Berthe is the living picture of her mother, without her mother's militant spirit; she is a refined, wittier replica of her mother – 'and more feminine,' as Laurence remarks with a touch of melancholy. She had been unwilling to marry her daughter before she reached her twenties. The family savings, wisely administered by the aged d'Hauteserre, invested in Government stock, constituted a dowry of eighty thousand francs per annum for Berthe, who, in 1833, was twenty.

Round about this time the Princesse de Cadignan, desirous of marrying her son the Duc de Maufrigneuse, had brought him some months before into touch with the Marquise de Cinq-Cygne. Georges de Maufrigneuse was dining at her house three times a week, accompanied mother and daughter to the Théâtre des Italiens, and curvetted round their carriage when they went riding in the Bois de Boulogne. It then became evident to Faubourg Saint-Germain society that Georges was in love with Berthe. But no one could quite decide whether Madame de Cinq-Cygne was wanting to make her daughter a duchess and wait for her to become a princess, or whether it was the Princesse de Cadignan who wanted to capture so fine a dowry for her son; whether the celebrated Diane de Cadignan was paying court to the provincial aristocracy, or whether the provincial aristocracy was fighting shy of Madame de Cadignan's reputation, tastes and extravagant expenditure. Desiring not to prejudice her son's interests, the Princess, taking to piety, had put a screen round her private life and used to spend the summer months in her Geneva villa.

One evening, Madame la Princesse de Cadignan was entertaining the Marquise d'Espard and Monsieur de Marsay, the

1. Passed in 1824: an attempt made by the government of Charles X to compensate the nobility for their confiscated lands.

President of the Council. This was the last time she was to set eyes on this former lover of hers, for he was to die the next year. Rastignac, Under-Secretary of State in de Marsay's ministry, two ambassadors, two celebrated orators who were still in the Upper House, the aged Duc de Lenoncourt and the Duc de Navarreins, the Comte de Vandenesse and his young wife, and d'Arthez the poet, were all present and formed a somewhat heterogeneous assembly whose composition can easily be explained: it was a question of obtaining an official permit for the Prince de Cadignan to return to France. De Marsay, as Prime Minister, was reluctant to grant this on his own responsibility and had come to tell the Princess that the matter was in competent hands: an old man well versed in political manoeuvres was to provide a solution in the course of the evening.

The Marquise and Mademoiselle de Cinq-Cygne were announced. Laurence, a woman of uncompromising principles, was less surprised than shocked to see the most illustrious representatives of the legitimate monarchy, belonging to both the Upper and the Lower House, chatting with the Prime Minister of Louis-Philippe (whom she never called by any other title than His Grace the Duke of Orleans), listening to him and laughing with him. De Marsay, like a lamp flickering out, was casting forth his last brilliant gleams. In this salon he was happy to forget his ministerial worries. The Marquise de Cinq-Cygne tolerated de Marsay in much the same way as the Austrian Court, it is said, tolerated Napoleon's emissary the Comte de Sainte-Aulaire: the man of the world allowed the Minister to get by. But she started up as if her chair had been of red-hot iron when she heard Monsieur le Comte de Gondreville announced.

'Adieu, Madame,' she said in curt tones to the Princess. The Princess said in a low voice to de Marsay: 'You have probably wrecked Georges's marriage.'

The man who had been a solicitor's clerk at Arcis, member of the Legislative Assembly, a Thermidorian, a Tribune, a Councillor of State, a Count and Senator of the Empire, a peer under Louis XVIII, a peer of France once again under the July Monarchy, gave an obsequious bow to the Princesse de Cadignan.

'Have no fear about the permit, fair lady. We don't make war on princes,' he said, sitting down next to her.

Malin had enjoyed the esteem of Louis XVIII, who drew some profit from his long experience. He had been of much help in overthrowing the Decazes ministry and had strongly supported Villèle. Coldly received by Charles X, he had shared Talleyrand's rancour against him. He was now in great favour with the twelfth government he has had the privilege of serving – or disserving – since 1793 and will probably disserve this one too. But fifteen months earlier he had severed his thirty-six-year-old friendship with our most famous diplomat – Talleyrand. It was on this same evening that he uttered the following sarcasm against the great diplomat: 'Do you know why he is so hostile to the Duc de Bordeaux? . . . The Pretender is too young.'

'That's a singular warning to give to young people!' Rastignac retorted.

De Marsay, who had been lost in thought since the remark made by the Princess, took no notice of these pleasantries. He was slyly watching Gondreville and evidently was waiting for the old man, who always retired early, to leave before he himself began to talk. All the other people present, who had witnessed Madame de Cinq-Cygne's departure, likewise kept silent. Gondreville had not recognized the marquise and was ignorant of the motives for this general reserve; but his knowledge of affairs and political etiquette had given him tact. For that matter he was a man of perception: he could see that his presence was found embarrassing and he left. As the old man of seventy slowly walked out, de Marsay stood by the mantelpiece and studied him with an air suggestive of deep reflection.

'I was wrong, Madame, not to have told you the name of my go-between,' the Prime Minister at last said as he heard Gondreville's carriage rolling away. 'But I will atone for my shortcomings and show you how to make your peace with the Cinq-Cygnes. It's more than thirty years ago since the episode I am going to relate occurred. It's as stale news as the death of Henri IV; but between ourselves it's certainly, despite the proverb, a scrap of history that people know least about, like many other historical catastrophes. I assure you, moreover, that it would be no less interesting even if it did not concern the marquise. In short, it throws light on an event famous in the annals of our time, Napoleon's crossing of the Mont Saint-Bernard. Their Excellencies the Ambassadors will see that, in the matter of deep scheming, our politicians of today fall far short of the Machiavellis whom the popular ebullience of 1793 threw up above the Revolutionary tempests, and some of whom, to quote the ballad, have "come safe into port." In order to be somebody in the France of today, one must have been tossed about in the storms of that period.'

'But it seems to me', said the Princess with a smile, 'that in this respect your own position leaves nothing to be desired.'

A smile hovered over the lips of this well-bred company, and de Marsay could not help joining in. The ambassadors were all agog to hear de Marsay's story; he was seized with a fit of coughing, and silence fell.

'One June night in 1800,' said the Prime Minister, 'at about three in the morning, just as the candles were paling in the light of dawn, two men who were tired of playing *bouillotte*, or were only playing it to keep other people occupied, left the salon in the Ministry for Foreign Affairs and went into a boudoir. These two men – one is dead, the other has at least one foot in the grave[2] – were both of them exceptional, each in his own way. Both had been priests and both had abjured their faith; both of them were married. One had been a mere Oratorian, the other had worn the episcopal mitre. The first was named Fouché; I needn't tell you the name of the second, but they were then both of them simple French citizens – only not so simple as all that. When they were seen to enter the boudoir, the people left in the salon manifested a little curiosity. They were followed by a third person. This man, whose name was Sieyès, thought himself more able than the two others; you all know that he too had been in the Church before the Revolution. The man who walked with a limp was then Minister for Foreign Affairs, Fouché was Minister of General Police, Sieyès had resigned from the Consulate. A

2. This is a sarcastic reference to Talleyrand's lameness, which dated from childhood.

small, cold, dour-faced man left his seat and joined the other three, saying out loud in front of someone who quoted his phrase to me: "I'm afraid of priests with aces up their sleeves." He was Minister for War – Carnot. His remark did not disturb the two Consuls who were still playing cards in the salon. These two, Cambacérès and Lebrun, were then at the mercy of their Ministers, who were infinitely more capable than they were. Almost all of these men are dead, and we owe them no deference. They belong to history, and the history of that night is a terrible one. I'm telling it you, because I'm the only one who knows it, because Louis XVIII didn't tell it to poor Madame de Cinq-Cygne, and because the present government doesn't care whether she knows it or not. The four men sat down. The lame one insisted on locking the door before one word was spoken; he even bolted it – so they say. Only well-bred persons take these little precautions. The three priests had the same sallow and impassive faces as when you knew them. Only Carnot had any colour. And he, the soldier, was the first to speak: "What are you conferring about?"

' "About France," Prince Talleyrand must have said – I admire him as one of the most extraordinary men of our time.

' "About the Republic," Fouché certainly said. "About power," Sieyès probably said.'

They all looked at one another. By voice, look and gesture de Marsay had admirably depicted the three men.

'The three priests understood one another perfectly,' de Marsay resumed. 'Carnot no doubt looked at his colleagues and the ex-Consul with a fairly dignified air. I think that under the surface he felt a bit dumbfounded. "Do you believe Bonaparte will succeed?" Sieyès asked him. "You can expect anything of Bonaparte," the Minister for War replied. "He has succeeded in crossing the Alps." "At present," said Talleyrand with calculated deliberation, "he's staking his all." "Come now, let's have it out," said Fouché. "What shall we do if the First Consul is defeated? Is it possible to create a new army? Shall we remain his humble servants?" "The Republic is a thing of the past," observed Sieyès. "He's Consul for ten years." "He has greater power than Cromwell had," the bishop added, "and he didn't vote for the King's death."

"He's our master," said Fouché. "If he loses the battle, shall we keep him or return to pure republican government?" "France", Carnot rejoindered sententiously, "can only resist him by showing the same vigour as the National Convention." "I agree with Carnot," said Sieyès. "If Bonaparte comes back defeated we must finish him off; he has shown his hand too clearly during the last seven months!" "He has the Army on his side," said Carnot with a thoughtful air. "We shall have the people!" cried Fouché. "You're quick on the mark," said Talleyrand in the deep bass voice he still preserves; and this made the Oratorian retire into himself.

'At this juncture a former member of the Convention showed his face. "Let's be frank," he said. "If Bonaparte is victorious we shall worship him. If he's beaten we shall bury him!"

' "So you were here all the time, Malin," the master of the house continued without a tremor. "You will be one of us." And he motioned him to sit down.

'It was through this circumstance that the man in question, a back-bencher in the Convention, became what we see he still is at this moment. Malin was discreet, and the two Ministers were loyal to him; but the whole conspiracy and its organization hinged on him.

'"This man Bonaparte has not yet known defeat!" cried Carnot in a tone of conviction, "and he has just gone one better than Hannibal."

'"If he comes to grief, the new Directory is here already," Sieyès slyly insinuated, indicating that there were five of them. "And," said the Foreign Minister, "we are all interested in the continuance of the French Revolution, since we have all three unfrocked ourselves; and General Carnot is a regicide. And you," he said to Malin, "you are in possession of an emigrant's estate." "All our interests are identical," Sieyès categorically stated, "and our interests coincide with the interests of the country." "A rare thing!" said the diplomat with a smile. "We must get going," said Fouché. "The battle is being fought. The Austrians outnumber our forces. Genoa has surrendered, and Masséna made the mistake of sailing to Antibes, so that he's not certain or being able to join up with Bonaparte, who will thus be reduced to his own resources." "Who told you this?" asked Carnot. "It's reliable," Fouché replied. "You'll get the news when the Stock Exchange opens." '

De Marsay smiled and paused a moment. 'These men were not mincing matters,' he said. ' "We can't wait for the news of disaster to come," Fouché went on, "before we organize clubs, stir up patriotic feeling and alter the constitution. We must have our 18 Brumaire ready." "Let us leave that to the Minister of Police," said the diplomat, "and distrust Lucien." (Lucien Bonaparte was then Home Secretary.) "I will spike his guns," said Fouché. "Gentlemen," cried Sieyès, "our new Directory will no longer be subject to anarchical changes. We will organize an oligarchy, a Senate with life members and an elected chamber which we can control; for we must profit by past mistakes." "With this mode of government," said the bishop, "I shall make a peace treaty." "Find me a dependable man to get in touch with Moreau, for our army in Germany will be all we can rely on!" cried Carnot, who had remained plunged in profound meditation.

'As a matter of fact,' de Marsay continued after a pause, 'these men were right, gentlemen! In this crisis they rose to the occasion. I would have done the same.'

De Marsay continued his story. ' "Gentlemen," Sieyès exclaimed in grave and solemn tones. The meaning of this exclamation was perfectly understood: every face expressed the same fidelity and the same promise, that of absolute silence and unswerving loyalty to each other in case Bonaparte returned in triumph. "We all know what we have to do," Fouché added.

'Sieyès had just quietly drawn back the bolt, his keen priestly ear having done him good service. Lucien entered: "Good news, gentlemen! A messenger has brought Madame Bonaparte a note from the First Consul: he has started his campaign with a victory at Montebello." The three ministers looked at one another. "A battle on a general scale?" cried Carnot. "No, an engagement in which Lannes has covered himself with glory. It was a bloody business. Having been attacked by an army of eighteen thousand against ten thousand men, he was saved by a division sent as reinforcement. Ott is on the run. In short the Austrian line of communication is cut." "When was the battle fought?" asked Carnot. "On the eighth," said Lucien. "Today's the thirteenth," the War Minister continued, making his calculations. "Well, it certainly looks as if the destinies of France are being played out at this very moment." (In fact, the battle of Marengo began at dawn on 14 June.) "Four mortal days of waiting!" said Lucien. "Mortal?" the Home Secretary coldly repeated, with a questioning air. "Four days," said Fouché.

'An eye-witness has assured me', de Marsay continued, 'that the two Consuls only learned these details as all six persons were re-entering the salon at four in the morning. Fouché was the first to leave. And here is what this man, with his infernal, underground activity, contrived. He was a man of deep, unequalled, unsuspected genius, a genius undoubtedly as great as Philip II, Tiberius and Caesar Borgia. His conduct at the time of the Walcheren expedition was that of a consummate soldier, a great politician, a far-sighted administrator. Fouché was the only real minister Napoleon ever had. As you know, Napoleon feared him at that time. Fouché, Masséna and Prince Talleyrand are the three greatest men, with the strongest brain-power on diplomacy, war and government, that I have ever known. If Napoleon had frankly associated them with his work, Europe would no longer exist, but only a vast French Empire. Fouché only broke with Napoleon when he saw Sieyès and Prince Talleyrand set aside.

'In the course of three days Fouché, whilst concealing the hand which stirred up the embers of disaffection, organized the wide-spread restlessness which weighed on the whole of France and revived the republican fervour of 1793. In order to throw light on this dark corner of our history, I must tell you that this agitation which he instigated, pulling as he did all the strings in the former Montagne party, produced the republican plots which threatened the First Consul's life after his victory at Marengo. It was Fouché's consciousness of the evil he himself had conjured up that enabled him to point out to Bonaparte (who had held a contrary opinion) that the republicans were more deeply involved than the royalists in these conspiracies. Fouché was an admirable judge of men. He counted on Sieyès because of his disappointed ambition, on Talleyrand because he was a great aristocrat, on Carnot because of his profound integrity. But he feared the man we have seen here this evening, and this is the way he twisted him round his little finger: at this time Malin was just simply Malin, the man who was in touch with Louis XVIII. The Minister of Police forced him to draw up the proclamations of the proposed revolutionary governments, its acts and decrees and its outlawry of the sedition-mongers of 18 Brumaire. What is more, it was this reluctant accomplice who had them printed in a sufficient number of copies and kept them ready in bales in his house. The man who printed them was arrested as a conspirator, for they had chosen a printer who supported the Revolution, and the police only released him two months later. He died in 1816, still thinking that it had been a conspiracy of the Montagne party. One of the most curious scenes enacted by Fouché's police was incontestably that caused by the first dispatch delivered to the most famous banker of that period, one which announced that the battle of Marengo had been lost. Fortune, if you remember, did not declare itself for Napoleon until about seven in the evening. At midday the agent whom the financial magnate of the time had sent to the theatre of war considered that the French army was annihilated and hurriedly dispatched a messenger with this news. The Minister of Police sent for the bill-stickers and town-criers, and one of his henchmen was arriving with a lorry laden with printed sheets when the evening messenger, who had travelled with incredible speed, came to broadcast the news of the triumph which made all France mad with joy. There were considerable losses on the Stock Exchange. But the crowd of bill-stickers and criers who were to have proclaimed Bonaparte's outlawry and political extinction were held in check and had to wait for the printing of posters proclaiming and glorifying the First Consul's victory.

'Gondreville, on whose shoulders all responsibility for the conspiracy might well fall if it came to light, was so terrified that he loaded the bales on to carts and went with them by night to Gondreville, where no doubt he buried these sinister documents in the cellars of the château he had bought under the name of a man – he later had him appointed president of an Imperial court – a man named . . . Marion. Then he returned to

Paris in time to congratulate the First Consul. As you know, after the battle of Marengo, Napoleon rushed from Italy to France with startling speed; but it is certain, for those thoroughly acquainted with the secret history of that period, that his prompt return was due to a message from Lucien. The Home Secretary had some inkling of the attitude taken up by the Montagne party and, without knowing from what quarter the wind was blowing, feared that a storm was gathering. He had no reason for suspecting the three ministers, and attributed this commotion to the hatred aroused by his brother on 18 Brumaire and the firm belief then held by the remnant of the men of 1793 that he would meet with irreparable failure in Italy. The shouts of "Death to the tyrant!" at Saint-Cloud still echoed in Lucien's ears.

'The battle of Marengo kept Napoleon in the plains of Lombardy until 25 June. He was back in France on 2 July. Just imagine the faces of the five conspirators as they congratulated the First Consul, at the Tuileries, on his victory! In the grand salon itself Fouché told the Tribune – for the Malin you have just seen was a Tribune for a short time – to wait awhile, for all was not yet over. In fact, it seemed to Monsieur de Talleyrand and Fouché that Bonaparte was not so indissolubly wedded as they were to the anti-Bourbon cause, and for their own safety they bound him fast to it by means of the Duc d'Enghien affair. The execution of that prince is connected, by ramifications which may be traced out, with the plot that had been hatched at the Ministry of Foreign Affairs at the time of the Marengo campaign. Today it is certainly clear, to anyone who has been in touch with knowledgeable persons, that Bonaparte was tricked like a child by Monsieur de Talleyrand and Fouché, who were intent on irrevocably embroiling him with the Bourbon dynasty, whose ambassadors were at that moment trying to win the First Consul over to their cause.'

One of the important persons listening to de Marsay then interposed. 'Talleyrand was playing whist in the salon of Madame de Luynes. At three in the morning, he pulled out his watch, interrupted the game, suddenly broke off the subject of conversation, and asked if the Prince de Condé had any other son than the Duc d'Enghien. So absurd a question, coming from Monsieur de Talleyrand, aroused the greatest surprise. "Why do you ask a question to which you so well know the answer?" someone said to him. "Just in order to tell you that at this very moment the House of Condé has come to an end." Monsieur de Talleyrand had been in the house of the Duc de Luynes since the early evening, and undoubtedly knew that it was impossible for Bonaparte to show mercy to the Duc d'Enghien.'

'But,' said Rastignac to de Marsay, 'I don't see how Madame de Cinq-Cygne comes into all this.'

'Ah! You were so young then, my dear friend, that I was forgetting the conclusion. You know about the abduction of the Comte de Gondreville which eventually brought about the death of the two Simeuses and Robert, the elder brother of Adrien d'Hauteserre, who, by his marriage with Mademoiselle de Cinq-Cygne, became Comte and then Marquis de Cinq-Cygne?'

At the request of various persons to whom the adventure was unknown, de Marsay told the story of the trial, informing them that the five masked men were ruffians of the Imperial General Police, who were ordered to destroy the bales of printed notices, which in fact Malin had come to burn now that he believed that the Empire was firmly established. 'I suspect Fouché', he said, 'of having at the same time ordered a search for proofs of the correspondence between Malin de Gondreville and Louis XVIII, with whom he had always had an understanding, even during the Reign of Terror. But one element in this dreadful affair was a vengeful passion on the part of the agent in charge – he's still alive, a great man in his way, though in a subordinate position, an irreplaceable man, one who has distinguished himself by some astonishing feats. It appears that Mademoiselle de Cinq-Cygne had given him rough treatment when he had come on a previous occasion to arrest the Simeuses.

'There, Madame, you now have the secret of the affair. You can explain it to the Marquise de Cinq-Cygne and make her understand why Louis XVIII kept quiet about it.'

Paris, January 1841